CASANOVA'S SECRET WIFE

Casanova's Secret Wife

BARBARA LYNN-DAVIS

KENSINGTON BOOKS
www.kensingtonbooks.com

KENSINGTON BOOKS are published by

Kensington Publishing Corp.
119 West 40th Street
New York, NY 10018

All Kensington titles, imprints, and distributed lines are available at special quantity discounts for bulk purchases for sales promotion, premiums, fund-raising, educational, or institutional use.

Special book excerpts or customized printings can also be created to fit specific needs. For details, write or phone the office of the Kensington Sales Manager: Kensington Publishing Corp., 119 West 40th Street, New York, NY 10018. Attn. Sales Department. Phone: 1-800-221-2647.

Kensington and the K logo Reg. U.S. Pat. & TM Off.

eISBN-13: 978-1-4967-1232-5
eISBN-10: 1-4967-1232-3
First Kensington Electronic Edition: August 2017

ISBN-13: 978-1-4967-1231-8
ISBN-10: 1-4967-1231-5
First Kensington Trade Paperback Printing: August 2017

10 9 8 7 6 5 4 3 2 1

Printed in the United States of America

For Patricia Fortini Brown,
who poured her love
for Venice into me

CHAPTER I

The Island of Murano in the Lagoon of Venice
March of 1774

Caterina Capreta perched on a chair in the chilly room where it seemed no spring came. She forced herself to meet the frightening gaze of Abbess Marina Morosini, her old friend and rival, who sat behind an elaborate scroll-leg desk. Gilt bronze vines climbed up its shiny redwood legs, as if it were on fire.

The abbess gave a nod. "Caterina, I am pleased you have returned to visit us at the convent. How long has it been?"

Caterina couldn't help staring at Marina's ruined beauty. Her waxy skin pulled tight across her cheekbones. Her eyes, once blue-green, had lost their color. She was dressed in a black tunic, black veil, and white wimple that covered her ears, neck, and hair. All the forbidden vanities Marina had indulged in when she was young to the veil—the jeweled hairpins, long fingernails, even the rose perfume that had seemed to breathe from the very folds of her garments—were gone.

Caterina's mouth was dry, but she forced herself to speak. "I believe it is almost twenty years."

Marina sipped water from a goblet. "Twenty years ... yes ... such a long time. As I explained in my letter, a situation has arisen at the convent that brought you to mind."

"I'm flattered you still think of me," Caterina said. As if Marina could ever forget her. "But I can't imagine how I might be of any help—you are the abbess now, after all. And I know so little about spiritual matters." Caterina bowed her head, as if warding off a coming blow.

"I haven't asked you here to counsel me on spiritual matters," Marina said, barely hiding her irritation. "I have an unfortunate problem on my hands with a young boarder—sixteen years old. She was brought here by her father a month ago. The mother is dead. He offered me a sack of gold *zecchini* to take her in. How could I refuse?"

Caterina dared to look up but said nothing, knowing how these things went. The girls weren't so much left off at the convents for religious reasons, as for safekeeping.

"Only she is pregnant. He neglected to tell me that part." Marina's voice was mocking. "Instead, he sat in that chair showing me old coins and cameos he collects out of the ground. He called himself an antiquarian. He was on his way to Constantinople and said he couldn't possibly take his daughter there—given the depravity of the heathens. He pleaded for my help."

At the mention of a pregnancy, Caterina's gut had started to ache. But she remained silent, hoping she was wrong about where this was heading.

"I can't keep Leda at Santa Maria degli Angeli any longer," Marina announced, confirming her fears. "It would cause a scandal. Of course you understand."

Caterina nodded. Of course she did.

"I need to remove her from the convent until the thing is done. So I asked myself—who would be willing to take in a girl in Leda's situation—quietly, and with discretion? And then, I thought of you."

"Marina," Caterina begged. In her mind she was already grabbing for the thick oak door, running to the dock, and slipping into a boat for home. "You think too highly of me. I'm sure she would do better here."

Marina simply waited for the foolishness of Caterina's words to disappear like a bad smell. Then she smiled for the first time. Her teeth had a greenish cast, like the lagoon.

"My angel. May I call you that?"

Caterina felt the cruel jab hidden in Marina's words. Someone else, long ago, had first called her an *angel.* And somewhere, far away, perhaps he still saw her that way.

"We share a long history, yes?" A glimmer of Marina's old spark had returned. "I remember when you were just fourteen. Such an innocent! Or so we all thought."

Caterina laughed nervously and stared at the floor to hide her hot face. Her heart began to pound in her head.

"I learned otherwise," Marina said, "and I've protected your secret all these years. Who knows why?" She sighed. "There was nothing to be gained by revenge; all was lost anyway. I let you be."

Caterina sat like a piece of marble in her chair. She could hear lagoon water outside the windows lapping at the mossy stones.

"Now, old friend," Marina pressed, "I ask you a favor. It is only for a short time—I would guess not more than six months. Remember that the girl is no more of a fool than you—we— once were."

Caterina looked up to meet her faded eyes, which looked softer now at the memory of long ago.

"Will you help her?"

"Of course." Caterina's defeat was complete, but she said it with strength, as if this was her wish.

"Good." Marina smiled green at her again. "Leda is waiting in her room, ready to go."

CHAPTER 2

Within the hour, Caterina was back in a gondola heading home toward Venice, but this time she had company. The lagoon was choppy, stirred up by a late March wind. Caterina stayed warm inside the cabin, but Leda sat right on the planks of the boat. Her dress—rose-colored cotton and not nearly warm enough for the time of year—rippled in the wind. Caterina watched the girl stare out across the water, as though unaware of her or the two gondoliers who rowed them. She appeared to let herself go where the wind and tide took her.

Leda's hair was ratty brown. In the sunlight on the open water, it looked oddly purple—could she have dyed it? She wore a strange gold pendant at her neck, strung on a black velvet choker. It was a thick square, and carved with designs Caterina could not make out. She did not hold her back straight, and her belly was slightly swollen. But Caterina saw how the gondoliers stared at her as though she was a great beauty. It was her eyes—they were English or Irish blue, suggesting someplace deep, and far away.

Leda was noble-born, a member of the Strozzi family in Florence. Phillida was her real name—Marina had told her this as they walked the convent hallways to fetch the wayward girl. The Greek name had been chosen by her father. But "Leda" was all she could pronounce of it as a child, and the shorter name had stuck. *Leda,* Caterina mused as she watched the girl now in the boat. Zeus had desired mythological Leda so strongly he had mounted her in the guise of a curling swan.

About an hour later, they arrived at Caterina's house along the wide, sunny *fondamenta* that faced the island of Giudecca. The spell of the ride now over, the gondoliers rudely tossed Leda's satchels onto the pavement in front of the door and left. A trunk with the rest of her belongings would be arriving in another day or two.

Leda turned her back on the satchels and stood idle while Caterina got her key out. She trailed Caterina inside, and only then did Caterina realize that the bags remained on the pavement, forgotten.

"I have no servants, Leda. If you want your clothes, you will have to carry up your bags yourself."

Leda looked interested for the first time since they had met. "Why do you have no servants? The house looks rich enough. At home, we have fourteen, including my tutors."

Caterina sensed she didn't say this to insult her. Leda was simply being honest. So she responded in kind.

"No servants. I don't need an audience in my life."

Leda studied her, then went back out and took the lightest satchel in hand. Caterina gave her a few more things, then loaded herself up like a donkey.

Selfish girl. When would she be gone?

Caterina gave Leda supper but said she wasn't hungry herself. It was a lie; she was starving. Out of sight, she devoured a few spoonfuls of pasta and bean soup right from the pot and gobbled some hard bread like a peasant. Thick soup slid down her chin and dripped onto her chemise. She was ashamed of her gluttony, but she did not want to share a meal with this stranger. She told Leda she was going to sleep early.

Caterina decided to give Leda her bedroom, and moved into the small spare room down the hall. Her own bedroom was the most inviting in the house, with a Moorish-style, double-arched window that looked out to the Giudecca Canal. Sunlight filled this room every hour before dark, and Caterina had long enjoyed clocking her days as they passed with each slow sunset. There were two narrow beds whose headboards echoed the arches of the windows, each one painted green and brushed with gold.

Caterina moved out of her own bedroom partly to be kind. She did not want Leda to be miserable in the spare room with one tiny window. She also did not want Leda rummaging through the letters that she kept in the spare room. True, she could have simply moved the ivory box where she kept them locked up. But the small room had come to feel inhabited by their magic all these years. As if the box had released some of its secrets into the air. Tonight, more than ever, it felt this way. The visit to Santa Maria degli Angeli had stirred up unwelcome memories.

"Signora?" Caterina heard Leda whisper in the doorway of the small room. The shutters had been pulled tight, and everywhere was black. She realized she had fallen asleep but was awake now, and hungry.

"Signora?" A little louder now.

Caterina did not answer her.

The next morning was Sunday, and Caterina invited Leda to go to Mass with her at San Gregorio nearby. She had awakened in a more generous spirit.

"But who will you say I am?" Leda asked, placing a hand on her belly and taking a seat on the bed.

Caterina didn't have a ready answer. Oh, she had once been a quick-thinking girl, but that part of her was long gone.

Leda came up with an idea. "We can say I am your niece. Your niece from Florence who—"

"—no, *not* my niece. If you knew my brother, you'd know why. Any mention of him and we will stir up a hornets' nest of gossip."

"Then I will be myself," Leda said. "Leda Strozzi, abandoned first by my lover, then my father, and now by the abbess. You can say you are simply a link on a chain."

The naked honesty startled Caterina. "Come, Leda. We will say . . . that are you are . . . Bastiano's cousin, recently widowed. It's a dull story. No one will ask more."

"Who is Bastiano?"

"Oh—" Caterina turned away to fetch a pair of earrings from her table mirror drawer. "My husband." She wondered if Leda would be nosy, and ask more.

"You have a husband, Signora? But where is he? Is this his room?" She started to giggle. "Did I sleep in his bed?"

Caterina tried to explain. "I do have a husband. He stays mostly on the floor below us. And—he often goes to Padua on business."

Leda stared at her: She was probably remembering the way her own lover touched her, wondering how a husband could bear to stay somewhere else. Caterina dropped her eyes.

"Signora—" Leda changed the subject, abruptly. "Will you help me dress my hair?"

"Of course!" Caterina replied.

She wondered if Leda was attempting to be kind, to distract her from the facts that were accumulating about her life: a mostly absent husband, no servants. There was not even a songbird in the house. All was still, as if entombed.

Caterina placed Leda in a chair facing the water and began to brush that curious hair of hers. She might not have brushed it often, but it looked as though she had tried to cut it herself. And it was clearly dyed: with berry juice? She didn't ask. She was enjoying their anonymity from each other, Leda's back to her, each of them lost in her own separate world.

She realized she needed to switch to a comb if she ever hoped to get the knots out. She tugged at each clump carefully, holding the top part at the roots to lessen the pulling. Still, Leda's head jerked as she did her work.

Caterina's mind started to go places.

How long is this girl going to stay with me? Six months, as Marina promised? Or longer? What are Marina's promises worth, anyway?

Marina. Caterina pulled at the girl's hair harder.

Leda took out a handkerchief and blew her nose. Caterina launched into a fresh panic. *Lord, is this girl going to make me sick? Is that Marina's real purpose? Like when the Florentines threw rotten donkey flesh and even their own excrement over the city walls of Siena to sicken everyone?* She continued to comb furiously. Leda blew her nose again. Caterina felt repulsed.

She looked out to the water, suddenly longing for freedom. Only then did she notice Leda's shoulders heaving.

"Leda! Are you crying? Am I hurting you?" By instinct, she threw her arms around the girl from behind.

"It's alright, Signora," Leda said, clasping her hand. Tears came, but she managed a smile. "I'm sure it looks beautiful."

Ashamed of herself, Caterina gently swept back two thick pieces of the girl's hair, and held them in place with a stickpin she pulled out from her own thinning tresses. The pin had an enameled ball at its tip, and its vibrant colors, wrapped in a web of gold wire, matched the purple tint in Leda's hair. Caterina noticed that Leda never went to the mirror to see how she looked: She was without vanity, and more beautiful for it.

On their way to church, Leda linked her arm with hers, as she saw Venetian women do. Caterina let her.

"Leda," Caterina asked her a few nights later, "that morning when I made you cry. Was it because I had hurt you, or because you are sad?"

They were at supper together in the main room of Caterina's house. Leda mopped up the last of the spaghetti and anchovies with bread and stuffed sauce-soaked pieces into her mouth. Caterina was pleased to see, at least, she liked her cooking.

"Oh, Signora—I don't know what to say—"

"Are you missing . . . the man . . . who . . . ?" Caterina gestured at her own stomach because she couldn't find the right words.

Leda shook her head. But then she started to cry.

Caterina immediately regretted what she had unleashed. But Leda caught herself and wiped her cheeks roughly with a napkin. After, her face was covered with pink splotches and her eyes shone.

"I'm sorry," Leda said. "You would not understand."

"Of course I would!" Caterina fought for her place at the table of lovers.

"No, Signora." Leda flushed. "Your husband sleeps in another part of your house. You come and go as if he is not even here—"

"—but he is not here! I told you, he is in Padua."

"But, Signora, you never speak about him, never say his name just to say it, never smile just to hear it." She smiled now. She was clearly saying someone's name to herself.

"Leda," Caterina said, "Bastiano is nineteen years older than I am. But it's not only years. He's the kind of man who—" She looked at her favorite painting, the one hanging right over them. "If he was looking at that painting—the Virgin in a field at sunset, her hand on a rabbit, her Son reaching for it and showing His innocent tenderness—Bastiano would say to me, '*What's that frame made out of? Walnut?*'"

Leda giggled and then cried a little more. Her emotions were everywhere tonight. Caterina couldn't help laughing a little, too. Even the most disappointing things in life could be comical, given enough time.

But she was ready to leave off talking about Bastiano.

"There was another man," she confided. "When I was even younger than you are."

Why was she doing this? It wasn't to help Leda; she didn't fool herself about that. No, it was for herself. She was greedy to revisit a place where the ground was still sweet.

She rose from the table and went into the small room that was now her bedroom. Her ivory box sat on the nightstand, its smooth surfaces reflecting the moonlight that slivered in from the window. The key she always kept strung around her waist. It was red-brown with rust, and so was the lock on the box. And for the first time in many years, she opened her box, twisting the key with a shaking hand.

There they were, stacked inside: all her dusty letters, filled with old love stories. Letters from her cousin. Letters from her lover. Letters that were not really letters, more journals she had written for herself. She fingered a few pages near the top, checking to see that the words were all still there. Strange how old possessions wait in time, wait for you to remember them.

She took just a few letters from the early days to Leda, to aid her memory. And she began to talk to the girl. But she knew just where to stop. She was careful to leave the darkest stories of her past safely locked up.

CHAPTER 3

Venice, May of 1753
Twenty Years Before

"Caterina!" my brother Pier Antonio called. The words floated up to the loggia at the back of our house, where I sat most days. "Come down! There is someone I want you to meet!"

I was delighted to find my boredom interrupted. My world at this time was no more than a series of boxes: my loggia, which looked over a high-walled garden . . . the garden, with its back wall facing a tiny courtyard, Campiello Barbaro. A narrow canal ran alongside the house and emptied into the Grand Canal.

Running downstairs, I tripped on my own heeled slipper. I stopped just before reaching the doors to the *pòrtego* to adjust the bodice of my green floral dress, which had slipped, and neaten the curls at my neck.

Walking in, I saw a tall man in his late twenties standing by the windows and talking to my mother. The room stretched from one end of the house to the other, and was filled with gloomy paintings and heavy gilded furniture. When my mother saw me, she gave the man a curtsy and quietly departed. Amor, her little white dog, followed behind. Near the doors, my mother gave me an encouraging smile.

"*Mademoiselle,*" the tall—and strikingly handsome—man exclaimed as I came closer, startling me by speaking in French. "Your mother and brother cannot stop praising you! I told them I had to meet you myself." His eyes took me in appreciatively from head to toe, and he bowed deeply.

"Signor Casanova is backing me in my new business enterprise, Caterina." My brother strutted into the room holding some papers. "Soon we'll be supplying the whole city with beef, and I will make him a rich man."

Signor Casanova looked like he might be suppressing a smile. I was relieved he didn't take my brother too seriously. No one got rich from any of Pier Antonio's business schemes.

I resisted revealing my own disdain. Pier Antonio was more than twice my age—I was fourteen, he was thirty-two—and had been a liar all his life. My father had been right to kick him out of the house. But now that the cat was away on business, Pier Antonio had simply walked all over my mouse of a mother and moved back in.

"Can you entertain our guest while I write up our contract?" my brother asked me. He spoke too quickly, and rarely looked anyone in the eyes.

"Certainly," I answered.

"Come join me, then," Signor Casanova said, gesturing over to a sofa. I took a seat, and he sat a respectful distance from me. "It is my good fortune to find you at home."

"Oh, I am always at home." Stupid. I had just made myself as interesting as a chair.

He gave me a kind smile. "Then you make others seek you out. That is the clever way to do it."

Our eyes met, and I smiled back gratefully. I dropped my gaze, then peeked up to study him more. His skin was swarthy, and his black eyes had a fiery light. He wore a sapphire-blue waistcoat with exotic birds sewn all over it, and on his fingers, several jeweled rings.

"I've just come back to Venice after several years abroad," he explained. "I was lucky enough to meet your brother, and even luckier now to meet you." He leaned in closer, and my heart started to beat furiously at his nearness.

"Where did you travel?" I asked, moving a bit away and also changing the conversation away from myself. What did I know about the world? I rarely went out, except with my mother—and usually, to church.

"Paris, for two years. Then Dresden, and lastly Vienna. A splendid city, but I was ready to come home."

I wondered if he had run out of money, which would explain what he was doing now with my brother. But I left it unsaid.

"Tell me about Paris!" I begged instead. "Did you ever see the king? Louis XV? It's said he is very handsome."

"He is. Like a god. He makes you believe in the idea of majesty just looking at him."

"And the queen? A beauty, too?"

"Oh, no! She is old and very religious. She dresses badly, and wears big Polish bonnets."

I laughed gaily. His eyes lingered on the curve of my lips.

"The court ladies are all ugly, too," he went on, clearly warming to my laughter. "They wear heels a half-foot high to look taller, and teeter about with their knees bent like this—" He jumped up and did a ridiculous imitation.

I squealed. "Signor Casanova—"

"Giacomo—"

"Giacomo, if you say such preposterous things, you will stop the sun in its orbit!"

"What?" He stopped his funny walking and sat down again.

"Oh, it's a saying of my mother's—she's from Dalmatia. If you hear a crazy thing, you say it is so crazy it will stop the sun in its orbit."

"My innocent, do you still believe that the sun orbits the

earth?" He looked at me with a surprised smile. "I was taught the same nonsense—*the earth is suspended motionless at the center of the universe*. But this idea has been soundly disproved. A book by Niccolò Copernico has turned the cosmos inside out—" Here, he drew with his long fingers in the air, showing me the earth being moved out of position. "The sun now sits at the center of all things."

I was embarrassed by my ignorance. In just a few minutes, he had altered my view of the heavens and set the whole world spinning.

I looked into my lap. "I apologize, Signor Casanova. I know as much about the world as a caged bird. I'm sure you are very bored."

"Not at all," he said. "I find you perfectly charming." I blushed at this news, and he seized the opportunity to take my hand.

"Oh!" I pulled it back, not displeased—only surprised at his boldness.

My brother came back into the room, and Signor Casanova made polite excuses. Suddenly, he had to go.

He left without signing the contract. He was clever that way—oh, I saw that many times after. He got what he wanted, but he never got drawn in too far. What was it he once said?

Cheating is a sin, honest cunning is simply prudence.

CHAPTER 4

That night it rained. The next morning was damp and cloudy. I was keeping busy in my father's study. It was my favorite room in the house—at least, when he was away. With its Turkish carpets and leather-bound books, it was a comforting room to be in. One whole wall was decorated with *intarsia,* panels made from cut and fitted pieces of different types of wood. The art was so lifelike, it fooled the eye. There were inlaid pictures of musical instruments, a half-empty hourglass, even a squirrel that looked like it might scamper down onto the floor. The woodwork was very old—you can be sure my father had not commissioned this kind of whimsy.

Rows of his account books lined the shelves. His business was dull, in my fourteen-year-old opinion. He traded in wine and olive oil along the Adriatic and Ionian seacoasts.

I pulled down a big book of maps from a shelf. Then, a painted Book of Hours from my mother's collection of devotional books.

I sighed. Thinking of my mother always made me sad. She had been changed in the head from the time my younger brother, Sebastiano, had died. That had been seven years ago, when he was five. Now it was as if she lived with ghosts in her head.

I heard a strong knock at our land door and startled. I tiptoed as far down the hallway as I could without being seen.

"*Buon giorno, Signora.*" The voice I had been dreaming of all morning—downstairs!

"*Buon giorno, Signor Casanova,*" my mother said. "It is a pleasure to see you again. Are you looking for Pier Antonio?"

"I am."

My heart sank. What did he want with that rat?

"I'm sorry. He is out. I don't know when he will be back." That was the truth. We never knew Pier Antonio's comings and goings, day or night.

"*Bene, Signora.*" A pause. "May I see the *signorina,* then? Pier Antonio asked me to deliver a message to her if he was not home when I came by."

I bit my finger with excitement. Would my mother let him in?

"*Certo, Signor Casanova.*"

Of course, she should have sent him away. That's what my father would have done. But she chose to give me this small happiness. I think she knew I was lonely—we both were back then, I now realize.

I ran back to the study. Breathless, I set myself up at a small table and pretended to study the Book of Hours.

My mother showed Giacomo in with a slightly nervous smile. She left the door open on her way out, and I suspected she would stay in the next room, embroidering and listening.

"*Buon giorno,* Caterina," Giacomo called. "What are you reading?" Sunlight beamed in through the window and fell on his light green silk jacket. He sat down and peered over the colorful pages.

"Oh—" He was immediately disappointed. "Prayers."

"I like to read the stories about the saints," I said, trying to make it sound interesting.

"Truly?" He pulled a chair next to mine. "Saintly lives are the most boring kind."

I needed a moment to collect myself after this insight.

"I take it you have not been leading a boring, saintly life?" I teased.

He laughed out loud. "Far from it. Life is happiness when we let ourselves enjoy its pleasures: good health, a purse full of money, and love." He moved his leg against mine, and I could feel the watch in his breeches pocket press against my thigh.

"This is your recipe for happiness?" I asked. His eyes were dancing. His joy made me smile.

"It is. There are misfortunes, of course, as I should be the first to know. But the very existence of these misfortunes proves that the sum of good is greater."

"Misfortunes?" I asked, curious whether there was something more to him than fine clothes, jewels, and a handsome face. But he was not about to let me find out. He was already on his feet, changing the subject.

"Is there nothing to read in this whole library but account books and books on religion?" he questioned, taking inventory of the shelves. "No poetry, no novels?"

"Nothing else," I answered, blushing. "My father doesn't let me read anything else."

"You deserve more than this library offers," he said, shaking his head in disapproval. "Impressive as it seems at first, it is impoverished. It is my duty to bring you something to delight your mind."

"What?" I asked eagerly. "Something you have written yourself?"

"I have the modest start of a career in literature," he said, bowing slightly. "Last year, my translation of a French opera into Italian verse was staged in Dresden."

"How impressive!" I exclaimed, clapping my hands together.

"Not really," he said, keeping a straight face. "Only my mother seemed to like it."

"Oh—" I stammered, both amused and embarrassed at his

theatrical failure. "I'm sure you are a gifted writer. Perhaps the music was simply bad."

"How adorable you are, my angel," he sighed, seeming almost regretful of the fact. He sat back down and took my hands in his. "I envy the man destined to be your husband."

I heard a tinkling of metal on the floor. My mother's scissors, dropping from her hands next door? I pulled away.

"You shouldn't," I whispered, apology in my voice.

"I understand," he said, exhaling deeply. He ran a hand through his hair, which was expertly dressed and scented with jasmine pomade. "You are right, of course. I should probably not have come, but I found myself unable to resist."

Hearing this, a loving flame rose from my soul and spread to my whole face.

"You will come see me again?" I asked. "I am so very lonely . . . and you cheer me immensely." I dared to place my hand lightly on his forearm. He moved it to his chest, where I could feel his heart beating wildly, and the warmth of his skin beneath his shirt.

"I will," he said, rising and staring down at me with eyes that seemed torn with some decision.

"I shouldn't, Caterina. But I will."

CHAPTER 5

"I hope you realize you will not hold his interest for long."

Pier Antonio spoke to me as we made our way toward Campo Santa Margherita a few days later. We had told our mother we were going to Mass together, and she had believed it—kissing us lightly on our cheeks before we set off.

"Why not?" I argued with my brother. "Giacomo seems quite taken with me."

"He's used to more excitement." Pier Antonio gave me a sly glance. "Not a fourteen-year-old girl who still says her bedtime prayers at night."

"What do you know?" I snapped, watching him put his hands together and imitate my fervent praying.

"Don't misunderstand me—" He laughed. "I want him to fall in love with you. It ties him even more to my business interests. But—don't expect too much." I blushed deeply, embarrassed by his meaning.

"We can all change for the better," I reminded him, repeating a phrase often spoken by our parish priest, Father Ludovico.

"We can all change, huh?" Pier Antonio mocked me. "Tell me more—since you know so much about men."

I chose to keep my mouth shut the rest of the way.

A few minutes later, we arrived at a tavern. I had always been curious where Pier Antonio spent his time, and now I got to see for myself. That is, once I adjusted to the dim interior, lit only by a couple of half-shuttered windows. The whole place smelled of cheap wine: sweet, like apricots and figs. Unkempt men and a few obviously low women sat at tables playing cards. As out-of-place and uneasy as I felt, no one seemed to notice me much. The glimmering piles of silver *zecchini* commanded everyone's attention.

Pier Antonio led me toward a partition that blocked off the rear of the room. Behind this, Giacomo sat waiting for me.

He sprang up the instant he saw me. "Finally!" He deluged my hand with kisses. I relaxed immediately, feeling reassured at my decision to come.

Looking up, I saw with dismay that Signora Castello was also there. She was my brother's mistress. She lay on a sofa against a side wall and blew me a kiss. I ignored the detestable woman. She was married to some unfortunate, who must have been so bad she preferred my brother.

Pier Antonio went over to her. Her dress was partly up, and he greeted her by putting his hand on her bare thigh, above her stockings and garters.

"I've brought you a gift," said Giacomo, distracting me from the unsavory scene. He presented me with a pair of long, leather gloves. They were bright blue with a black geometric pattern on them. They matched nothing I owned, and particularly not the painted Indian cotton dress I was wearing that day, with its delicate flowers and sprigs. I even wondered—after the ugly conversation I'd had with my brother—whether he had bought the gloves for someone else, then decided to give them to me.

"How—unusual they are!" I stammered, slipping them on. The fit was perfect.

"The color reminded me of a beautiful caged bird," Giacomo said, taking my gloved hand and kissing my wrist. His mouth traveled luxuriously up and down my arm, to the inside of my bare elbows and back to the tips of my waiting fingers.

I blushed with pleasure. How poisoned was my thinking! The gloves were clearly meant for me. I vowed to become the kind of woman who would wear such gloves: beautiful, vibrant, and unusual.

"Go on!" my brother cried out, taunting us from the sofa. "She wants a real lover's kiss!" Pier Antonio groped Signora Castello and gave her the kind of kiss he meant. She answered by pushing him back and climbing on top of him. He lifted her breasts out of her chemise and cupped them in his hands. She began to unbutton his breeches, greedily reaching in.

I turned my face to the wall, horrified at what was unfolding. But a large gilt mirror faced me. I could still see everything, could hear my brother's grunts of pleasure.

My face was burning, and I think I said something stupid to the wall about my new gloves.

The next thing I knew, Giacomo had turned me around. He used his body to block my view. He urged me to forget what I was seeing, to think only of him. To remember I was better than all of this.

He kissed my black curls and my white powdered face, and told me I was his angel.

CHAPTER 6

"He did not."

"Yes. He did."

"Your brother made love to a woman with you in the same room?" My cousin Zulietta's small, rosy mouth hung open at my news. She looked like a fish, which caused me to giggle.

"It's not funny, Caterina. It's—horrible!" Zulietta picked up the red chalk she had been using to sketch a bouquet of lilies we had cut from the garden. We sat in the *pòrtego* of my house, near the windows for good light.

"Yes—it is horrible. But don't you see how considerate Giacomo was toward me? He shielded my view of them!"

"Simply because Pier Antonio is black does not make Signor Casanova white," she said, setting down the chalk.

I scowled. Zulietta was my cousin, and my closest friend. But she was sixteen, and believed that those two extra years gave her the right to guide me in the world.

"Why are you behaving like this, Caterina?" She looked at me worriedly, soft shadows beneath her dark honey–colored eyes. A few ringlets of her auburn hair, carefully curled, framed her heart-shaped face.

"Like what?"

"You are being disobedient. You know perfectly well what is planned for your future." She smoothed her red and pink rose–embroidered skirt, making sure not one thread was out of place. "One day, you will marry a successful merchant and lead an honorable, comfortable life."

"That may be true—but in the meantime, I'm playing a little." I winked at her, but she was not amused.

Her voice dropped to a whisper. "Why risk doing this behind your father's back? I'm sure he will . . . he will choose someone well-suited to you when the time comes." But she lowered her eyes when she said this last part, as if she did not entirely believe it herself.

" 'Well-suited' to me?" I snapped. "I bet he will choose some old man and I will be miserable." How trapped I felt! By my father—and now, even by Zulietta.

Zulietta smiled at me sadly. I think she understood why I was fighting back. Neither of us liked my father much. In fact, we were terrified of him. When we were children, whenever we heard his footsteps coming up the stairs, we would hide in an empty linen chest.

"Giacomo is a perfect choice," I continued, sensing Zulietta's mood had changed. "He is courteous, and kind—"

"And handsome," Zulietta broke in, shaking her head, but I saw she was fighting a smile.

"And handsome!" I chirped happily. I picked up a sofa pillow and hugged it tightly.

Zulietta went back to her drawing. Her style was meticulous: Every detail had to be captured and set down correctly on her paper.

"Be careful, Caterina," she said after a few minutes. "I do worry—what Signor Casanova might be expecting from you."

"I will be *fine*." I said it quickly and without thinking. I was on a new path, heading into a new land. No one was going to hold me back. Not even the cousin and friend who loved me most.

CHAPTER 7

Night. I was sure I heard my name being called beneath my bedroom window. Running to check, I saw no one. I tiptoed barefoot down the two flights of cold stone steps and out into the garden. I didn't need a lantern, because the moon was full. It was huge, hanging in the sky.

At the far edge of the garden was a back door we had not used in years. It was overgrown with leaves and vines. In the moonlight, half-hidden, I spied a folded piece of cream paper poking through a crack in the wood. I ran to retrieve it, plucking it out eagerly. Something sweet released its fragrance at my touch.

Tucking my secret message into the folds of my nightgown, I raced back through the garden, up the steps, and back into my bedroom. I locked the door and began to read.

> *My beautiful angel—your skin white like*
> *alabaster, your black eyes reflecting only sweetness,*
> *your curious and lively spirit—*
> *As promised, I have copied out something for*

you to read. It is a poem by Dante. It tells the story of a pilgrim, a wanderer. He is the poet, who travels down to hell and then up to paradise in a journey inspired by his muse, Beatrice.

In this verse I've copied out for you, the poet finds two lovers wrapped in each other's arms for eternity. Their names are Paolo and Francesca, and he asks them for the story of their early love. How did they recognize its first signs?

But tell me, in the time of gentle sighs,
with what, and in what way did Love allow you
to recognize your still uncertain longings?

Someday I will share the rest of the poem with you, and tell you about their fate together. But tonight, I simply want to ask, when will I be made a happy man and see you alone . . . ?

G.C.

I held Giacomo's words to my heart and kissed the top of the page. "Soon," I whispered to him in the moonlit night. "Soon."

CHAPTER 8

Venice, 1774

Caterina tried to gauge Leda's reaction to her story. She wanted the girl to see her in a new way: the beautiful younger woman she had been, the desire she had inspired.

"Very sweet," Leda said. She yawned. "What time is it?"

"Late." Caterina felt disappointment close in around her. The main room where they sat, enlarged all day by views to the water, appeared black and small.

Caterina collected her letters from the table and headed back to the spare bedroom. She carried the pile with no particular care while Leda could still see her, but as soon as she turned down the hallway, she hugged them closer. These letters were alive to her still. Now that they were out, it felt impossible to put them back in a locked box. Instead, she lit a candle on the nightstand and tucked them under her pillow. She was almost certain she would not be able to sleep well that night.

"Signora," Leda's voice surprised her in her doorway. Caterina wasn't sure how many minutes had passed. She felt years away, drifting in a dream.

"Do you want to hear how I met my lover—Filippo?" Leda

settled herself on the bed right on top of Caterina's nightgown. Lord, she was a funny girl. There was something unpolished about her, despite her wealthy upbringing. Caterina gave her a welcoming smile.

"It was a few weeks before Christmas," Leda began, her words rushing out in a new way Caterina had not heard before. "Filippo plays the harpsichord, and my father had invited him to perform at a party. He arrived in a gold silk suit. But I noticed his jacket was rumpled—as if this was the only one he owned and he pulled it out each night to play. Oh, Signora—he is handsome! Black hair, soft eyes, and a little mole right here." She pointed just above her mouth. Caterina nodded, wanting to share in the memory.

"He started to play," Leda continued, her own eyes shining in the candlelight. "I fell in love watching his hands fly over the keys. When the music finally ended, Filippo stood up and—I don't know how, Signora, but he told me afterward he had felt my stare—he came over to me. One of his eyes is just a tiny bit crossed"—this Leda briefly tried to imitate—"so when he looks at you, it is as if you are the only person in the room. No one else matters. No one else is there."

Caterina remembered the feeling. She had felt it, too, for a time, at least. She forced a smile to encourage Leda to continue.

"Filippo was born in Naples," Leda went on. "His mother was a well-known singer. He traveled the world with her as a boy—Italy, France, England. Only she had recently died, and he did not know his father. He was alone! My heart went out to him."

Leda looked at Caterina for approval of her feelings, and Caterina gave it by putting a hand to her own heart. Still, Leda grew quiet and fingered the gold pendant at her neck. It glowed mysteriously in the night.

"Was that necklace a gift from Filippo?" Caterina ventured.

Leda looked surprised. "This?" she asked, holding the thick gold square between her fingers. "It was my mother's."

"Oh!" Caterina regretted she had brought up this subject, when Leda had been happily telling her about her lover. But she seemed to want to talk about this, too.

"It shows Saint George spearing the dragon—can you see it?" Leda asked. She leaned in so that Caterina could inspect it more closely. Caterina held the candlestick nearby. Now she could make out a knight dressed in armor with a foot resting on a vanquished dragon.

"And inside"—Leda flipped over the pendant—"is a piece of the saint's lance encased behind crystal."

"It's . . . lovely," said Caterina, softly running a finger along the frame. Now that she understood it, it was. "Have you worn it since you lost your mother?"

"Yes," said Leda, her words coming less rushed now. "She died from smallpox a year after I was born. She had gone to visit her family in London, fell sick, and never returned home."

"Oh, Leda," Caterina said, stroking the nightgown beneath the girl because she thought it might make her uncomfortable to give her the hug she felt she needed. "I'm so sorry."

"The family in England sent me her necklace to wear about a year later. I remember my father fastening it on me—it's my earliest memory. He said, 'Corraggio, *Leda. Like Saint George.*'"

"Saint George was your mother's patron saint?" Caterina asked.

"Yes." Leda smiled. "Georgiana was her name."

"I'm sure she was a beauty—like you," Caterina offered, wanting to lift Leda's spirits.

Leda smiled at her weakly. "I don't think she'd be very proud of me now, Signora."

"Nonsense," said Caterina firmly. She wasn't sure where her strong response was coming from. "Of course she would be very proud. You mustn't think these kinds of hurtful thoughts about yourself."

CHAPTER 9

In early April, Bastiano returned to Venice. Caterina heard him before she saw him, shuffling around in the rooms downstairs. Coughing. Sneezing loudly. She went down to greet him and told him about Leda so that he would not say something awkward when he first saw her.

He kissed Caterina on the forehead.

"We have a visitor!" she said cheerfully. "Leda Strozzi, from Florence. She is a boarder at my old convent, and I was asked to help her. She needs a place to stay for a while."

"To stay? Why?"

"Oh, she is a beautiful girl. You'll see." Caterina tried a new approach. Distract him. "But she fell sick and—"

"You remind me. I need to go to the pharmacy for some things."

The pharmacy was Bastiano's favorite place in the city. His nose. His stomach. His feet. These parts of his aging body chronically needed help.

"Does the girl—Lisa, is it?—does Lisa want to come along?"

"Leda."

"Leda. Do you think she wants to go? We can all take a gondola. I have a blister on my toe."

Caterina brought Leda downstairs to join Bastiano in the waiting gondola. She saw the color rise in her husband's wrinkled face when he saw the girl. As she had expected. Leda was a beauty in her loose blue cotton dress, eyes shining in the sunlight. Bastiano hopped up in the boat and helped her in, before the gondolier had a chance to assist her.

"Welcome! Welcome, Leda!" he said, patting her back and almost losing his footing.

Leda smiled indulgently at him. Caterina chuckled a little to herself. She did not feel jealous. She knew his attention to Leda was innocent. And besides, she had never loved him as a wife.

The pharmacy *Vecchia* was in Campo San Luca. The square was always bustling with activity, just off the Grand Canal and near the Rialto Bridge. But today, the three of them could hear a roaring crowd even before the gondolier made the turn to dock.

"What is happening?" Caterina asked.

"It is the Festival of the Old Wife today," the gondolier said. "A long tradition at the *Vecchia* pharmacy." Caterina saw him steal an admiring glance at Leda.

"Oh, Lord," Caterina said. Any day was an excuse for a festival in Venice. She was not in the mood for a noisy crowd. Could she ask Bastiano to go to another pharmacy?

The gondolier gave a final heave and turned the beak of the boat toward the mooring poles.

Too late.

They got out and walked down the narrow street that led into the square. Leda ran ahead, drawn by the music and cheering. Caterina took Bastiano's arm—he was limping from his blister—and played the part of a good wife.

Spring sunlight warmed them as they entered the square. The pharmacy at the far end was blocked from view by a temporary wood stage. On it sat a large puppet of an old woman, the Old Wife. They pushed closer to see her better. Her face was made of leather: brown and creased. Her lips and cheeks were painted red. Her hair was a mess of fishing nets, and covered by a flopping cotton cap.

The Old Wife was hideous, but two young actors on the stage whose faces had been whitened by flour paid her burlesque attention. They knelt and kissed her hands and feet; they danced and pranced around her. How attractive they were, Caterina thought, with their lean, stocking-clad legs and black hair smoothed by pomade. She watched their antics for a while, then dropped Bastiano's arm. After too long touching her husband, it felt uncomfortable to keep it up.

One of the actors spotted someone in the crowd and motioned for her to come onstage. He held his hands to his heart, begging ardently. He kicked the Old Wife to the floor. The crowd shouted encouragement, while a jangle of out-of-tune instruments played. Finally, a girl was thrust onto the stage. It was Leda! Her dress had come off her shoulder, and she was almost doubled over laughing. She looked happier than Caterina had seen her before—like the sixteen-year-old girl that she was.

The young man led Leda to sit where the Old Wife had been. He took her hand and kissed it, making an exaggerated bow. The crowd shouted more now, ecstatic. Beauty Triumphs over Old Age. The other young man sawed the Old Wife in two, and candy and confetti poured out. Children scrambled to grab for the sweets, pulling the puppet's body open like wolves.

The crowd began to thin, and Bastiano made his way over to the pharmacy. Caterina waited outside, leaning on the wooden stage. She didn't like pharmacies, or anything to do with illness. The two handsome actors walked by, laughing. They were sweating from their exertions, and it had streaked the flour on their faces. A memory took hold in Caterina's mind, and she stood there frozen. She followed them with her eyes, thinking about a night long ago when Giacomo had disguised himself with a floured face.

She swallowed hard to banish the memory, and bowed her head. Bile rose in her throat.

Bastiano joined them upstairs for supper that night. Caterina could never quite understand what he gained from meals with other people: He simply filled his plate and shoveled the food in. Still, it was sweet how he offered Leda sorbet after, and when Leda said yes, he shuffled downstairs to scoop it from where he kept it packed in ice.

The three ate their sorbet greedily—Bastiano always chose unusual flavors, like pomegranate, or pistachio. Leda's face was pink and sunburned from the day spent outside, and she seemed content. Her cares were far away from her for now.

Finally, to Caterina's relief, Bastiano went downstairs to bed. He always seemed like a heavy coat to her—in summer when she wanted nothing on.

Leda gave Caterina an inviting smile from across the table. Caterina sensed what she wanted. Or was it more what Caterina, herself, wanted? To not be an Old Wife for the rest of her life? To remember her time of gentle sighs?

"Do you want to hear more?" she asked Leda. The girl nodded.

Caterina went to get some letters from the ivory box in her bedroom. The silent pile told her whole story. But she took out just a few more letters to share, inhaling the scent of their sweet pages and clutching them close.

CHAPTER 10

Venice, 1753

My next time to see Giacomo came when Carnival season started, the early days in June. When I was growing up, Carnival had always been marked by a little fair outside my church in Campo San Gregorio. Masked boys and girls would dance the *furlana*, floral garlands were hung all about, and the air was fragrant with roasting nuts. But later, I realized that Carnival was mostly about hiding who you were—man or woman, rich or poor—from the world for a while. To be who you were not, to live the life you craved.

The theaters in Venice were only allowed to play during Carnival time. I had never been to an opera or ballet. Now Pier Antonio invited me to go with him. The secret between us was that Giacomo would meet us at Teatro San Samuele.

My mother was as gullible as ever.

"What opera is playing?" she asked. We stood in the kitchen, and she offered my brother a warm cinnamon doughnut wrapped in a linen napkin.

"*The Upside-Down World,*" he answered. He grabbed the

doughnut from her hand, popped it in his mouth, and snickered until he was choking on the crumbs. I imagine he was thinking she was fairly upside down herself.

She loved him more than he ever deserved.

Zulietta came to my house the afternoon of the performance to lend me a dress. She was a little plumper than I was, but this was easily solved by pulling the dress laces tighter. And she knew I had always adored this particular gown. It was sage-colored silk, with dragonflies sewn all over in gold thread. The thread looped around to show the insects' patterns of flight.

"I shouldn't be helping you look so beautiful tonight," she said as she finished tying the bodice. The dress still smelled of her sweetness—like orange blossoms.

She reached into her pocket and pulled out a miniature jewel box. "Close your eyes and hold out your hand." She dropped some trinkets into my palm.

I opened my eyes. Six dragonflies sat there, hairpins to match the dress. "Oh! They are precious!" I said. "Will you put them in?"

Zulietta motioned for me to sit down in front of the mirror. She arranged the dragonflies, light pink, yellow, and green glass, to shine in my hair. I felt her gentleness, and pure love for me.

"You are sure that Pier Antonio will stay with you all night?" she asked. "Do not let him out of your sight."

"Of course," I reassured her. This was obviously a little game we were playing. We both knew Pier Antonio was not the kind of brother who protected anyone's reputation.

"Be careful, *cara*," she said as she examined me in the mirror. I stood and hugged her.

"What did I tell you?" I asked, grasping both her hands.

"That you will be *fine?*"

"Exactly."

She gave me a worried look, and squeezed my hands until I finally eased them away.

*   *   *

It was near midnight when Pier Antonio and I left our house and headed up the Grand Canal. I tied on a simple black leather mask in the cabin of our gondola. A couple of the glass dragonflies fell out of my hair and landed on the velvet seat. I caught them up and pinned them back in. It was as if they were alive, flying in the night.

I opened the shutters to take in the scene around me. It was warm, and everyone had gathered on their balconies to watch the parade of boats on the Grand Canal. Silk banners and carpets hung on the balustrades. Our gondolier began to sing "If You Love Me" ("*But if you think I should love only you...*"), and the next line came answering back from someone in the watery darkness ("*Shepherd, you are surely deceiving yourself....*"). I was in high spirits, singing along.

"Stop here!" Pier Antonio called out to the gondolier.

"What are you doing?" I turned to him. "Where are we?"

"The Ridotto," he said.

"You are—stopping to play cards?" I asked. "Are you not coming to the opera with me?"

He slapped a purse of coins bulging in his breeches pocket and laughed. "Oh, no! Giacomo has paid me well to send you on to him alone." He left me behind in the cabin and jumped out onto the wet pavement.

So—I had been bought for the night. I felt like a courtesan. But at the same time, it made me feel strangely valuable. Desired.

"How will I get back into the house?" I cried out to my brother through the open window, suddenly remembering.

"Oh, right," Pier Antonio called back. "I told *mama* I lost my key. She's going to leave the waterside door open." He gave me a mock bow and strode away.

What a good-for-nothing! The gondolier stared at me, waiting. "*À Teatro San Samuele,*" I commanded him. "*Voga!*"

The boat slipped on through the night. I sat back on the soft seat and hugged myself for comfort. My hands were clammy, and I wiped them on my dress. Zulietta's dress. What would she think if she saw me now? Alone outside my home for the first time in my life, headed to meet my lover?

My heart was fluttering. I had little idea what lay ahead. But—Giacomo was waiting for me.

CHAPTER 11

"Ah. Finally. We are truly alone."

Giacomo greeted me by the lantern-lit steps in front of the theater. He wore the traditional Venetian costume for Carnival: a long, black cloak and hood that hid his head and shoulders, black tricorn hat, and white, angled mask that resembled a beaked bird. This, he had pulled aside so that—along with recognizing his unusual height—I would be able to find him in the swarming crowd.

I felt alive to the tips of my fingers at the sight of him in the menacing disguise. He took my hand in his—large, warm, and commanding—and led me inside.

Teatro San Samuele struck me as resembling a huge golden jewel box. I had never seen anything so splendid, even in church. Candles with gold-orange flames burned everywhere, throwing light on four tiers of gilded boxes rising from the stage. Thousands of gold stars sparkled on a sapphire blue–painted ceiling.

We started upstairs. Up and up, all the way to the fourth tier.

"Why—so—high?" I asked, becoming short of breath. I regretted having laced my dress so tight.

"I will show you," he said, leading me over to a balcony edge.

We peered down into the pit. I could see peddlers moving among crowded benches hawking wine, sausages, fruit, nuts, and seeds. Cries in imitation of cocks and hens rose up, laughter, and shouts. Seeds and pieces of fruit were being thrown about for fun, and there seemed to be some sort of contest as to who could make a bigger fool of himself.

"*Men are apes on the outside, swine on the inside,*" said Giacomo, keeping a straight face. "It's a line from the Bible." I gave him a disapproving look, but could not suppress an amused grin.

"I adore your dimples when you smile," he said, touching my cheek just below my mask. After he dropped his hand, I could still feel the sweet echoes of his fingers on my skin. I touched my cheek, as if I could seal the feeling in, forever.

We went to find our private box. It was stifling inside, high up and surrounded by what seemed like thousands of burning candles. A waiter came to offer us sorbet, which we eagerly bought. Giacomo removed his cloak and mask, but I left my own mask on, fearing I might be recognized by someone who knew my father.

"Is this your first time at the opera since your return to Venice?" I asked him.

"It is," Giacomo said, savoring his lemon sorbet and offering me a taste from the delicate spoon. I had ordered my favorite, blood orange.

"I chose this opera for you because the soprano, Agata Ricci, is a crowd favorite," he explained. "We might be lucky and see doves let loose by her admirers at the end, with bells tied around their necks so they make their own music as they fly . . ." His voice trailed off and he gazed out to the stage, as if remembering something.

"I take it you've been to this theater before?" I ventured.

"Why, yes." He regarded me. "Many times. In fact—I used to be a musician, a fiddler in this very orchestra."

"Oh!" I was not sure how to react. To be an acclaimed musician, that was one thing. Society admired a master in his art. But a fiddler?

"I was terrible," he continued, as if reading my mind. "I earned a *scudo* a day scraping away at my violin."

I laughed, because I adored how Giacomo laughed at himself without appearing obviously to do so. But I was also beginning to sense he was hiding failures, losses, and regrets.

"All that is behind me," he was quick to reassure me. "I've become a different man."

Nothing about him was adding up. Who were his family, and why did he never speak of them? How did he go from being a fiddler, to someone my brother would approach for money?

"How is it your fortune changed?" I dared to ask him.

"I will tell you," he answered, smiling at me a bit wickedly. "One night changed the entire course of my life."

"Truly?"

"Truly. I was twenty-one years old at the time. I'd been playing in an orchestra at Ca' Soranzo, for a wedding. I left maybe an hour before dawn. As I went downstairs I saw a man in a red toga—a Venetian senator—drop a letter on the ground as he was taking a handkerchief out of his pocket. I retrieved the letter, and, returning the favor, the senator offered me a ride home.

"Three minutes after I take a seat in his gondola he begs me to shake his left arm. 'I am numb,' he tells me. 'I feel as if I've lost my arm.' I shake him with all my strength but now he tells me he feels he has lost his leg. I hold a lantern close to his face and see that his mouth has curled to his left ear." Giacomo put a finger in his mouth and pulled his lip aside to show me. I pretended I was disgusted, but actually, he was as handsome as ever.

"The senator was near dead by the time we reached his house. I carried him upstairs with the help of a servant. We fetched a doctor to bleed him. Two other friends arrived, and I learned that the senator's name was Matteo Bragadin. His friends told me I was free to go, but I felt it was my duty to stay."

I nodded. I learned later that Giacomo had a kind heart for the sick and unfortunate. Which did not mean he didn't make people sick and unfortunate; only that he did his best to stop misery if he felt it was in his power.

"The next morning," he continued, "the doctor applied a mercury salve to Signor Bragadin's chest. The aim was to cause a violent brain disturbance, which would then move to other parts of the body and revive the circulation of fluids." Giacomo shook his head at the idiocy, and I breathed in, transfixed.

"By midnight, Signor Bragadin was on fire and very agitated. I saw death in his eyes. I told his friends we had to deliver him from the thing that was killing him! Without even waiting for their response—I washed off the mercury salve. In three or four minutes Signor Bragadin was relieved, and fell into a deep sleep."

Che consolazione, I breathed out. Relieved to hear that Giacomo had not killed a nobleman.

"The doctor came the next morning and was pleased to see his patient thriving. But when he learned what I had done—interfering with his cure—he called me a charlatan. Signor Bragadin dismissed him. He said that a violinist clearly knew more than all the doctors in Venice!"

We laughed together over the happy ending. Giacomo's dark eyes glittered in the candlelight. He was bewitching.

"From this time on, Signor Bragadin has listened to me as if I were an oracle sent to lead him." He paused here, taking measure of my reaction.

"As if you have something of the . . . supernatural in you?" I asked, trying not to lose myself in his fiery eyes.

He nodded. I felt he was daring me to make sense of it. Was I supposed to believe in his magical abilities? I couldn't tell. But I learned later what was true.

"He rewarded me with rooms in his house, a servant, a gondola, and a generous allowance," Giacomo finished. "He has adopted me like a son."

"Ah—" I smiled. Now many things made sense: his fine clothes, jewels, and self-confidence. "But it is more than good fortune that vaulted you into the place of a nobleman," I noted. "Your own judgment, wits, and daring allowed you to alter your destiny."

"*Bene,*" he said. "That is one way to see it. A flattering view. I like seeing myself through your eyes." He leaned in and gave me a soft kiss on the lips. Our first kiss—long and ineffably sweet. His warm mouth tasted like lemon syrup. "You make me a better man, Caterina," he whispered into my ear, and my heart soared.

By now, the candles around us had started to burn out. Only two oil lamps remained to light the stage. The strings began to play.

The Upside-Down World is a comic opera about a reversed society. Men are willing—if incompetent—slaves to the women they love. They knit clothes, bring hot chocolate in bed, even empty the chamber pots. At one point, a man runs onto the stage with a pair of knitting needles, singing: "*I have been knitting very fast and in three months I have knit half a stocking!*" We laughed hardest at that part.

The late-night hours passed. Amorous feelings grew up like vines around our box. In the midst of an *aria* about being powerless in the sea of love, Giacomo slid his chair behind mine. From this hidden spot, he laid kisses on the back of my neck. I shivered with delight.

He reached around with his hands, his fingers playing at the lace edge of my bodice, in and out. One time in, they caught something. He pulled it out for me to see. It was one of the shiny glass dragonflies—a pink one—that must have fallen into my dress in the gondola on the way to the theater. It had been hiding all this time, waiting to be found.

He kissed it, and I could feel him smiling hot against my skin. He let the insect trace some golden loops of thread, as if in slow flight. No destination. Just happy to be on me. Then it flew back in. Giacomo untied my dress and followed the dragonfly in with a hungry hand.

My breathing was coming very fast. I couldn't stop it. I didn't want to; I wanted to drown in whatever I was feeling. Maybe we could be seen, I thought, maybe I could even be heard over the singing, moaning with pleasure, but I didn't care. I felt greedy, crazy with longing.

He moved a hand under my skirts. And I became a slave to love.

CHAPTER 12

"Don't take me home yet—please." I sighed, leaning my head against his shoulder as we left the theater. There were maybe two hours left until dawn, I judged. Campo San Samuele was still alive with lantern lights and throngs of theatergoers, but soon enough, it would be just us beneath a starry sky.

"Shall we take a walk?" he suggested, kissing me on the temple. I giggled, feeling playful and more content than I ever had before. This, I guessed, was love.

"I will take you on a tour," he announced, giving me a deep, sweeping bow in his black cloak. He tied on his beaked mask again. "Something like the Grand Tour of Europe, only maybe not as grand. It will be a secret tour of this part of Venice."

"Secret?" I was intrigued.

"Secret," he responded, taking my hand and steering us to a narrow street that led out of the square.

The reassuring lamplights and noises of the crowd soon faded behind us. At the end of this street he turned down another, this one even more cramped and dark. Every house was locked and shuttered. Giacomo kept us walking as quickly as cats. "Just a little farther," he called softly over his shoulder. I had paused to look behind, fearing some stranger with a knife.

Giacomo stopped suddenly and I practically fell into him, laughing at my clumsiness. "Shh." He began laughing, too. "We'll wake the whole neighborhood."

He took a powder tinderbox out of his pocket and knelt down. I could hear the fast scraping of steel on flint, and soon saw sparks. He lit a small candle. When he stood and held it above our heads, I saw we were in front of a grated iron entrance door. Everything smelled damp, as if no one had opened the door in a long time.

"Where are we?" I asked. Looking higher up, I saw a plain brick-and-stucco house. Nothing like my own splendid home, which was covered in porphyry, rose and green marble brought to Venice from as far away as Egypt.

"This is where I was born," announced Giacomo.

"Oh!" I made an effort to sound admiring.

I heard him take a long breath, perhaps steadying himself. "My mother was the only child of a shoemaker. My father—an actor—was performing with his troupe at Teatro San Samuele. He caught sight of her here, sixteen and a perfect beauty, and fell in love. Nine months later, I was born."

He blew out the candle and I stood very still, listening. I could make out his black cloak, the white mask he now untied from his face. His eyes were glittering—a gambler's eyes. Taking a gamble he could be honest with me.

"I lived here until I was eight years old," he continued. "I was a pitiful child, with a disease that baffled everyone. I bled profusely from my nose. As a result, I was extremely weak. I had no appetite, was unable to apply myself to anything, and looked like an idiot."

"I do not believe it," I interjected. "That sounds nothing like you."

"All true," he insisted, keeping his usual straight face. "I was cured by a witch."

"Giacomo!" I protested, incredulous.

"Well—that part might not be true. I can't be sure. All I know is, my grandmother—whose pet I was—took me to a witch to cure me. This witch lived in a hovel on Murano. She locked me in a chest, recited spells over me, sang, wept, and thumped on the lid. I had no idea what was going on but was too stupid to be afraid. Somehow this encounter cured me. I bled less and less. Within the month, my wits improved and I finally learned to read."

"Do you think it was a miracle?" I asked, becoming excited.

"I have no belief in miracles, my angel. The greatest power God gives us is reason."

"Oh," I agreed, feeling disappointed. "Well—miracle or not, *che consolazione,* that it all ended well."

"Ah—almost," he said, taking the back of my hand to his mouth and kissing it softly. "My father died six weeks later. A sudden abscess in the brain."

"Oh, Giacomo!" I threw my arms around him. He bent his head over mine, and I kissed his cheeks. I found myself crying for him, my tears eventually mingling with his. I knew about grief, having comforted my mother.

"And your mother—was she forced to remarry?" I asked, when he had collected himself.

"My mother was left a widow at twenty-five, with six children. She had to make a living." He sounded bitter, but I couldn't tell if he was angry at her, or only the circumstances. "She became an actress and—still young and marvelously beautiful—was in high demand. Within the year, she left for Saint Petersburg, and then accepted a lifetime engagement in Dresden."

"Who raised you, then?" I asked, feeling anxious for him.

"My grandmother, Marzia. Every few years my mother would return to Venice and make a dazzling appearance, but my grandmother was the one who took care of me. She died ten years ago. And when that happened, my mother sold the house and everything in it. By then I was eighteen years old—a grown man—but I took it all quite badly. I went completely to the dogs. I wasn't ready to lose my home, and go to live in a boardinghouse."

"Good God," I said, understanding these were the misfortunes—at least some of them—Giacomo had alluded to in my father's study.

We began walking back toward the square in slow silence. Giacomo had wanted to show me his home, but it had made him pensive, and sad. I took his hand to comfort him.

After a few minutes, we passed the east end of the church of San Samuele. "And here"—Giacomo gestured broadly, becoming cheerful again—"is the site of my fine—if short-lived—career as a preacher!"

"No!" I retorted.

"Yes, my angel," he responded, making a mock blessing over me. "I was destined to be the greatest preacher of the century. Or so my mother and grandmother believed, when—at only fifteen years old, and studying ecclesiastical law in Padua—I was given the honor of delivering a sermon right here on the pulpit."

He spied a pile of empty vegetable crates outside a shuttered shop, grabbed one, set it down, and stepped on top with a flourish. It could not support his weight for more than a moment, and he quickly leapt off. I was laughing merrily: He was ridiculous.

"Unfortunately, before this most important debut, I enjoyed myself with a huge meal and lots of wine. I stood up in front of everyone in church, went blank, and—whether in fright or to save myself further humiliation—I fainted."

"Oh, my!" was all I could say, losing myself in laughter. "I could have told you myself you are not fit for an ecclesiastical career!"

"You are very intelligent, Caterina," he said. "I wish I were half as observant about myself. I wasted four more years chasing after a position in the Church. But it was not suited to my temperament."

At this, he grabbed me and pinched my behind. I pretended to slap him in outrage. He responded by catching my hand in the air and kissing my palm. Our lovemaking becoming real, he pressed me against the curved apse wall of the church. The sky had become cloudy, with only a few stars glimmering above. He deluged my neck and bosom with kisses, to which I surrendered with the sweetest moans.

"Aren't you happy you gave up the life of a priest?" I teased, pulling him even closer by the top of his breeches.

"Extremely," he breathed, pressing against me with a moaning gasp. "A man cannot change who he is."

CHAPTER 13

"Caterina—no!"

Zulietta jumped up from the turf seat where we sat in my garden the next afternoon and paced anxiously.

"Why are you upset?" I asked. "Nobody saw us!"

"How do you know?" She sat back down and started picking at the tufts of chamomile that covered the seat. The soft, thready leaves released a smell like fresh apples.

"We were seated high up," I explained again, "in the fourth tier—"

"Exactly," said Zulietta. "The fourth tier of any theater is notorious, Caterina. It is where men take their mistresses for all kinds of—of things they should not be doing. Are you so easily won?"

I shrugged my shoulders and blushed. Zulietta looked at me with disapproval.

"Cousin," I said, "please do not worry about me. Giacomo is a good match. My heart tells me that."

"I think," Zulietta said, "that other parts of your body are telling you that."

I did not know what more to say. Yes, Zulietta was older. But she had not yet discovered this sweet new world. Already that morning, I had taken a big pillow in my arms and imagined it was Giacomo, kissing it over and over. The furies of love had built to a frenzy. I had touched myself very lightly at the end, feeling a cascade of pleasure.

"Are you—jealous of me?" I asked.

Zulietta jumped up again and put her hands on her hips. She reminded me of a chiding washwoman at the well—Stop splashing the water! Stop—stop—

"I am not jealous, Caterina. I am scared for you. If you let him up your skirts, soon enough, no better man will want to have you."

"There is no better man for me!" I insisted.

"I do not trust him," Zulietta said. "He has no profession. What is he after? An innocent girl—and her sizable dowry? Ten thousand *zecchini* is a lot of money."

"He does not need money," I shot back. "Can you not believe he would love me without it?" I was shaking with hurt, and sudden doubt.

Zulietta fell silent. She came over and put her arm around me. "I'm sorry," she whispered in my ear. "Of course I do."

Reassured, I laid my head on her shoulder. "Are you starting to wonder . . ." I asked her, "what man your father will choose for you?" I wanted to make peace between us.

"I am." Her voice sounded faraway. "He tells me he has something clever in mind. Maybe"—she paused—"a nobleman."

"How is that possible?" I lifted my head in surprise. Yes, Zulietta was very wealthy. Her father was a merchant, like mine. He dealt in exotic silks and spices. Still, ours were not noble families. And nobles only married other nobles.

"I don't understand it, either," she said. "He tells me there is an official process that makes it possible for a very few. You apply to the magistrates of the *Avogaria di Comun,* and make the case that you are worthy of a prestigious marriage. The doge must approve it." She cast down her eyes. Zulietta was modest, but her father was always grasping. He wanted his only child to have everything.

"*Bene*—" I said, "if anyone is worthy of making such a marriage, you are!" I meant it sincerely. She was not a great beauty, but she possessed the manners and grace of someone higher born.

We heard the bells of San Gregorio start to clang nearby.

"Are you going to Mass?" she asked me.

"Oh—I went this morning with my mother." It was a small lie. I did not feel like going to church.

"Of course," she said, rising. "How late I am!"

We walked arm in arm across the crushed shell path toward the main door of the garden. On our way, I glanced at the back door and spied a folded piece of paper waiting for me in the same place where Giacomo had left me the poem. I hurriedly said goodbye to Zulietta, my heart jumping. I ran across the lawn and plucked my secret message from the blooming vines.

Beautiful Caterina, you move the sun and other stars for me.

I stopped and stared up at the blue midday sky. By now, I knew that the sun did not move. But it made the words even better. *I* was the one who moved the heavens for my lover, the sun and all the stars.

CHAPTER 14

I decided to pawn some jewelry. If I wanted to see Giacomo alone again, I needed money. I didn't want him to have to empty his pockets each time he wanted to see me—and Pier Antonio would not help us unless he got something in return. After all, he was chronically in debt. He had recently been denounced for bad credit in one of the Lion's Mouths at the doge's palace. These are special wall slots Venetians use to report wrongdoings.

I owned quite a lot of jewelry because my father often brought me gifts from faraway ports. I kept these trinkets in an ivory box by my bed, the same one where I keep . . . other precious things now. I was very young when my father gave me the box and told me it was made from a real elephant in the land of Africa. I have always treasured it.

I opened the box and fingered the jewels inside, finding forgotten things. Ornate cuff bracelets, gemstone rings I never wore. But I began to feel uneasy. If I pawned these gifts from my father, would I invite the Evil Eye on myself? Closing the box, I went over to my dressing table mirror. Inside one of its drawers, I kept a pile of fans.

I rummaged through the pile, opening each fan. Some had rips or stains or broken handles. But I already knew in my heart the one I was going to sell. It had once belonged to my grandmother—my father's mother. I had never known her.

It was a magnificent fan, this one. Not parchment, but silk. I had been told it came from Russia. The handles were mother-of-pearl, inlaid with tiny crushed diamonds. Its painting was very fine, too, showing pairs of lovers in a garden. How happy they looked! I wanted to be just like them. Alone with my lover under a leafy tree, my cheeks turning pink as he whispered secrets in my ear.

I folded the fan and dropped it into the pocket beneath my skirts. I rushed to find a pair of flat leather slippers, so that I could move about quickly. I needed to hurry, before my mother discovered I was gone.

I slipped out our land door and ran toward the church of the Salute at the tip of the city to hail a gondola. I found several boats gathered there, waiting for passengers. I stepped into one, hid in the cabin, and drew the shutters closed. The Jewish *ghetto* was where you went to pawn things, every Venetian knew that.

It was a long ride north, about a half hour. The boat finally docked near a hinged wooden bridge. I'd heard about this bridge—used to shut in the Jews at night. It lay open now in the sunlight, guarded by a watchman peering down from a small square window. I walked across this bridge and down into a narrow passageway. Rats scurried near the dark, damp walls. I shuddered and hurried through as fast as I could.

I found myself in a large public square surrounded by tall, crumbling buildings. There was no church, as in every other square I knew. And where were the synagogues? I saw no sign of them, though I'd heard they were set high up, to be near the sky and stars.

I saw dark-skinned Jews in turbans, Jews in high black hats,

Jews (or were they Christians?) in fashionable tricorn hats. A man dressed in rags was selling dented pots out of a basket as if these were his last worldly goods. Under the arcades, women darned old clothes in the shade. Pawnshops lined the square on every side, and I noticed a pharmacy, as well, the *Casa degli Speziali*. Next door was a pawnshop that appeared to have the finest things for sale. I made my way there.

The sign over the door read *Vivante* in gold. When I entered, the place smelled like old books, and dust. A girl no older than I was stood behind the counter.

"Oh—*scusì*—do you—" I lost my courage.

"*Buon giorno, Signorina.* Is there something you wish to buy?" She was an exquisite girl, small in stature, with brown wavy hair and almond-shaped eyes.

"To sell," I said. I took out the fan and opened it up for her.

"Oh—how beautiful!" She picked it up and pretended to fan herself like a *nobildonna*. We both giggled.

"Papa!" she called out. A bearded Jew came out from a back room. He was small, like his daughter. He held a soiled rag and his fingers were black from tarnish.

"See this fan that the *signorina* has brought to us!"

He put out his hand to inspect it, but the girl held it back. It was too precious to be touched by dirty hands; she knew that.

He realized it, too, and smiled at her.

"Elia, hold it open for me then." His eyes brightened at the sight of the diamonds. "Ah." He stroked his beard with his black fingers. "Did you want a loan for it, or to sell it?"

I was confused. I had never pawned anything before, and didn't understand the choice he was giving me.

"I can give you one hundred silver *zecchini* as a loan," he explained. "This way, when you are ready to repay me—with a little interest, not much—you can have your fan back."

"And if I sell it?"

"One hundred fifty *zecchini*."

"I will sell it," I said without hesitation.

What did I care if I ever got the fan back again? I just wanted to leave that rat-filled *ghetto* with as much money as possible. And I hoped I would not have to come back anytime soon.

CHAPTER 15

"That's it?" my brother said when I handed him the silver coins. "Five *zecchini?*"

"By God, how much more do I have to give you?" I snapped. "All I want is a copy of your key so I can let myself back in."

"Seven *zecchini,*" he said. "I also have to lie about where I'm taking you. What if I am discovered?" He put a hand to his heart and batted his eyes at me, innocently. My blood burned.

"Fine. Seven. Now, I want that key." Ahead of me I saw an entire night alone with my lover, and nothing was going to stand in my way.

Pier Antonio told my mother we were going to a choir concert at the famous Pietà orphanage, in the neighborhood of Castello. But instead, he would take me across the lagoon to the garden of San Biagio, on Giudecca.

Many times before, I had walked along the edge of the city on my mother's arm, or holding her hand, and stared out to this long, green island across the water. I had often wondered, what secrets hid behind those high garden walls? What lay at the feet of the tall cypress trees, waving in the wind? I was about to find out.

We left our house a few hours after *pranzo*, the day still hot. I was quite satisfied with my choice of dress: a yellow silk gown with painted flowers on it, to capture the look of a bright garden. I tried to ignore Pier Antonio as much as possible in the boat—he was busy cleaning his teeth and fingernails with a toothpick. Nauseating.

The lagoon current was against us. By the time we neared the tip of Giudecca, almost an hour later, our gondolier's white shirt was drenched with sweat.

My heart soared when I spied Giacomo, waiting for me. He was leaning against a stone statue next to a wide iron entrance gate. The sun was lower now, creating deep shadows across the pavement. As we got closer, I could see that the statue was of Pan, the Roman god of desire. And, true enough, Giacomo had attracted desiring company, a mother and golden-haired daughter, busy fanning and fawning.

I felt a sting of jealousy. Oh, it was the first of many times. But, seeing me approaching, he gave them a quick bow and went down to the mooring poles to meet us.

"Here she is, delivered with her seal unbroken!" called out my brother as our gondola bumped into place. I flushed, feeling suddenly very warm. I yearned to loosen the ribbons of my bodice, but after that comment, how could I?

Giacomo regarded Pier Antonio with disdain and lifted me out of the boat. He put his arm around my waist and led me away. He did not even acknowledge my brother.

"I don't know how I restrain myself from cutting his throat," he hissed in my ear as we walked to the gate. I could not get any words out. Instead, I held on to his arm tightly. He wore no jacket or waistcoat that day, and beneath his linen shirt I was aware of his muscular strength for the first time. I felt safe.

Once inside the garden, I forgot immediately about my bad mood, and my rotten brother. I had never seen—or imagined—such a large and beautiful place! Wide brick paths were flanked by tall evergreen hedges. Hidden behind these were hundreds of beds of roses, a sea of pinks and yellows.

We wandered down the central path, which was intersected by gushing fountains—a rarity in Venice. Along the way, inspired by the roses, I presumed, Giacomo began to sing a verse about the rose, and desire. It sounded old-fashioned to me, which made it all the more amusing as his voice rose:

Queen Venus's ardent torch does fire
The Lover's bosom with desire
So fervid that he dares the Rose
To kiss, in faith 'twill heal his woes.

Each time he reached the words *To kiss,* he would lean in and kiss my temple or cheek, until I was giggling and singing along. Strolling couples coming the other way smiled and blew kisses to us as they passed by.

Finally, we reached the edge of the garden facing the open lagoon, the air salty and fresh. The day was closing, the sun still strong but getting ready to descend into the water. Giacomo led me to a bench shaded by an arbor covered with sweet jasmine.

He sat down and pulled me onto his lap. I nuzzled his warm, powerful neck and laid my head on his chest, delighting in hearing his beating heart beneath my ear. He was one of those people you can't ever imagine growing old, or even dying. They are forever strong, sensual, and vital.

"I have some presents for you, my angel," he said, reaching into a pocket of his breeches and pulling out a pair of ribbon garters. They were pink silk with a French verse embroidered across them, in red.

I dripped the smooth ribbons over my fingers, marveling at their luxury. I remembered the plain white garters I was wearing and could not wait to replace them with these finer French ones.

"What do the words mean?" I asked Giacomo.

"Imagine the garters are speaking," he explained, fingering them as if they were fond companions. "They say, '*In seeing every day the jewel of Caterina's beauty, Tell it that Love bids it be true.*'"

"Oh—" I stammered, blushing furiously. I imagined a set of spying eyes up my skirts. "I will—go put them on!" I sprang off his lap and hid behind a nearby hedge. I untied my old garters and threw them in the dirt.

Giacomo followed, peeking behind the dense wall of leaves. "You ran away before I could give you your second gift," he called. He came and knelt close by me in the grass and began to gently pull off my stockings. From his other pocket he produced a pair of new pearl-gray stockings, more finely spun than any I had ever seen. These, he rolled slowly onto my feet, over my ankles, my calves, my thighs. He began to shake, almost violently.

"Why do you tremble?" I asked, reaching to touch his cheek. This was always my favorite part of his face: sculpted so finely by God.

"My desire makes me lose control," he said, tying the garters above my knees and kissing a soft circle around them.

I melted back onto the grass with my skirts still partly up and he climbed over me. Our desire felt like something alive between us—too strong for me to resist. I ran my fingers through his hair, and he kissed my neck and bare shoulders.

"Come," he whispered, his lips suspended just over mine. "Let's find the *casino* I have rented for us. The sun is almost down."

I obeyed, grateful—once I had come to my senses—he had

the strength of mind to exert control over us. I sat up and re-arranged my skirts. Giacomo clasped both my hands and helped me up off the grass.

We came out from behind the tall hedges. The other couples I had seen before in the garden had all vanished. The sky had turned dark blue-gray, and the hedges loomed in the coming night. I turned back to watch the last sliver of the orange sun lowering, still burning, into the water.

Giacomo reached for my hand. I gave it willingly. I felt I was about to change the course of my life—and I was ready.

CHAPTER 16

Our *casino* sat by the water's edge. I'd heard about these little pleasure houses found all around Venice—but never been inside one, of course. This one was built in the Roman style, with a deep porch and four slender marble columns framing the entryway. An old servant woman greeted us and told us to call her when we wanted supper. But food was the last thing on our minds! Giacomo pulled me up the well-worn stone stairs. My excited laughter echoed all around us.

We stepped into a cozy room that was furnished with a rustic table and two chairs, and a bed laid out with clean linen sheets. Giacomo picked up where we had left off in the garden, pushing me toward the bed with hungry kisses.

But so fast! Suddenly, I was a dove in the talons of a hawk.

"I beg you!" I cried out, pulling myself away. "You kiss me as if you will hurt me!"

"Forgive me!" He dropped to his knees, looking anguished. "You are young—I know—and I forgot myself—"

I took pity on him and timidly offered my hand. He pressed his palm against mine. We intertwined our fingers.

Stealthily, with his other hand, he reached beneath my skirts to fondle my ribbon garters. He pressed his body against mine, whispering, "Please." By God, I was in danger of losing all reason! Still, from somewhere deep in my mind, Zulietta's warning words came back to me. *"Are you so easily won?"*

I pulled his hand away.

"Now, my love," I teased him gently, "you know that my jewel is only for my husband."

"As one day I shall be!" he said, lifting my skirts again and kissing the very jewel I had just said he could not have.

"But no—" I took a few steps back and sat down on the bed. All of a sudden, from some deep well I did not know I had, I started to cry.

"My angel!" He came and knelt before me again, taking my hands and trying to undo the violence of his initial approach. "I disgust myself that I have made you cry."

"No—no," I comforted him, cupping his beloved face in my hands. "It is nothing you have done. It's—it's my father. He has plans to marry me to a merchant—and all I want is for *you* to be my husband."

There. I'd said it. The truth had come out. I hadn't even quite known it myself until I said the words.

The room became silent, and Giacomo very still. Finally, he spoke.

"I've known about your father's plans all along." He sighed deeply. "Pier Antonio told me, soon after I met you. I knew I should stay away—there was no way to win. Tell you I love you, and be kicked aside by your father. Try to steal your love, and ruin you. You have wisely stopped us from going any further."

He stood up and began smoothing his wrinkled shirt. The top button of his breeches had come undone. Had I done that?

"Giacomo—no!" I begged. Why follow all the stupid rules, when they were clearly making me miserable? "We should—we can make ourselves happy. There must be a way. What stops us?" *Fear,* my mind called out, my heart beating wildly.

He approached the bed and sat back down beside me. I turned to face him, my eyes searching his. He looked into mine as if he could never have enough of seeing me.

"My angel," he said, taking my hand and bathing it in kisses. "Are you sure that I love you? Do you trust me never to fail you?"

"I am certain of it." I pushed away any memory of the sting I'd felt when I saw that mother and daughter circling him by the garden gate. "You are my one true happiness."

"Then let us marry here tonight," he declared. "We don't need any documents or witnesses except God to pledge our faith and unite our destinies. Later, we can do all of this publicly in a church ceremony—but here and now, we can make ourselves happy."

I was turned upside down. I could hardly breathe. His words were everything that I secretly wanted. Only one part did not feel quite right. At least not yet.

"I have sometimes wondered," I questioned him, "whether— given your opinions about religion—you are an atheist. Now you say that God is the only witness we need for our marriage vows. Am I to believe you?"

He nodded and laughed out loud, as if pleased to find himself cornered by me. "You are clever, Caterina—there's no denying that. I have often been accused of being an atheist, but I'm far from it. I am simply a freethinker. I have no faith in the institutions of religion, but I have faith in God Himself." His voice became as soothing as water over rock, and his glittering eyes locked with mine. "My angel, I believe we can have no more worthy witness to our marriage vows than our Creator, who knows our intentions are pure."

I forced myself to look away and reflect on his words. What he said made some sense to me. I had never considered the Church apart from God. But now, as I gazed around me, the holiness of the very room we were in became visible. The early dark, when no candles had been lit. The soft shadows that fell over everything, including ourselves. I knew in that moment that we were safe together in God's love.

I turned and pressed my upright palm against Giacomo's, to signal I was ready. And I began in a low voice that gained strength as I spoke: "Giacomo Casanova . . . I promise God and you . . . that from this moment until death I will be your faithful wife, and that I will say the same to—to my father, to the priest who will bless us in the Church, and to the whole world."

He smiled, his face deeply flushed. It struck me he looked happier than I'd ever seen him. And he repeated the same vow to me: "Caterina Capreta, I promise God and you that from this moment until death I will be your faithful husband, and that I will say the same to your father, to the priest who will bless us in the Church, and to the whole world."

We gazed at each other . . . for how long? Long enough that I will never forget the feeling. Being so entirely desired, and desiring him to oblivion. And then we embraced—happy, laughing, and ecstatic at what we had done.

Did I become a real wife in this moment? In my heart, yes— I did.

"And now, to complete our marriage ceremony—" Giacomo said, pushing me down on the bed and eagerly untying the silk ribbons of my bodice. He loosened my chemise and covered my exposed bosom with kisses.

"Does a husband not undress, as well?" I asked, obeying the promptings of instinct and starting on the buttons of his breeches. He helped me undress him in less than a minute.

"My nightingale—it is sighing for you." He guided my hand to show me the place where he deserved mercy, and moved his fingers between my legs. I surrendered to the most supreme degree of pleasure that ever seized my senses.

"Is it true you really belong to me?" I cried, clasping him to me, more completely happy than I had ever been in my life.

"Yes, my divine angel," he assured me, "and what we are about to do will make our love immortal."

He reached for something out of the night table drawer. With a trembling hand, he rolled on a thin skin sheath. I had never seen one before.

"What is it?" I asked, struggling up and alarmed.

"To protect you, my angel." I had little idea what he meant, but lay back with complete trust in him.

We fit our bodies together. I felt sudden, disappointing pain. Tears filled my eyes.

"Hymen only hurts the first time," he reassured me. He covered my face with kisses. More tender now, less urgent. I learned that night the tongue has powers far beyond speech!

We made love for hours. By early dawn, when I left him, standing in the pink-gray light outside my house in Venice, I had become another person.

CHAPTER 17

"Are you mad at me?" I asked Zulietta the next day.

I had told her everything, whispering the last part in her ear. My face was as hot as a furnace. I tried to appear serious, but kept smiling.

"No—I'm not mad at you." But her rosy mouth tightened as she folded a stack of dresses.

We were in her bedroom packing her traveling chest. Her family had rented a villa in Asolo for the summer. I had been so lost in my own affairs that I had nearly forgotten the date of her departure. I kept that guilty secret to myself.

"In fact," Zulietta continued with a forced smile, "I am happy for you."

"Do you mean that?"

"I do." She nodded, as if still busy convincing herself. "You and Signor Casanova . . ."

"Giacomo," I said, smiling even more.

"Yes—Giacomo. You and Giacomo have taken vows before God to be husband and wife. You . . . are husband and wife."

"You already said that."

"Oh." She stood stock-still, searching for more words. She sat down on the bed. I sensed a storm coming.

"Caterina—" she burst out. "How can I leave you in the grips of this man? What will you do while I am gone?" She began to cry. "I've let this happen—indulging you—"

"No!" I threw my arms around her. "I am so happy, Zulietta. Please be happy for me. I know what I am doing."

"Oh, Caterina," she said. "I only wish that were true. Promise me that one day you really will be married in front of a priest—and your father?"

"Of course! Very soon."

"And promise me," she said in a halting voice, "that until then, Giacomo will wear his . . . sheaths? You are too young to risk becoming pregnant."

"I will." I meant it sincerely. I wanted to be a wife, not a mother.

She nodded and stood up, smoothing her skirts. "I am sure he loves you," she offered, quietly. She gave me an affectionate smile, but fear was written in it.

I was not sure if she believed her own words. But I knew she wanted me to believe them, to tell me I was loved.

It was a relief to have told Zulietta everything. Things only felt true and real in my life when I shared them with her. She was my anchor. But with her leaving me now—honestly, I was not at all sure where I was going to end up.

CHAPTER 18

Venice, 1774

"*B*ene, Caterina," Leda whispered at the dining table where they had been talking well into the night, "you were a wife."

Caterina noticed this was the first time the girl had used her name. The intimacy made her realize she had probably said too much. She lit a candle between them, to break the spell of the past.

"You know I am a wife," she said, intentionally misreading what Leda had meant.

"But a real wife," Leda persisted. "Like your Giacomo said. No church, no contract, no family. Only your lover, who loves you."

Caterina noticed she spoke as if that love was somehow still alive. Maybe it was—for Leda.

"Let's get back to your story," Caterina said, wanting to change the subject. She had taken this girl into her confidence; in fairness, Leda should do the same. "You were at your father's party and Filippo played the harpsichord. He was alone. Your heart went out to him . . ."

"Oh—" Leda was happily reminded. "Filippo and I started

talking, talking at the party. All the time he was undressing me with his eyes. I could feel what he wanted. I knew it like a cat licks her kittens." She gave Caterina a mischievous smile. "We slipped outside while no one was looking. At least I don't think we were seen—who knows? I didn't care, just as you didn't care in your opera box. It was a winter night, but warm. We fell onto the ground in the garden. I gave myself to him all at once— by the shrubs, lit by the lanterns. When we got back to the party, I could still feel the heat of his body on me, my legs dripping."

Caterina was fairly shocked by this behavior. Leda was all impulse and little reason. But who was she to judge?

"We were able to meet many times after, at his lodgings," Leda chatted on. "I told my father I went out for music lessons— which was partly true, because Filippo would always play the harpsichord and sing for me."

> *Queen Venus's ardent torch does fire*
> *The Lover's bosom with desire*
> *So fervid, that he dares the Rose*
> *To kiss, in faith 'twill heal his woes.*

Caterina's mind played the memory of its own song. She had the feeling it might play all night for her now.

"I was pregnant in a month," Leda announced, which startled Caterina back to reality. "I thought it took longer!"

"No," Caterina said quietly, blowing out the candle to signal it was time for bed. "It can all happen . . . very fast."

CHAPTER 19

April 23. Caterina had been waiting for this day. She went to fetch Leda from her bedroom, as it was getting late. She could hear women greeting passersby from open windows—*S'ciao bella!*—newspaper sellers calling out—*Gazzetta Veneta! Osservatore!*—and cries of "*Oe! Gondola!*" as boatmen navigated the crowded waterways. All Venice was coming alive, and she didn't want to miss it.

"You're still in bed?" Caterina asked, disappointed to find Leda awake, but wrapped in a cocoon of sheets and blankets. She threw open the shutters, and bright sunlight poured in.

"I think . . . I will skip church today," Leda said, turning her head to hug her pillow. They had been attending morning Mass at San Gregorio just about every day. Caterina had grown to like the routine very much. Sitting in the hard chairs, with a new friend close by.

"Come," she urged. "I've planned a small surprise."

"I'm really not in the mood. I'm sorry."

"I understand that you're not." Leda looked at her, puzzled. "Just come," Caterina urged again, walking over to the chest of drawers and picking up Leda's velvet and gold pendant choker. She dangled it gently over her fingers and brought it near the bed. Leda sat up, and Caterina attached the clasp around her neck.

Armed with her courage, Leda got up.

They arrived in Campo San Gregorio, where parishioners were starting to gather for the service. Leda was still not saying much, her arms folded around herself. Distractedly, she walked up to the black wood church doors. Only when she looked back did she stop and see Caterina had not followed.

"We're not going in today," Caterina called from near the wellhead at the center of the square. "Follow me."

Now Leda became interested.

"Where are we going, then?" she asked, coming back.

Caterina smiled mysteriously and guided them down a narrow street, whose buildings seemed to grow tighter and tighter as they walked. At the end, they burst into Campo della Salute, at the tip of the island.

"Here?" Leda asked, still confused.

"One more stop," said Caterina, lifting her arm to hail a gondola. The gondolier helped them both into the boat. After about two minutes rocking across the water, they arrived.

"Why are we hopping from church to church today?" asked Leda, staring at the white marble exterior of the second church they had visited in less than ten minutes. "Are we hiding from someone? God?" she teased, smiling for the first time all morning.

Caterina took her hand and led her up the steps. This church was built in the Roman style, with four thick columns mounted on bases and not one, but two superimposed pediments. It looked very different from most of the churches in Venice—especially Caterina's beloved San Gregorio, a confection of warm bricks and pink and white marble. This one was ordered, almost severe.

The bronze doors were sealed shut and Caterina rang the bell. Leda looked at her, furrowing her brow and pretending to be about to run back down the steps.

A black-cowled monk opened the door. He was lean, about fifty years old, with a beaked nose and sharp eyes.

"Signora Marsigli," he greeted Caterina, bowing slightly. "*Ecco la signorina,*" he said, turning to Leda. She looked surprised he knew who she was. The monk gestured them inside.

Caterina was awed at the sight of the church interior once again, its clear light flooding in from two stories of semicircular windows. Massive gray stone piers rose up, framing white walls uncluttered by any art. The space, she felt sure, was filled by God's pure glory as much as any other place on earth.

"Leda"—Caterina turned to her to explain—"as you know, today is the Feast Day of Saint George—your mother's saint day." Leda nodded, bringing her fingers to her pendant. "I asked the good *Frate* for a favor—permission to bring you to this special place dedicated to her saint. I know how much you miss your mother. Perhaps you would like to pray to her here."

Leda gave Caterina a sad but grateful smile. She wiped her fingers under her eyes.

"*Grazie,*" she managed to say.

The monk led them silently up a dark, snail-shaped staircase.

"*Ecco,*" he said, unlocking the door of a large upstairs room. It was as brightly lit as the church below. Along three walls were carved dark wood choir stalls—a chapel, also a meeting room, perhaps. Over the altar at the head of the room, lit by a few candles, was a painting of a knight charging a winged dragon. Clad in shining armor and sitting astride a galloping horse, he pierced the dragon with a long lance to its throat. Blood poured from its mouth and down its haunches. Leda gave a little gasp, immediately recognizing triumphant Saint George, and approached the painting.

"*Bene.*" The monk nodded and closed the door behind him.

Leda dropped to her knees on the marble platform before the altar, crossed herself, and buried her head deep in her hands. Caterina watched her for a few minutes, saw her shoulders moving up and down softly. But she resisted going closer. This was Leda's day—time with her real mother, Georgiana.

"Caterina." Leda finally looked up, her face wet with tears.

"Yes, sweetheart," Caterina answered, not knowing where the endearment came from. It just slipped out.

"Will you come light a candle with me?"

"Of course." Caterina approached. Together, both kneeling, they held a golden candle at its base and lit its wick in a burning flame.

"*Coraggio,*" said Leda, setting it back into its holder. Caterina noticed now how the painting took on an eerie glow in the increased candlelight. She could see several dismembered body parts—the dragon's victims—littered in the desert landscape of the foreground.

"Shall we go back to San Gregorio?" she asked, helping Leda up before the girl could look any closer at the unnerving painting. "Perhaps we can still get to Mass on time."

"No," said Leda, surprisingly lighter in mood. She took Caterina's arm as they exited the secret room. Down the snail-shaped staircase—*Mille grazie!*—to the monk at the doors, outside onto the glistening marble steps. The sun reflecting off the water greeted them warmly. "Such a beautiful day!" Leda exclaimed.

"Shall we just walk, then?" Caterina offered.

"Walk—and talk," Leda said, with a sideways glance at her. "I want to know . . . why are you Signora Marsigli, and not Signora Casanova?"

"Oh!" said Caterina, surprised. And strangely pleased. *Signora Casanova.* How she had wished. How they had tried.

CHAPTER 20

Venice, 1753

It is an odd feeling when someone you ought to love by blood—but do not love that much—goes away. You miss them in a sharp, shallow way. So it was with my brother. He was arrested one morning soon after I had taken my secret marriage vows.

The pounding came at our waterside door at daybreak. My mother was the first one downstairs. I followed close behind, standing at the top of the steps in my nightgown. When she opened the door, about fifteen policemen flooded in. It is well-known in Venice that ridiculous numbers of police are used for any arrest—which is amusing, since most Venetians are cowards. Certainly, my brother was. He let my mother handle the situation, while he hid in the rooms above us. I could hear Amor barking wildly across the whole house.

"*Buon giorno—Signora Capreta?*" the chief officer said.

"*Sì,*" my mother answered. Her face had the pallor of marble dust.

"Is your son Pier Antonio Capreta? Does he live here with you?"

"*Sì—non*. Only sometimes. He is—I do not know if he is here now." She glanced up at me, terrified.

"Signora Capreta, we are here to arrest your son for nonpayment of debts." He waved a pile of promissory notes in the air.

"Oh—that is not possible," my mother insisted. "I gave him money to pay his creditors just last week. His accounts are settled." Lord, she would have given him her last pair of shoes if he had asked. "Pier Antonio can explain all of this to you."

"Good. Then he is at home." The officer managed to outwit my mother quickly enough. He motioned for some officers to go to our land doors to prevent any escape. Others pushed past me and inside to the main floor of the house. Doors banged until they found him in the area of my bedroom. I would find out soon enough that he had taken all the money I had gotten by selling the fan.

They brought him downstairs, still in his dressing gown. My mother cried at the sight of him. I turned away.

"Signora, he will be in the New Prisons," the same officer reassured her. She heaved her relief. At least he would not be in the Wells of the Doge's Palace, where everyone knew stinking lagoon water lapped all around the prisoners. Or in the Leads above, with its sweltering lead roof. The New Prisons had been built in another building, reached by a high stone bridge. The cells all faced a central courtyard that offered fresh air and light.

"You can bring him furniture and a few necessary things later today," the officer said, continuing to try to calm her. But her crying told me she wasn't taking anything in.

"Caterina!" I heard my brother's voice yell up to me. "Send me a bed, shirts, stockings, slippers, razors . . ."

"No razors! They are not allowed!" The officers pushed him toward the open door to the canal.

". . . handkerchiefs, combs, a mirror . . ."

His list was still echoing up to me as a gondola took him away.

CHAPTER 21

The truth was, Pier Antonio's arrest was good news for me. Suddenly his room was empty and I could use it for myself. It was located in a corner on the top floor of the house. He had chosen this room for himself, and now I saw the wisdom in it. It lay well away from the ears of my mother and father.

My father. I knew he would start for home any day, once he got news from my mother about my brother's arrest. I had to act quickly. I could risk sneaking Giacomo into Pier Antonio's room with just my mother at home—but not my father. I did not dare.

I sent Giacomo a message. Our washing girl delivered it for me. I told him to come at midnight, when I was fairly sure my mother would be asleep. Still, we had to be careful. She was a poor sleeper, especially in the days after my brother's arrest, when she would wander the house at strange hours and drop off to sleep on the sofas.

As dusk descended over the city, I took a bath scented with jasmine oil and sprinkled more on a clean linen chemise, trimmed with needle lace. I combed and curled my hair. Powder and rouge were out of the question. If my mother came in to say good night, it would look too suspicious.

To pass the time, I reread Zulietta's first letter from Asolo to me, which had arrived that morning. She was terribly excited to tell me that her father had arranged for her to meet Giorgio Contarini, eldest son of one of the oldest noble families in Venice, in just a few days. He was staying at a nearby villa on the mainland near Vicenza.

> *The Contarini are rich in houses and villas, I'm*
> *sure, but they probably don't have enough money*
> *to live the lavish lifestyle they require. A match*
> *with my family solves this problem. I'm not fooling*
> *myself that our union would be based on much*
> *more than this, but still, I am confident love*
> *between us could grow richly in time.*

I folded the letter back into its envelope, shaking my head. Oh, I did not agree! Love did not grow slowly in time . . . love seized your senses immediately. What you wanted, what was right for you—these two were surely the same, and your heart led you strongly to it. No one else could find love for you. Certainly not a clueless father.

Once the stars rose high, I slipped downstairs to unlatch the land door for Giacomo. Of course, I trotted to the back garden door to see if he had left me any secret message. He had. It was written on a single sheet, pushed into the crack of the wood. The paper was curled, as if it had once been wet.

> *My beautiful angel, C.—*
> *I am in ecstasy with the sweet pleasure of wait-*
> *ing for you! I have eaten nothing today but a salad*
> *dressed with vinegar and the whites of six fresh*
> *eggs. Why eggs? So you can collect the whites from*

me in your hand tonight. Oh . . . thinking of your
delicate hand relieving me . . . I cannot resist . . .
one white I have just collected into my own impa-
tient hand. I rub it here as proof of my immortal
love for you!

I held the crinkled note in my hands, astounded by his desire smeared at the bottom of the page. It made me long to be filled with all of him, to be possessed and to possess him entirely.

CHAPTER 22

The first of his egg whites that night I did collect in my hand. But for the next ones to come, I had new and different ideas.

We lay in my brother's bed, calmed from the initial furies of love. Even though Pier Antonio was gone, the room still smelled of bad wine. Drafts of his worthless contracts lay in piles on the desk and on several chairs. But no matter to us. Our love made the place the happiest one on earth.

"Giacomo—my husband," I said, lighting a candle on the nightstand, "I want to ask . . . will you do something for me?"

"Anything. I have four egg whites left." His tone was light, and teasing.

"I only need one." I did not know how he would react to my surprising request, and so I buried my face in his chest, which was loosely covered by his unbuttoned linen shirt.

"What is it you need from me?" he asked. I felt his heartbeat quicken against my cheek before I raised my head.

"I want you to make me pregnant," I declared. A hot blush spread across my face, but I tried to appear sure of myself by steadily holding his stare.

He sat up against the pillows and let out a deep exhale. "Caterina, do you think that is wise?"

"Wise?" I repeated, sitting up, as well, and covering myself with a sheet. Was anything I had done since I met him *wise*?

"Well, think of it," I urged. What had begun as a deep longing—a desire to give him something, to create something together—did, in fact, make some sense as a plan. "If my father refuses to let me marry you, saying I am too young, or you are not a rich merchant, he will surely change his mind when he sees me with a big belly!"

Giacomo laughed out loud. "I can only imagine his reaction when he learns his son is in prison and his daughter has a child on the way. He will be dragging us to the priest."

"True!" I cried out, giggling and elated. "I am a genius."

"Yes—you are. A beautiful, irresistible genius." His voice was full of admiration. "But, Caterina—are you sure you want to do this?"

"I am," I said, without hesitating. Any caution I ever had fell away as I dreamed of the child I wanted to bring into the world. A son—whose dark, joy-filled eyes would tell all Venice of our union.

Giacomo put his hands behind his head and regarded me closely. His black, lively eyes gleamed in the candlelight.

"Do you imagine . . ." he asked after a while, "that your father will give us your dowry money? Is it possible he would withhold it to be vengeful?"

"Of course he will give it to us!" I promised, having no idea what my father might actually do. And I wondered, my mind racing, how important is my money to you? Is this what Zulietta had warned me about? *What is he after? An innocent girl—and her sizable dowry?*

"Money is not important to me," I said, watching his face.

"Ah," he said, chuckling without any humor. "Only the rich have the luxury of saying that."

"Giacomo!" I burst out, hurt he was dividing us. I waited for him to explain himself.

"No matter, my angel," he said, quickly assuaging my troubled mind. He took both my hands and kissed them softly, one, then the other. "I promise to provide you—and our child— with every comfort we shall ever need."

I smiled and embraced him. I buried the panic I had briefly felt over the dowry. Talking about money, and my father, made me feel as if he was in the room with us. And I did not want him there.

"Do you understand," Giacomo asked me now, changing the uncomfortable subject between us, "that your becoming a mother may take some weeks or even months to accomplish?"

"What do you mean?" My surprised pleasure at hearing myself called a "mother" for the first time was followed by immediate confusion. "Without your sheath to protect me—won't I become pregnant tonight?"

He laughed gently, tracing each of my dimples with his thumb. "No, it can take many acts for this miracle to happen." He pulled me down to kiss him.

"All the better," I said, returning his kiss.

He leaned to snuff out the candle. I moved to sit astride him, a novel position. Where had I gotten this idea? Oh yes—my brother's mistress at the tavern. I had not forgotten.

CHAPTER 23

One night, lying in his arms in our secret room, I asked him, "Giacomo, has there ever been anyone else you called your wife before me?"

I felt his arm muscles tighten beneath me before he spoke. "Why do you ask, my angel? Are you becoming jealous?"

"No—no!" I insisted. Actually, I was lying to him, for the first time. "I only want to know," I continued, creeping again toward the information I badly wanted, "have you ever loved anyone else enough to ask her to be your wife?"

"Caterina," he said, his voice sounding tense as he adjusted himself to sit upright on the pillows, "I make it a rule never to speak to one lover about another. Each is perfect in herself, and brings me complete happiness in the time we are together."

He reached for his watch on the night table, noted the time, and started to get dressed. As he was pulling on his black stockings, I slid behind him, my arms around his back.

"But, my husband," I said, my voice playful, kissing his neck, his ear, "you have not answered my question."

"Caterina," he replied, unable to resist smiling, "am I to be a fool and break my own rule for you?"

"Of course you are," I teased, taking his hand and pulling him back onto the bed. "Tell me . . . about her."

He sighed deeply, surrendering to me. "There has only been one other I have ever loved—almost"—he caught himself—"as much as you. Her name was Henriette. I lived with her for a short time in Parma. She was French, and had run away from her husband. Henriette charmed me with her gentle nature, and when she played the cello for me—as she did every day—the human voice of that passionate instrument captured my heart." His voice trailed off, as if he were still hearing her play.

"Go on," I prompted, though his words were as painful to me as knives would have been.

"It was necessary to keep Henriette hidden—no one could know who she was. But after a few months, we were tempted to go to a concert at a Frenchman's house in Parma. On a whim, Henriette took the cello between her knees and played for everyone. The applause for her deafened the orchestra." He paused, looked at me with a wistful smile. "Do you know, I was so overcome with her talent that night, I wept in the garden?"

I was startled to see his eyes were shining with tears.

"After that, we grew reckless. In the end, she was recognized by a count—Count d'Antoine"—Giacomo practically spat out his name—"at another party outside Parma. He forced her to return to her husband in France." He stared at the wall, lost in the past. "I traveled with her as far as Geneva and—miserable—said good-bye."

"You never saw her again?" I pressed.

"No." Giacomo turned back to look at me. His face was slack. "At the time, I told myself our separation would be brief. But she knew better. When I got back to our room at the inn in Geneva, I found a message from her etched into one of the window-panes. She must have used the point of her diamond ring. It read: *You will forget Henriette, too.*"

"And—have you?" I asked, my voice strangled.

"The wound has healed with time, as is only natural. Still—
you see I have not forgotten her." He changed course then,
melting my anxiety with a disarming smile. "To answer your
question, my curious angel. I never called Henriette my wife.
You are my only one."

He pulled me onto his lap and covered me in kisses, whispering into my ear, "*Je suis a vous de tout mon coeur.*"

Whereas I had always adored his French before, now it made
me burn with envy to hear it. I asked myself, *Who is he really
thinking about when he says he belongs to me with all his heart?*

CHAPTER 24

A few days later, I received a most upsetting letter from Zulietta, sent from the villa where she had gone with her family to visit her possible match, Giorgio Contarini. They planned to stay there a few weeks, in the airy hills around Vicenza; the whole summer had no doubt been planned by Zulietta's father to put Giorgio within reach. As I said, he was always grasping.

Zulietta reported that Giorgio Contarini was unexpectedly handsome. She had assumed she would have to marry someone who looked like a goat in order to gain entrance into the noble class. But Giorgio was fair, with neatly curled light blond hair and green eyes. His mother was the daughter of a German merchant who had settled in Venice at the beginning of the century. Clearly, marrying into the merchant class for money was something the Contarini family had been doing for a while.

So, Giorgio was acceptably handsome. He was also shy, not saying much to her during their first meal together—a long family *pranzo* eaten in the frescoed dining room of the villa. I sat on my own bed rereading her letter, the foul summer smells of the canal beneath my window drifting into my room. Her description of the villa felt like the fresh breeze I craved:

The pòrtego is the best part, painted as if the
walls are transparent and look out onto a real land-
scape. Painted columns appear to hold up the
vaulted ceiling, and between them are scenes of
peasants herding their flocks, lakes, waterfalls,
ruins, harbors—all giving the room a delightful,
open-window effect.

I looked at my own four walls, clothed in deep pink damask.
In the darkness, the pattern of the rich fabric looked like black,
climbing serpents. Mosquitoes lurked on the ceiling, drawn in
by the burning lamp. Not such a delightful scene.

But after her promising beginning, Zulietta's letter took a
bizarre turn. Giorgio had surprised her by asking her up to his
bedroom:

"I have some special possessions to show you," he
whispered in my ear after our meal.

I expected someone might try to stop us from
going upstairs alone, but our fathers were off hunt-
ing for the rest of the afternoon, and our mothers
had gone outside to the terrace. I decided I should
show interest in his collection. I agreed to slip up-
stairs with him.

Once inside his bedroom—he shut the door, which
made me very uneasy, so I stayed by it—Giorgio
threw himself down on the enormous bed at the cen-
ter of his room. He lay on his stomach and lifted the
cover off a chest at the foot of the bed. Inside were
folded linens. But he dug his hand in deeper and
with infinite tenderness, pulled out a doll.

It was from Naples, he explained, once used in a
crèche. It was maybe half an arm in length, dressed
in a white lace smock, with painted blue eyes and a
mass of yellow hair. I thought, as I stood there

*dumbfounded, how eerie it is, that this doll is
trapped in a chest day and night, smothered by
linens, eyes wide awake and staring.*

*Giorgio showed me a whole collection of crèche
figurines—exotic kings and ragged shepherds, sheep
and oxen and camels—until they were strewn
across the bed. Then, once he had assembled them
all, he forgot I was in the room, and went about
playing with his toys. He talked to them, he had
them act out little scenes. I tiptoed toward the door
and silently released the latch. I wonder how long
it was before he realized I had gone.*

Oh, I did not like the sound of this. Zulietta had been worried about me, about my taking risks and going behind my father's back—but who was this idiot her father had picked out for her?

I folded the letter and went straight to my desk. The hour was getting late, but I wrote furiously in the flickering lamplight.

*Zulietta—Giorgio Contarini is clearly soft in the head.
Stay away from him. Please.*

CHAPTER 25

It was to be our last night together in my brother's room. News had arrived that morning that my father was docked in Ravenna. He would be home within a day or two.

"Come—" Giacomo whispered, holding out his hand to me. We slipped through my back garden door and out into the waiting night.

"Tell me where we are going?" I asked, trotting to keep up with him. I had thrown a black cloak over my chemise, but otherwise, was dressed for bed.

We headed west in the city. In Venice, when someone asks directions, often the answer is *"sempre diritto."* Always straight. But what is straight in Venice? Nothing. It is a maze of wonder.

We reached Rio San Trovaso, which I knew well, and turned down the street. Its wide canal shone in the moonlight, and I could make out the silhouettes of gondolas propped upside down at the boat repair shop. But why had we come?

"Almost there," said Giacomo, leading us closer to the church of San Trovaso.

"It will be locked!" I exclaimed. "And why are we here—to

pray?" True, we did need prayers for ourselves right now. We had promised we would say our marriage vows to my father, the priest, and the whole world one day. And that day was now upon us. However we told my father, he would realize how I had been behaving while he was gone. He had left me a child, and I had secretly grown up. I was terrified to face him.

Giacomo stopped at the church bell tower and, warning me with a finger to his mouth, pushed open its door. My eyes widened—I was amazed it was open in the middle of the night. We entered, and found ourselves inside a small, dark vestibule, ahead of which I knew must be hundreds of stairs. Giacomo groped along the wall and located a hanging lantern. He lit it, and his face shone magnificently in its glow. How handsome he was. I would follow him anywhere.

"I will race you," he teased. I answered by scampering past him, holding my chemise hem and cloak in my hands. He ran up several steps to catch up, but, giggling, I ran up more. He pretended to be out of breath, clutching his stomach. "Mercy!" he called.

"None!" I called back, covering more steps. Round and round we went, the lantern casting golden shadows on the brick walls around us.

Finally, panting and laughing, we reached the top of the tower. I saw its huge bronze bell before us.

"Why have you brought me here, my love?" I asked again.

"It's a place I used to come," he explained. "Remember when I told you, before I met Signor Bragadin, how I had gone to the dogs? I had a group of friends, and we used to spend our nights terrorizing everyone. We would summon priests to the beds of healthy people; we would untie gondolas, leaving them to float aimlessly in canals. And one thing we also liked to do—ring church bells to warn of fires, in the middle of the night."

"Fires that were not burning?" I asked, smiling and shaking my head at him.

"Of course," he responded, giving my nose a playful tap. "Imagine the relief of waking up and learning your house is not burning down. As I see it, we brought people comfort they otherwise would not have had."

"You are terrible," I told him. But I felt the opposite. *You are dangerous, unpredictable, and exciting. I refuse to go back to the boring series of boxes I was living in before I met you.*

He placed the lantern on the floor and together we stepped outside to look over the balustrade in the direction of Piazza San Marco. Its lights were still burning. If I strained my ears, I could hear music playing from the outdoor cafés. I wondered if we would ever walk in the great square together, arm in arm, like true lovers.

"I have brought you here," Giacomo said, taking my hand and pressing it to his lips, "to tell you my plan. It is as ambitious as this tower is high—but I am confident it will work."

My heart began to beat excitedly. I forgot my earlier fears. I wanted only success and was ready to hear how it would happen.

"Our problem," he explained, "is to convince your father I am worthy of your hand, and that your dowry will be safe. I must offer a means to guarantee it."

"Guarantee it?" I had no idea what he meant.

Giacomo kept explaining. "A dowry belongs to a wife and her heirs, although her husband has temporary use of it. But what if I were to lose it all? A guarantee means there is no risk to your father, as the amount is backed by other wealth."

"But, who has this other wealth?"

Giacomo smiled, a sudden flash of white. He always kept his mouth impeccably clean, and scented with eau de cologne. "Signor Bragadin, naturally."

"But how will we convince him to take this huge risk for us?" I pressed, feeling unconvinced myself.

Giacomo took my hand and held it against his cheek. His

skin was surprisingly hot, and his eyes had taken on a strange glow.

"What if I told you," he said, "that I am . . . a magician of sorts?"

"A magician?" I pulled my hand away, afraid to trust what sounded like nonsense.

"Yes. Someone with special powers. To conjure spirits."

"Spirits?" The dangerous word hung in the air. I knew that any sort of sorcery was forbidden in Venice. It was said that the State Inquisitors had spies all over the city to root it out.

"Signor Bragadin is kind, learned—but quite meek," Giacomo explained. "He has suffered many stormy affairs in his life. His own brother once accused him of poisoning him. At this point, he has given up women, is very religious, and has surrendered himself to fate—which I control."

"You control his fate?"

"I do—in a fashion. He and his circle of friends are fascinated by the Jewish *cabbala*. Its mysteries hold them spellbound, like wishing children." He put a hand to his heart, in the way of fervent believers.

"And you think, with a little of this magic, Signor Bragadin will be convinced to promise away ten thousand *zecchini* to my father—a stranger?"

"I am certain of it," declared Giacomo. "If Paralis—that is the name of the Oracle I conjure to guide him—tells him to do it, he will do it."

"Paralis? Who is he? Is he real?" I was becoming increasingly confused.

Giacomo's black eyes glittered in the moonlight. "Paralis is a ghost who responds only to my prayers."

"A ghost? Can you see him?"

"Oh—I can see him. But no one else can." He gave me a wicked smile.

My brow furrowed. "But is it not wrong to—"

"Caterina"—he stopped me—"it is the only way. Think of it as taking money destined to be spent on follies by others, and changing its application to ourselves."

I smiled to appease him, but I still felt confused. Was this all just an elaborate trick, garbed in black magic? Where did my trust in him begin—and end?

"Good," he said, noting my smile. "You understand what must be done." He turned to face the balustrade and began speaking to the sky, opening his arms and seeming to conjure the spirits right there: "*Let me deceive, let me appear just and good; cover my sins with darkness and my stealth with a cloud.*"

"What was that?" I asked, suddenly shivering. The clouds had shifted, and the night was becoming deep, and cool.

"More ancient wisdom. Come"—he reached to take my hand—"it is time for bed."

He led me home, and I kept my hand warm in his pocket. Deep inside, I felt a small scrap of paper, and curious—with my own stealth—I plucked it from him just before giving him warm kisses at my garden door.

Once back in my bedroom, I unfolded the tiny piece of paper.

How to keep C.'s father from seeing me as I am?
I am nothing, but believe I am something.

In that moment, I realized Giacomo risked more than I had imagined in asking for my hand. He feared becoming unmasked, and being seen for who he was.

CHAPTER 26

Wh
hat was this *cabbala* that held my fate? Was it truly sorcery? And who was Giacomo: conjurer, or fake? I felt I had to know.

My mother had been running around like a chicken since news had arrived that my father would be home. Many things were left undone while he was gone. Now bedclothes had to be washed, the kitchen scrubbed and mopped, dog hair pulled off the chairs. I drew her attention to a velvet bed curtain with the hem out and offered to take it to be mended.

"No—no. What tailor sews on Sunday? I will do it myself." She did not suggest I sew it. We both knew I was hopeless at tasks that required any patience.

"I can take it to the *ghetto*," I said. "There are many—I've *heard* there are many tailors there." Almost slipped.

"The *ghetto*?" Amor was barking and ran around us in circles. Something from the kitchen smelled like it was scorching.

"I'll be back within the hour," I pressed. "And the curtain will hang as it should and not look like it belongs in a bad inn." My mother rushed to the kitchen, and I took that as my answer. I was one step closer to speaking with the only Jew I knew.

I had the washing girl unfasten the ripped curtain for me, and I bunched the dusty thing in my arms. I nearly tripped on it as I ran downstairs. I gathered it into a tight bundle and walked briskly to the tip of the city, to find a gondola and head north to the *ghetto*.

As it was Sunday, the waterways were mostly clear and we arrived in less than the usual time. I hurried across the lowered drawbridge, through the dark, humid tunnel, and back into the hazy summer sunshine. The main square was crowded, and the storefronts were all open, as Sunday is not a day of rest for the Jews. I dumped the curtain with the first tailor I found and continued on to the Vivante pawnshop.

Elia looked up—startled—when I burst through the door. Her face brightened when she saw me.

"Oh, Signorina! We do not have your fan anymore. It sold quickly. Or—did you have in mind to pawn something else?"

"No, Signorina Elia." I hoped she would be flattered I remembered her name. She was. I saw her smile, and flush a little. "I—have a question to ask you. Something I need a Jew"—no, that sounded bad—"something that relates to your religion."

"Of course," she said, studying me. I noticed her lashes were lush charcoal black. "What is it?"

I was breathless from rushing, and now, from fear at what I might learn. I approached the counter. "I have a friend—" I began, "he is more a friend of my brother's—who tells me he understands the mysteries of the *cabbala*. He uses it to—to guide men toward making certain decisions. But how can he do this? What exactly is it?"

Elia's almond-shaped eyes flashed briefly at my mention of the *cabbala*. She studied me a bit longer, as if assessing the depth and sincerity of my questions.

"Wait here," she finally said, and disappeared into the back room. A customer walked in while she was gone, but I told him to come back. I did not need any spies.

Elia came back with a large book. I could see it was old, its leather cover worn and dried out.

"This is the *Zohar*," she said, laying it on the counter. "It was left here by someone who hoped to buy it back from us. But that was long ago." She seemed a little sad as she opened it up, running her fingers along the browned pages with reverence. I imagined that she had known its owner. "The *Zohar* contains the key to the *cabbala*," she continued, "written down by Rabbi Bar Yochai in the time of the Romans."

All I saw were letters I could not read.

"Is it in Hebrew?" I asked.

"Hebrew and Aramaic. But I can explain it to you. Not the full wisdom of the *cabbala*—of course! I am not a scholar. But I understand the code."

She reached for a nearby pen and scrap of paper. "In the Hebrew language," she began, "each letter of the alphabet is also a number. So *Aleph,* our first letter"—she drew it out—"is equal to one, *Beit,* our second letter, is equal to two, and so on. In this way, any word in the Torah and Talmud can be calculated as a sum of its letters. And once you have that number, another word with the same value can be substituted for it. New meanings can be found. This is the essence of the *cabbala*."

"Do you know how to do this yourself?" I asked.

"I play with it sometimes when I have nothing to do at the shop. My uncle—he is a learned physician, and owns the pharmacy next door—taught me how to do some simple calculations." She wrote out two Hebrew words. "See how the letters of the word for 'love'—*ahbah*—and for 'unity'—*echad*—both add up to thirteen. What does that mean, do you think?"

I was surprised to hear the questioning turned back on me.

"Love . . . and unity," Elia prompted me. "Think about how these two ideas connect to each other."

"Love . . . unifies us all?" I attempted. "Or, unity is necessary for love to exist?"

CASANOVA'S SECRET WIFE 95

"Exactly." She smiled. "The meanings of the *cabbala* are many. There is no one answer to anything. This is the essence of its brilliance, and mystery."

"As to your friend," she said, gently closing the book, "the *cabbala* is a tool to look more deeply into God's words. It is not meant to guide men in their worldly affairs, or to make someone rich."

"And—an Oracle?" I asked, feeling I was about to jump off a cliff. "Have you ever heard of an Oracle named Paralis?"

Elia knit her lovely eyebrows, clearly confused. She did not answer me immediately. I sensed she was reluctant to destroy my belief in my friend. Then she murmured, "No."

No Oracle named Paralis.

Giacomo, then, was a fake. A glittering-eyed trickster.

But—but did it even matter? Maybe I loved him even more for being willing to take on such a risk to marry me. My life entwined with his felt more dangerous, forbidden, and thrilling.

I glanced at the tall clock in the shop and saw that time had gotten away from me. I thanked Elia and rushed into the sun-drenched square, back through the tunnel—tripping in my hurry, and sending long, ringed rat tails scurrying along the walls—and across the drawbridge. I hailed a waiting gondola and slipped inside its black cabin.

Only when we made the turn into the Grand Canal did I realize I had forgotten the bed curtain at the tailor.

And when I got home—my father was there.

CHAPTER 27

Venice, 1774

Deep clangs rolled from church towers all over the city and the morning air sang. Caterina stirred *risi e bisi* in the kitchen. It was springtime—time for fresh peas. It was also her cousin Zulietta's favorite dish, and Caterina wanted this day to be a happy one. She had invited Zulietta to visit from the mainland where she lived near Vicenza, in order to meet Leda.

Caterina had been vague with her cousin about why the girl was staying with her. She had shared the main truths: that Leda had come from the convent, that she was expecting a baby, that an old friend had asked Caterina for help. But she had skipped key details, wanting to avoid too much scrutiny from her cousin.

Leda sat in her favorite armchair by the windows, sketching. At some point she had found paper and pens in the house, and had taken to drawing a few hours a day. She would show Caterina sketches of lonely, empty gondolas, mangled street cats, gypsies—all sorts of sights she saw from the windows. Drawing kept her busy, and that was a good thing. Caterina hoped this visit from Zulietta would be good for Leda, too. To meet another mother.

"*Buon giorno! Carissima!*" Zulietta arrived at the door and kissed Caterina on both cheeks. Caterina hugged her tightly. She did not get to see Zulietta as much as she would have liked. It was a long, bumpy carriage ride from Vicenza, and then a boat trip across the lagoon. It was especially challenging for her to come with all three of her children. Today, she had only her youngest in her arms, one-year-old Ginevra. The baby had been a late, happy surprise for Zulietta.

Leda put aside her pen and paper and started to get up from her chair.

"No—no, *cara*, you stay there!" Zulietta insisted. "I will come to you!" She bounced over with Ginevra. The baby giggled with delight. How youthful Zulietta always seemed! Her skin was still soft, her brown eyes marvelously awake.

"I am happy to meet you!" she said to Leda, who stared at the baby as if a visitor from China had entered the room. "Caterina was hoping we could talk and—" But Zulietta already seemed to sense that any conversation about children was not going to go well.

"Do you like to draw?" she asked Leda, instead.

"Yes." Leda picked up her pen and went back to some distracted sketching.

Ginevra squirmed in Zulietta's arms. Zulietta set her down, and the little girl ran around the room and right into Caterina's knees. Caterina laughed and lifted her high into the air. Squeals of delight.

Leda looked up, her face green.

"I'm sorry—I am not feeling well." She ran to her bedroom. Caterina exchanged a concerned look with Zulietta and within seconds, they heard Leda retching. The window banged open, and they heard the sound of slop being tossed to the edge of the lagoon.

"I remember those days," said Zulietta with compassion.

But Caterina was sorely disappointed. Leda did not return for the meal.

* * *

"Why did you open your home to her?" Zulietta asked in a whisper. Leftover rice and peas sat in a cold clump in her bowl. Feeding Ginevra on her lap had taken most of her attention. Now the baby slid down to play and Caterina felt a little panicked not to have the child blocking real conversation between them.

"As I said—an old friend who is now abbess asked me for a favor," she said simply.

"Did she not consider it would be hard for you?"

"Hard?" Caterina's face felt suddenly warm. She drained her water glass.

"That it would stir up what you should not be forced to relive again? Your years at the convent?"

Oh—if Zulietta only knew how much it stirred up! But she had no idea. Caterina always wanted Zulietta to see only her best side. She had hidden a good deal of the rest, to be worthy of her cousin's love these many years.

"It is all so long ago, Zulietta, I hardly remember!" she lied. "And I enjoy Leda's company. Sometimes . . . with Bastiano away so much, I am lonely."

Zulietta nodded with warm, caring eyes, but Caterina knew her cousin had never been lonely in her life. She had gone from girl to wife to mother exactly—well, almost exactly—as society expected.

"Your old friend has done you a favor, then," Zulietta observed. "Caterina? You seem a thousand miles away right now."

"Do I? Oh—forgive me!" Caterina reached out to clasp her cousin's hand. She gave her a generous smile that reflected all of their years together.

Maybe Zulietta did not know her as well as she believed she did. But Caterina was grateful all the same, that this true old friend was the one constant thread in her life.

* * *

"What happened yesterday?" Caterina asked Leda the next morning. They sat together for tea and *biscotti*, the weak sun of a cloudy day warming them through the windows. Leda's appetite was back and she ate every cookie on the table.

"I felt sick," she said, some crumbs sticking to her lower lip. "Did you have a good time with your cousin?"

"Yes—not completely, no. I was disappointed you did not join us. She came here especially to meet you."

"Why? We would probably not get along."

"Why not?" Caterina felt stung.

"Your cousin—forgive me—is a sweet fool who was so manipulated by her father she couldn't even tell when she'd been matched up with an idiot. You had to tell her!"

"You don't know anything about her," Caterina snapped. She regretted now certain details she had shared about Zulietta. "No one is more kind and brave than she is! She—"

"Oh, I know the type," Leda interrupted her. "No will of their own, mindlessly following their fathers." Her voice was uncharacteristically sharp. "Fathers are all tyrants!"

Leda's cheeks had grown bright pink and hot. It was clear she was not even talking about Zulietta anymore.

"Do you consider your father to be a tyrant?" Caterina asked her, gently.

"You be the judge," Leda shot back. "When Filippo learned I was pregnant, he went immediately to my father. Filippo explained he wanted to marry me—only said he needed a few months to earn enough money for us to live on." Her hands started to tremble. "What did my father do? He handed Filippo a purse full of money and told him to disappear. The coward took it and ran out of Italy!"

Leda picked up her cup to drink some tea, but much of it splashed into her saucer and onto the tablecloth. After she had set down the cup, Caterina reached over to hold her hands.

"Can you imagine—" Leda asked, more calmly now, but in a

haunted voice that seemed to fill the room, "a father who would do such a thing? Put every obstacle in the way of the man who loves his daughter so that the love goes away?"

Caterina felt a strong urge to run away from the demons Leda's words were bringing back. But she steadied herself, for Leda.

"I can well imagine it," she said. "In fact . . . I lived it."

CHAPTER 28

Venice, 1753

"Caterina—where have you been?" my father demanded. He sat behind the huge mahogany desk in his study, gripping the clawed ends of his armchair. His gray beard had grown tangled and his fingernails were dirty. Too much time spent on a merchant ship.

"I—I'm sorry I wasn't here when you came home," I said, staying several paces away. "I was running an errand for *Mama*. She needed something mended." The air in the room felt heavy, as if I were suffocating inside the wool carpet. I was suddenly nauseated.

"I come home to a fair welcome," he said. "My son is in prison and my daughter running all over the city—"

"I was in the *ghetto*—"

"—oh, even better. The *ghetto*. A fine place. Did you stop to pray at one of their temples for good measure?"

I thought of Elia and hated him.

"Come," he said. I felt my whole body stiffen as he beckoned me forward. "I missed you. I brought you a present."

My heart beat faster in desire—I couldn't help it. You can always find a little affection for someone who brings you presents. I slowly approached.

He pulled out a small leather pouch and shook it onto the desk. Two extraordinary gold earrings shone in the afternoon light.

"They are from Crete," my father said. "The merchant who sold them to me says they are over a thousand years old."

I picked them up and admired them in my palm. They were irresistible, in the shape of crescent moons and covered with hundreds of tiny gold beads. My father noticed my pleasure.

"*Bene*—it is not so terrible to have me home."

I flushed. How easily I had been bought.

"You know you are your father's favorite girl, Caterina."

I was his only girl. How then could I be his favorite? But it was the closest he ever came to telling me that he loved me. I knew that was what he meant whenever he said it.

"And when I am ready, I will pay your brother's debts and let him come home," he continued. "We will all be together again."

"I am happy to hear it." I was. I didn't want to be alone with my father for long. Who needed that scrutiny? Let Pier Antonio be the bad child.

"Happy? I don't see what there is to be happy about." He sneered. "I have to redeem him from prison like some blackened silver from a Jew's pawnshop."

At those last words I felt dizzy. Could he somehow see through me? Know where I had just been?

"Oh—my brother is worth more than some old silver!" I stammered. What an idiotic thing to say. I turned to go, terrified of being exposed.

"Will you hand me my tray of mail?" he asked. It sat on a side table by the door. "I started opening it as soon as I got home, but the pile is endless."

"Of course." I went to get the large oval tray. On one side was a stack of sealed, unopened envelopes, and on the other, the laid-out sheets of letters he had already read. On top of the laid-out pile, I saw the signature of a man whose name I knew well: *Matteo Bragadin.* My heart jumped at the sight of it.

"Oh—I can't wait another minute to put on my new earrings!" I exclaimed, peering into the small circular mirror on the wall. It was from Flanders, a prized possession of my father's, the glass surrounded by miniature scenes of Christ's Passion painted on wood. "But I have to unfasten these pearls first—oh, it is stuck!"

While I fumbled with my earrings, I scanned the note on the tray below me as quickly as I could.

> *Most excellent Signor Capreta,*
> *Will you honor me with a meeting on Tuesday at my house, at 16:00? There is a matter of great importance I wish to discuss with you. A sort of business arrangement between us. It will be of mutual financial benefit, I assure you.*
> *Your most devoted and humble servant,*
>
> *N.H. Signor Matteo Bragadin*

By the time I walked over and handed my father the tray, my heart was beating so hard I thought I might faint.

Our plan had been launched.

CHAPTER 29

That night, while everyone slept, I snuck down to the garden. I figured Giacomo would leave me a message in our special place. It was our only way to communicate. My father was guarding me like a Turkish sultan might watch his favorite harem girl. I needed news—what had Signor Bragadin agreed to do for us?

I saw the deep red of a wax seal shining in the starlight as I approached the old back door. My heart soared, but I also felt terror. Giacomo had never sealed any message to me before. I knew this one must contain dangerous secrets. I pulled it from its hiding place and ran back inside and up the stairs. I dropped into a dark corner of my bedroom with the stub of a candle and started to read.

> *My waiting angel—*
> *The letter from Signor B. to your father has been sent. How did I do it? With a little magic in numbers. Signor B. has agreed to guarantee your dowry—and more. He will give us an annual income to live on.*

How can we fail now, my angel? The Oracle—
speaking through the mysteries of the cabbala—has
shown our love to be worthy of great gifts.
I love you with all my heart, my beautiful C.

Your G.

Maybe I did not believe in the magic, but I believed in my
Giacomo. Was he not brilliant, and bewitching? I saw no way
we could fail. I was going to marry him, my dowry would be
safe, and we would even be given an income to live on. My
dreams, once as fragile as blown glass, were all coming true.

There was nothing to do now, but wait.

CHAPTER 30

I hid in my bedroom most of the next day, alternately day-dreaming about my future and wringing my hands raw.

Actually, though my own fears and fantasies preoccupied me, I was increasingly worried about Zulietta. A letter from her had arrived while I had been out in the *ghetto*. I picked it up from my desk to read again.

> Oh, Caterina, the more time I spend with
> Giorgio Contarini, the more frightened I am about
> my future.
> Most of the time, he acts like a child, and wants
> to play cards or other games with me. But when
> he's had too much wine—which, in truth, is most
> days—he grows cruel. Today, after losing at check-
> ers, he threw the pieces across the room and
> stormed out to the kennels. Foolishly, I followed,
> thinking I could calm him, but not before he had
> let all the dogs out of their cages. Then, when they
> began to bark and run wild—confused, and

*overexcited, poor things—Giorgio began to kick
them into submission.*

*"No, Giorgio! Stop!" I screamed. Their howling
was heartbreaking. The kennel master came running, grabbed Giorgio, and twisted his arms
roughly behind his back to restrain him. All the
while Giorgio was shouting, "Release me, you ass!"
and "Hands off me, fool!"*

*I ran to the stables, weeping uncontrollably. I
went to the lower barn, thinking no one would find
me there. At first, I saw nothing in the darkness—
but soon, the smell of fresh hay and the sound of
buzzing flies began to soothe me. I heard soft
clomping and chewing in a far stall. I slowly
approached and came upon a big brown mare with
gentle black eyes shining.*

*"Hello! Are you all alone down here?" I whis-
pered. I let her sniff my hand, then petted her nose,
very softly, so as not to scare her. "What's your
name?" I asked. "Do you want to tell me?"*

*"That's Farfalle," I heard a man's voice answer
from somewhere behind me. I gasped and jumped
away, but the horse did not startle.*

*"Oh—I'm sorry—I should not be in here!" I
squinted to see who it was who had come down the
stairs. Somehow, in my preoccupation, I had not
heard anyone.*

*"It's perfectly alright," he said, in a voice that
immediately set me at ease. "She could use the company. Isn't that right, old girl?" He approached the
horse and gave her a pat on the neck. He shooed off
a fly that tried to settle on her forelock.*

*"Welcome—Zulietta, is it?" I was surprised he
knew my name. "I am Stefano Cavallini, the farrier."*

"The farrier?" I asked. I couldn't help admiring his muscled forearms, and the way he stood—as graceful as a gondolier on the prow of a boat.

"I forgot, Venetians know nothing about horses!" He laughed. "A farrier shoes the horses, but also takes care of them—almost like a physician. Farfalle here is my old friend, twenty-two years old."

The farrier appeared to be about the same age. "Have you looked after her all your life?" I asked.

"Almost." He smiled. "I was three years old, working with my father in this same barn, when she was born—I still remember." He paused. "Well—you don't want to know all about barn life, I'm sure. Here you are in your silk dress and slippers."

"Yes, here I am," I said, unable to take my eyes off him. Oh, goodness, Caterina, he is handsome. Not in the way of a nobleman. No fine clothes—of course. Not tall and refined. But short, compact, and strong. Broad, ruddy face, with a square jaw.

"Are you . . . hiding from someone?" he asked, cocking his head in the direction of the kennels. And I knew then, he knew. I did not even need to answer.

"Is this horse sick?" I asked him instead. "Why is she kept alone down here?"

"She's not sick, it's more that"—he stepped away from Farfalle and pretended to whisper to me, so the horse did not hear—"nobody in the family is interested in her anymore. She's slow. I worry they'll want me to do away with her, so I keep her down here. Out of sight. They forget she's even here." He stepped back to Farfalle and stroked her smooth withers. "Isn't that right, love? This way, you get Stefano's special care." He winked at me.

"Zulietta!" I heard yelling above us, in the main barn. Giorgio. My whole body went rigid, and I saw Stefano's eyes widen. "Zulietta—don't tell me you're in here!" Sounds of boots on the floorboards, and then clattering down the stairs.

"Here I am!" I called out, sounding ridiculously lighthearted. "I—I felt hot, so I came in for some shade." Didn't you once tell me, Caterina, I don't even know how to lie? True! I'm terrible at it. Luckily, Giorgio is a fool.

He approached us, scowling. My chest was rising and falling in fear, and I put my hand onto the stall door to steady myself.

"You like horses?" he asked me, but with a strange edge to his voice that was terrifying. I noticed he ignored Stefano, as if he were invisible.

"I—I do," I stammered. "Though in Venice, of course, there is not enough open land to keep horses—"

"Nonsense." His voice was cutting. "You can keep . . . this horse." He began to laugh, mocking me. "This old nag can be all yours."

"Oh, no—" I cast a desperate glance at Stefano, whose easy, cheerful face had gone pale. "I couldn't—she belongs here—I have nowhere to keep her in Venice, and I hardly know how to ride!"

"When you leave the villa, take her with you," he ordered me. "This one"—he indicated Stefano—"spends too much time on her. Why nurse a horse that is no good anymore? I should just shoot her—"

"I will gladly take her!" I cried out. I quickly

*glanced over to Stefano. He looked very sad, but
nodded almost imperceptibly in the shadows.
    "Thank you, my lord!" I said to Giorgio.
"Thank you! This is the best gift I have ever
received."*

Maybe it was my own nerves as much as her story, but I was
shaken and seething as I finished Zulietta's letter. I considered
the awful match made for her by her father, and my perfect one,
made without my father knowing about it at all. In the end, neither of us controlled our destinies. To be a daughter was to have
decisions taken right out of your hands.

CHAPTER 31

Oh, time passed slowly on Tuesday. Or rather, the hours crept by and then suddenly seemed to jump. Was it only ten o'clock? I had been awake since daylight. By God, it's already two o'clock in the afternoon? Only two hours until the meeting at Ca' Bragadin!

I sat at the dining room table with my parents. My father had been unusually cheerful throughout our midday meal. I could tell he imagined Signor Bragadin's *proposed business arrangement* was going to bring him wealth.

"You grew taller while I was away, Caterina," he remarked. "Shall we have some dresses made? It's been a while since— what's his name?—Signor Fazzoli?—came to the house with his books of plates to show you the fashions from Paris."

My mouth popped open. My father hated these kinds of frivolities. He usually called the dressmaker Signor Fenocchio behind his back. My brother had explained to me, this was slang for a man who loves other men.

"I don't need new dresses," I said, wanting somehow to save my wishes for the one I truly wanted my father to grant.

"But—thank you," I added, with what I hoped was an angelic smile.

"As you wish, *carissima*," he said, indulgently. "Maddalena," he addressed my mother now, who sat silently as if awaiting his next command, "I have a meeting this afternoon. With"—he paused for self-important emphasis—"a nobleman who wants to do business with me." At the mention of the meeting, I froze in my chair.

My mother smiled, her face wan. She never smiled broadly, fully, with joy and life in her eyes. "Let me help you get ready," she offered. "Your red silk suit would be best, I think." My father eyed her gratefully. For some reason, he only let her dress him. No servants. It was a private ritual between them, an old tenderness.

Left alone at the table, my worries began to crest. *How to keep C.'s father from seeing me as I am,* Giacomo had written on the secret slip of paper I had found. Did he plan to even show himself? Or hide behind Signor Bragadin's noble status, and money?

If Giacomo did show himself, that might not go well. I was sure my father would not take well to his soft hands, fine silks, and lack of a serious profession. My father was a hard, self-made man. Nothing for him had come easy—not as a sailor, sent to sea to make his own way at just seventeen; or later, when he lost his favorite child, Sebastiano, and my mother became ill with grief. But what if, instead, Giacomo hid from him? Then my father would see him as a coward, unworthy of his daughter's hand.

I left the table and returned to my bedroom, not wanting to face my father before he left. My panic would be too plainly visible.

Sitting down on the bed, I rubbed my sweaty palms on my skirt. I felt a sudden swell of nausea, and gagged into my chamber pot. No food came out, as I had eaten almost nothing at *pranzo.* Desperate for distraction, I snatched up Zulietta's letter from the night stand again. Her closing words caught my eye.

> *If I had 10,000* zecchini *of my own, dearest cousin, I would guarantee your dowry myself. Remember that I believe in you, and in Giacomo Casanova, too.*

Was Zulietta herself changing in the face of her terrible experiences with Giorgio Contarini? Her rigid sense of rules, loosening? She seemed ready to throw herself on the altar of love with me, despite her earlier doubts. Her encouraging words gave me strength.

I leaned out my window, and felt the late afternoon summer sun on my face. *Remember that I believe in you, and in Giacomo Casanova, too.* I decided to say Zulietta's words over and over, until my father came home. Like a prayer. I said them to the green waves below me; I said them to God above. I said them to my little painting of the Virgin on the wall; I said them through my tears. I said them and said them until my mouth got so dry the words came out in broken pieces. Finally, I lay down on the bed. I must have fallen asleep.

The door slammed downstairs, and I startled awake. I fumbled to find the watch I had hung at my waist, to track every minute. Two hours had passed, daylight faded.

My father was home.

CHAPTER 32

Opening my bedroom door a crack, I heard him call for my mother in a firm voice. She came running, Amor barking after her down the hallway. My father closed the door of his study on the dog and I could hear the *click-click* of her toenails on the *terrazzo* floor outside. That was how I felt, too: shut out and frantic. I needed to know what was happening.

I could hear no words, but I heard my mother start to cry. This was not necessarily a bad sign: Perhaps my father was telling her I was soon to marry. She would not expect it yet. She had lost Sebastiano when he was young; Pier Antonio was a gambler and a cheat. I was all she had—poor thing, she would miss me. I felt a seed of pity for her, but I dug that right out of my heart. I had my own plans, my own life to make happy.

Shoes on the steps. My father was on his way up, alone. I closed the door silently and ran back to my bed. My heart was beating wildly. Amor must have tried to follow, because I heard him shout her downstairs. I dropped to my knees to pray. It would please my father to find me this way—and I needed the strength of God right now.

The door burst open and I swung around. Oh! There are only a few times in your life when you see someone's face transformed before you, and this was one of those times. My father looked like some creature who stoked the fires in hell. His face was red; the veins on his forehead blue and bulging.

"So—ambushed, I was," he yelled across the room. "I go for what I thought was a business meeting, and a stranger tells me my daughter—who is a *child*—is ready to marry. Who? Who is she ready to marry? A coward who does not even show his face."

"Because—"

"Is he a merchant? No! He hides from me because he knows he is a good-for-nothing."

"That is not fair!" I cried, still on my knees. "You do not know him! He is a musician, and a writer—"

"*Basta!* Enough, Caterina." His eyes were burning. "You think I don't know all about him? I do. Years ago—the whole city was complaining. A prankster and a wastrel. And now here he is, preying on my only daughter, saying he wants to marry her. For money—I'm sure of it!"

Did no one believe Giacomo wanted to marry me for myself? *I* believed it.

"He is changed!" I pleaded. "He is—"

"If Signor Casanova wants to show me he is changed—let's see him try. When you reach eighteen years old—and *if* he has a well-established position—he can ask me again."

Four more years? Impossible.

"In the meantime—Caterina, I am sending you away."

"What! Where?" I stood up, grabbing for the bedpost. I felt that I was drowning, a huge wave about to take me under.

"To a convent. On Murano. Your aunt Gaia boarded there, and has often told me it would be a good place for you. The nuns can keep a better eye on you than I can here."

"No! No!" I ran to him and fell on my knees again, hands clasped, and crying. "I beg you—don't make me go!"

"Do not resist me, Caterina! This is what you need. I have been a poor father, maybe—letting you run loose when I am away. Your mother is too soft to look after you. And the result is the bad situation we are now in. There is no cure for it but some time away from that leech, Signor Casanova."

I stood up now and began to pound my fists on his chest. I screamed more than cried. I felt insane with rage. He threw me off and I saw his eyes were flooded with tears. He turned to go.

"Pack your things," he said on his way out. He did not turn back to look at me again. "You will leave tomorrow."

CHAPTER 33

I cried myself empty and fell into a short, black sleep. When I awoke, my mother was rubbing my back.

"*Figlia mia, figlia mia . . .*" I heard her say.

I realized suddenly how much I loved her. I did not ever want to leave the soft comfort of her. But I could not soothe her as she soothed me. I suppose this is what mothers do for daughters, but daughters rarely do in return. Instead, I pretended to be asleep. When she saw I would not talk to her, she kissed the back of my head and left.

I knew she loved me; I knew even my father—spit on him!— loved me. But I felt completely alone.

The sun had gone down. I lit a lamp. I was very hungry, but refused to eat. I wanted to need nothing, feel nothing anymore.

I began mechanically to pack my things. I knew boarders at convents did not have to wear a nun's habit. I laid all my dresses on the bed, too numb to choose among them. I decided to take them all, maybe run away one day. Run away with Giacomo. No dowry. No income. Only love.

When I was sure my mother and father had gone to bed, I

ran down to the garden. I was hoping for a last message from Giacomo in our secret place. But I found nothing. I slid my back down the length of the door, sat on the cold ground, and cried to the stars.

"Caterina!" I heard on the other side of the wall.

"Giacomo!" I jumped up, dizzy. I slid open the bolted lock and stepped into Campiello Barbaro. I still wore my dress from the day, rumpled. My eyes were swollen. But I never felt more adored, more alive than when I saw him that last night.

"You have heard?" I asked him. His shirt was sweaty and clinging to his back. His face was unshaven.

"I have heard it all," he said. "That is why I had to come. We have nothing left to lose."

"I *hate* him. I hate my father," I said.

"I hate only myself," he echoed, surprising me.

"Yourself? Why?" I threw my arms around him. "I love you more than ever. For trying. For keeping your promise to me." I buried myself in his warmth, and the delicious smell and feel of him.

"I should not have taken this step," he said, his voice full of self-loathing and regret. "I risked everything and I've ruined us." He began to weep.

"No—no!" I found myself comforting him. "We are not ruined. Never say that. I will wait for you. What is four years when you are in love? Will you wait for me?"

"Of course! I will wait until you are freed." He wiped his eyes.

"Did you know," he asked, and a ghost of his old mischievous smile came back, "one of my ancestors from Spain, Don Jacobe Casanova, abducted his lover from a convent the day after she took her vows—and fled with her to Rome?"

"To Rome, then," I said, finding some small strength.

"To Rome," he murmured, pressing a feverish kiss on my lips.

He began to kiss my face, my shoulders. I melted against the wall and, right there in the shadow of my father's house, let him hoist me up and take me. There was nothing left to lose.

After, we heard footsteps nearby and I froze. But neither of us moved apart. We could not bear it.

The footsteps receded. I could feel Giacomo's hot breath on my skin and his heart still beating fast. How was I going to survive without him near me like this?

"Do you know the name of the convent where you are being sent?" he whispered, tenderly kissing my forehead.

"No. My father has not told me. Somewhere on Murano."

Giacomo let go of me to take out a leather pouch from his pocket. "Here—the last of my winnings at cards. Take it. You will need it."

"What for—?" I asked. It was true, I had no money. Pier Antonio had taken everything on the day he left for prison.

"Find someone to help you," Giacomo urged, pressing the coins into my hand. "Have them tell me where you are."

I nodded. He held my face in his hands and I stood perfectly still, memorizing my last look at him.

"Oh, my love, my wife—" He convulsed, surrendering to despair, kissing my neck and, collapsing on his knees, desperately kissing my stomach, my wrists, my hands.

My sorrow was immense, as deep as the sea. But I was sure this was not the end. My father could not kill our love.

CHAPTER 34

I was up all night after Giacomo left. I could not sleep, knowing what I faced in the morning. Just before dawn I took some bread from the kitchen and decided to sit outside in my loggia for the last time. I wanted to see the sun rise over the city, see the domes of the churches, the clay-tiled roofs, the funnel-shaped chimney pots—the sights of my beloved Venice, and of home.

On my way upstairs from the kitchen, I stopped in the garden. The plants and tiny shells on the paths were moist with dew. The sky was turning pink—what was it I had once read about a pink sky? Something Aunt Gaia had read to us, when she used to tutor me and Zulietta as girls. *Rosy-fingered dawn.*

Oh! How I hated my aunt now. I could never forgive her for convincing my father to send me away to a convent. She would never send her own daughter there, I was sure. Her single treasure, Zulietta.

I was surprised to see a folded square of paper stuck in the crack of the old back door. My last message. Perhaps Giacomo had been unable to sleep, as well, burning a lamp at his desk and wandering the dark streets, alone. I ran to get the note, and then, breathless, hurried up three flights to reach the loggia. I began to read as the sun rose high.

> *My beloved angel—*
> *Do you still remember the verse by Dante I once*
> *sent you, about Paolo and Francesca? Here it is, the*
> *poet's plea to the lovers:*

> But tell me, in the time of gentle sighs,
> with what and in what way did Love allow you
> to recognize your still uncertain longings?

> *I promised you sometime I would tell you the*
> *rest of their story. And after saying good-bye to you*
> *tonight—plunged into misery!—I know this is the*
> *right time.*
> *Francesca's answer is that they were conquered*
> *by their desires while reading together the legend*
> *of Lancelot and Guinevere:*

> One day, to pass the time away, we read
> of Lancelot—how love had overcome him.
> We were alone, and we suspected nothing.

> And time and time again that reading led
> our eyes to meet, and made our faces pale,
> and yet one point alone defeated us.

> When we had read how the desired smile (*this is*
> *Guinevere, my love*)
> was kissed by one who was so true a lover,
> my Paolo, who never shall be parted from me,

> while all his body trembled, kissed my mouth.

> *Lancelot and Guinevere . . . Paolo and*
> *Francesca . . . their love was forbidden, eternal. As*
> *ours is. I kiss your desired smile a thousand times,*

*my love! And I will kiss you ten thousand more in
my mind while you are gone. Nothing shall part
you from me.*

I pressed the poem against my heart and took my last, long look out. *Nothing shall part you from me.* I vowed the same to Giacomo, wherever he was.

The birds had started to sing, and church bells to ring, when I finally rose to meet my fate.

CHAPTER 35

Venice, 1774

"But—where is he? Why is he not here with you?" Leda's face had gone as pale as the lovers in the poem. Caterina realized she had frightened her, the opposite of what she had meant to do.

"Giacomo had to leave Venice many years ago," she explained, intending to close the book on this story. "I doubt he will ever come back."

Caterina stared out the windows of the main room, where they sat together over their cold tea. The lagoon shone in the noonday sun, and the sight of so many gondolas and fishing boats made her realize the day was slipping by.

"The convent you were sent to," Leda whispered, "was it Santa Maria degli Angeli?"

"It was." Leda was beginning to get dangerously close to where their stories intersected: not only with the convent, but with Marina Morosini herself. Caterina itched to get away.

"It has gotten late," she said briskly, standing up from the table. "Soon the markets will close and we will have no food for *pranzo.*"

"Did Giacomo forget you—" Leda persisted, "forget about you while you were locked away in the convent?" Her striking blue eyes were wide with apprehension.

Caterina perched on the arm of her chair. She couldn't leave Leda like this, a rag wrung out on her story and terrified it would happen to her.

"Do you ever wish Filippo would come back for you?" Caterina asked her, speaking softly. Leda looked down and Caterina admired her long black eyelashes. They were wet with tears.

"All the time," Leda said, keeping her eyes hidden. "But he won't."

"You don't know that," Caterina reassured her. In the moment, she believed it because she wanted to believe it. For Leda.

She rose and kissed the top of the girl's head. Her hair was softer than she remembered. She felt a stirring in her heart, a sweet tenderness that almost hurt. She put on her cloak and left, noticing she felt a little shaky.

Out on the street, Caterina leaned against the chill stone of a doorjamb. She put a hand on her gut, trying to hold in all the memories coming up inside.

Caterina took a quick gondola ride across the Grand Canal and walked the rest of the way to the Rialto market. She avoided Piazza San Marco, with its cafés, and music, and cheerful crowds. Leda's questions echoed in her head. *Where is he? Why is he not here with you?* She was in danger of sinking too far into the past. It felt as though a strong spell had been cast over her. *It is all so many years gone, Caterina. Stop. Wake up.* She tried to pull herself back into the real world of stone and lapping water all around.

As she approached the market, she could smell fish, and soon she saw tables laid out with creatures of the sea. Men in bloody aprons were cleaning their catch. Caterina waited in a deep crowd of women to be served. She had decided she would make boiled stockfish for herself and Leda, with *polenta*. Yes, nothing brought you back into the present like fresh fish just pulled from the water. Their scales glistened like tiny mirrors, still reflecting their lost home.

She tried to move to the front of the crowd, but found herself pushed aside by rude maids and wives. Their sharp voices, their endless lists of wants: *"Dammi... e poi... e poi..."* The madness of the need to fill one's mouth each day.

Caterina started to feel vaguely queasy, and wandered away. More than anything, she longed for an altar. A place to sink to her knees. To lose herself in stillness. She walked on, remembering she was near the church of San Giovanni Crisostomo, where she had not been in years.

In less than ten minutes, she reached the side entrance to the stone church, hung with a burgundy velvet curtain. Inside, all was empty, echoing silence. Who could be bothered with prayers when it was almost mealtime? Caterina stumbled to the first altar she saw, near the transept, where dozens of candles had been lit. She dropped onto the prie dieu, buried her face in her hands, and surrendered to the noise of a thousand demons in her head.

"Did Giacomo forget you—forget about you while you were locked away in the convent?" What made her keep telling Leda more than she should—talking and talking? What good would ever come of it, for herself, or for Leda?

She looked up. Directly in front of her, she noticed a large painting of Saint Jerome on a rock in the wilderness. The dark gray stone columns of the actual church had been painted into the picture, so it looked like the church wall itself suddenly broke open to the outside air. She imagined herself climbing the rock and running into the distant mountains of the painting, under the dome of blue sky with its pink and gray clouds and soft, clear light.

A gypsy approached, startling her. She held a child swaddled in a coarse red cloth at her breast. The child was large, maybe two years old. The gypsy had hungry, deep brown eyes.

"*Vi prego . . . Signora.*" She put out her hand. Her nails were long and dirty. Caterina went against her better instincts and gave her a coin from her pocket. After, she patted the pocket under her skirts, protectively.

"*Il bambino, Signora . . .*" the gypsy begged for more. Softening, Caterina reached into her pocket and gave her another coin. The woman smiled to receive it, showing her buck teeth, and disappeared into the shadows.

Caterina's mind went from the gypsy mother to Leda. Her own strange, wandering girl. Waiting at home for her. Waiting for all the little things—like food, which she had forgotten to buy!—and needing bigger things, too. Like Caterina's care, and maybe love.

She crossed herself and rose to her feet. Leda needed her. And just as much, she was beginning to see that she needed Leda.

Caterina heard Leda running to the door as soon as she took out her key. Impulsive girl, she pulled it open so that Caterina flew forward inside. They both laughed at the farcical entrance, embracing for the first time since their lives had crossed two months before.

Yes, it was good to be home. Good to have someone who waited for you, and good—yes—to have someone to care for.

"I found some of your favorite cheese at the market," Caterina said to her. "The hard orange kind from the Veneto. You must be hungry!" She had not managed to buy much more, just a loaf of crusty white bread.

"You sit down," Leda said, guiding Caterina by the shoulders. "You look tired. I will make you a surprise."

She disappeared into the kitchen and soon Caterina smelled the best smell in the world: Turkish coffee. It was her favorite, the sweet blackness of it. When had Leda learned to make it? She must have been watching more than Caterina had realized.

Leda came to the table with the steaming copper coffeepot and some dishes. Caterina laid out the bread and cheese. Leda sat and, before she had even poured, broke off a heel of the bread. She gobbled it down, dropping flaky crumbs on the table.

"No coffee for you?" Caterina asked, noticing she had only brought one cup.

"Oh—no," Leda answered with a sudden blush. "It makes the baby wakeful now that the kicking has started."

"The kicking has started?" A huge smile rushed to Caterina's face at the news. This was a road she knew. It had ended for her too soon. But she started down it again with Leda.

CHAPTER 36

Murano, 1753

Stone, stone: That's mostly what I remember from my first day at Santa Maria degli Angeli. Cold stone floors in the dormitory, a bed like stone, the stony stare of Christ from an icon on the wall. I shivered and my teeth chattered, though it was high summer.

The abbess—Sister Paulina at that time—came to greet me in my room. She had pockmarked skin and a fat nose. We girls used to whisper she was part troll, because she was so ugly and short. Her whole body hardly reached up to my shoulders.

"The girls at Santa Maria degli Angeli are not allowed any visits from men—except your father, brother, and uncles," she told me. She held a pile of books stacked up to her chin. "No men pretending they are cousins. And no letters to, or from, home."

My eyes filled with tears. I felt sick. Visits from my father and brother? I would rather be alone.

"These books will help you pass the time," she said, stepping past me to unload them on a writing desk that sat in a dark corner. "You can copy out the passages that you find most inspiring."

I saw there were pens, ink, and a few sheets of paper on the desk. Oh, I was already thinking of other uses for these marvelous tools!

"*Grazie,* abbess. I will start now," I said, eagerly. What I really wanted was for her to leave me alone. I think she knew it: She gave me a sly look with her small, puffy eyes.

"Listen for the bells for prayers at Sext," she said. "After, we will eat." I guessed by her stout body that this was secretly her favorite time of day.

Once the door closed behind her, I went immediately to the writing desk. It was simply made, maybe by some poor monk at a nearby monastery, of knotty pine. Nothing like my luxurious and sweetly fragrant rosewood desk at home. Also, it faced the wall. I pulled the desk out carefully, a few feet, to sit under the single window. Doing this, I could look out to the lagoon, stretching like a shallow pool of tears between me and my Giacomo. Home. I was no more than three miles from Venice and could still see the bell tower of San Marco. But how to cross the distance? How to get a letter to him?

I sat down and began to write nonsense, pouring out my love. All the time, my eyes ran like sad fountains. Could Giacomo feel me thinking of him, I wondered—feel my words as if I spoke right into his heart? Would he ever hold the letter where my fingers brushed, as if joining our hands magically across the water? I willed myself to believe these things.

Prayer bells startled me out of my reverie. My fingers were covered with ink. I balled up what I had been writing. What good was any of it, in the light of reason? I was trapped. I sat and stared out at a few gondolas and fishing boats passing in the far distance. Wearily, as if I had grown old in just a few hours, I rose to go to church. I would pray to God to free me.

How ironic the convent was called Santa Maria degli Angeli. What angel would ever choose to make a home in that miserable place? The church—a pile of rough bricks. Inside—cold tombs, marked by creepy sculptures of nuns laid out sleeping in marble habits and clogs.

I kept my eyes down as I took a seat in the choir. From a quick glance up, I saw a sea of black-veiled and habited nuns around me, and, clustered together near the back, a group of brightly clothed younger girls. These were the boarders, I realized. As the prayers droned on, I sensed everyone's eyes were on me. I was probably the most interesting thing that had happened at the convent in a while: a change.

After the service ended I went with the others to the refectory, still keeping to myself, however. I wasn't ready to be anyone's new friend. To look up or speak was to sprout a root, and I preferred the soil of home.

I felt hot and nauseous at lunch. The meal was some sort of fried seafood, with legs. I avoided it. The nuns and boarders were all pressed together on benches at long tables. At one point, a beautiful nun of about twenty years old approached me. Turning to face her, I saw she was dressed in the usual black habit, but wore no veil. Instead, her chestnut-colored hair was twisted up in a fashionable style, and set with a lilac glass pin surrounded by pearls. Her brows were perfectly arched, etched and elegant, as if she took in everything and was surprised by nothing.

She gave the girl beside me a tap on the shoulder with a long fingernail and nudged her away using only her eyes. How clear and blue-green they were, in the sunlight that shone in from the high windows all around. The girl hastily got up, taking her seafood with her. The beautiful nun sat down.

We could not speak because someone was reading from the Bible while we ate. A boarder no more than twelve years old stood on a box at a lectern set up at the head of the room. A peeling and faded fresco of *The Last Supper* loomed above her as she recited the venerable Song of Solomon:

Let him kiss me with the kiss of his mouth:
for thy breasts are better than wine,
Smelling sweet of the best ointments.
Thy name is as oil poured out:
Therefore young maidens have loved thee.

Her young, high-pitched voice echoed in the huge refectory. Only recently I had been full of earnest faith, too. But now: *Let him kiss me? Thy breasts are better than wine?* I was hearing new things.

It was as if the beautiful nun by my side read my mind. She squeezed my knee under the table, her arm perfectly still beneath her habit. She continued to eat with her other hand.

I stifled a giggle. How good it felt to laugh at the ridiculous seriousness of the place, to feel I was not entirely alone. At the end of the meal she slipped me a note. I realized she must have seen me earlier in church and planned to seek me out. How flattering!

I held my secret in my palm and read it only when I got back to the dormitory.

Come to my room tonight.
—Sister Marina Morosini

CHAPTER 37

Marina Morosini's room was better than mine. It was about twice as large, and filled with her own furniture: a gilded bed with thick mattress, pink silk-cushioned sofa, Turkish carpets, even a bright yellow canary in a cage. She came from an old noble family. Her name told me that. I remembered several past doges of Venice had been named Morosini.

Why was she here? Surely, such a high-ranking family could afford a dowry. And if money was short, wouldn't this be the daughter they banked on for the marriage market? The beautiful one? It was no secret that many girls sent away to convents were defective in some way.

"*Enchantée!*" she said in French when I showed up and told her my name. She acted as if we were destined to be friends, clasping both my hands and kissing my cheeks. I followed her into her room, my eyes popping at all the luxury.

"You must smile for me, Caterina!" she said, taking a seat on the sofa and patting a cushion to beckon me next to her. "You may be unhappy now, but I will show you how to be happy here."

"How do you know I am unhappy?" I asked, still standing awkwardly. But of course every girl dumped at the convent was unhappy. Why wasn't she?

"Your eyes tell me you are sad," she said. "They are the windows into our souls. Do you . . . miss someone?" She patted the cushion again and gave me an inviting smile. This time, I came over to sit beside her.

"Hmm?" she asked me again.

"I do," I confessed, wanting to draw the warmth of my love over me. "I do miss someone, desperately."

"Tell me!" she urged "You can tell me all of your secrets."

"Oh—it is nothing," I said, keeping myself from an indiscretion I might regret.

"Of course it is something!" she pressed, taking my hand in hers. "Tell me."

How comforting it felt to hold hands, to have someone touch me, and seem to care about me. "I—I am secretly married!" I blurted out.

"A wife!" she exclaimed. "At—how old are you? Fifteen?"

"Fourteen." I blushed.

"Fourteen." She pulled away a little, as if considering me from afar. I watched her lips, which somehow looked damp with dew. Did she anoint them with some mysterious and costly oil?

"Well, it is no wonder someone has snatched you up already," she said, after a while. "How pretty you are, Caterina. Especially when you smile."

My heart started to flutter. The way she was studying me—admiring me as if she could eat me—made me feel uneasy. I realized I had probably said too much about myself, and should stop before I spilled more. I gathered my skirts to start to go. She reached for my hand again, keeping me with her.

"I imagine you would like to write to your husband, yes?" She dangled my most fervent wish. "To hear from him?"

"Oh—yes!" I said, melting at what she was offering. "*Gra-*

zie! Grazie, Marina!" Without thinking, I threw myself on her and embraced her. I noticed her heart beating fast against me.

"Caterina—" she said, color rising in her unblemished white cheeks, "only the stupid ones here follow all the rules. There are many ways around them." She smoothed her habit, which I had rumpled, moving closer to tell me secrets.

"Take the first rule—no letters to or from home. Easy. Any servant here past forty years old—they are called *converse*—has the privilege of leaving the convent to do business for the abbess."

"Why only the ones past forty?" I asked.

Marina laughed, then lightly touched my nose with her finger, as if noting my adorable innocence. "Because what trouble would they ever get themselves into? They are too old for trouble—at least the kind we want for ourselves!" She squeezed my arm in a conspiratorial way. "But that doesn't mean they don't want money. That lust lasts for life. A coin in the right hand, and off your letter goes to Venice. Another coin, and back comes a letter from your lov—husband, my dear."

"Can you tell me which *conversa* might go to Venice for me?" I was already springing up, remembering the letter I could now rescue and send. And thanks to Giacomo, I had a purse full of money to spend on the hundreds more I planned to write to him.

"Wait! Wait!" said Marina, reaching around my waist and guiding me back to the sofa again. "You are like a gazelle, ready to run off! Let me tell you a story, Caterina."

I settled back down, though my mind was jumping elsewhere.

"These *converse*, they don't only deliver letters. No—they are the very servants of young love! There was a nun at San Giacomo di Galizzia, nearby us on this island. She was frantic to see her lover again. Her *conversa* figured out that a storeroom that stood along the canal was the perfect place for a tryst. They began to dig a hole together in one of its side walls. They picked and picked away each night using garden tools. In a month they were finished."

"But wouldn't anyone who came into the storeroom see the hole?" I asked.

"No. They concealed it with a large stone that could be removed whenever they wanted. Her lover would come out and hide in there for days—sometimes weeks! Such a happy nun!"

I clapped my hands at her story. I was ready to go dig my own hole.

"Voilà. I have made you smile, Caterina. That is all I wanted."

She rose to lead me to the door. She was letting me know our time together was over. But somehow, now I did not want to leave. I felt pulled to stay near her. Her power over her situation, her mastery of the rules, her miraculous beauty: She had drawn me in. I could not bear returning to my lonely room.

"Come, Caterina. In only a few hours the bells for Matins will ring. Sitting in that cold church at dawn, you'll be sorry you stayed up gossiping with me!"

"Why are you here?" I asked her, suddenly. It was the question I had been wondering since I had first walked into the room. Or even, since I had first seen her in the refectory, wearing no veil, and jewels in her hair. "You seem—not to belong in a convent." I blushed at my bluntness.

"For my freedom," she said, smiling devilishly. "To do as I please."

This was not the answer I had expected to hear. But I sensed, for her, it was true.

CHAPTER 38

I found my bridge back home. Concetta was the *conversa* who took my first letter to Giacomo. She was a disagreeable fisherman's widow, always complaining.

"Signorina, stop your scrawling and give me your letter! The abbess will have my head on a plate if I am late getting back!" I had written a journal about seven pages long and was still scratching away when she snatched the last sheet from me.

"*Che pazzesca,*" she muttered as she left my room. *Crazy girl.*

She was right: I was crazy all that day from the excitement of my words reaching Giacomo, the anticipation of hearing back from him—maybe in only a few hours!

Concetta did not strike me as an eager servant of young love. All she cared about was the two silver coins I dropped in her palm. Then she had smiled, showing me several black holes where teeth were missing. She was not much past forty, with muscled arms still good for hard work. But she was rough, like an old sea sponge.

The hours spent waiting for her return to the convent—by God, they were endless. I joined some of the other boarders playing games in the refectory. The favorite was *biribissi,* a game of chance. Each player had a piece of paper printed with thirty-six pictures in squares. You placed your bet on one of the pictures, marking it with a glass bead. A girl wearing a blindfold drew cut-up tickets printed with these same pictures from a small leather purse. If she picked a picture you had marked with your bet, you won the other girls' beads. They were worth nothing, but all the girls wanted them.

The hunchbacked girl who wore the blindfold—Arcangela was her name—seemed to want to be my friend. One time, I noticed she eyed my bet on a picture of a pear, then drew a pear next from the purse. Maybe she had some secret way of knowing which ticket had what picture on it, like the way it was folded. She untied her blindfold and gave me a *please-love-me* smile. I offered her a small smile back. Pitiful girl, she was badly misshapen and also squinted with poor eyes.

I could not wait to get out of that place, which also smelled like old food. Impatience bit at me.

I saw Marina pass by the open doorway. I jumped up and abandoned the game and all the girls.

"Marina," I called, tripping after her down the hallway toward the dormitory.

"I am glad to see you made the wise choice," she said when I had caught up with her. She turned to warn me. "The boarders will all pretend they are your friends, but they will run to the abbess at any chance to tell her everything they know about you. Be careful."

"Oh—" I said. "You are right. I will avoid them."

"Yes, do." She stopped at the door to her room. A sly smile crept onto her face. "Do you know any French?"

I thought of the pink silk garters Giacomo had given me in

the garden of San Biagio. I heard him reading in my mind, felt his kisses circling my thighs.

"A little," I said, blushing.

"Then it is time to teach you more!" She reached for my hand and kissed it playfully, then pulled me inside. "It is the language of lovers!"

CHAPTER 39

The canary in Marina's room chirped to greet us. I took a seat on the sofa, my eyes catching on the unusual candlestick that stood on the table beside me. It was in the shape of a peacock, made of fine white clay, and brightly glazed in blue, green, and orange. It had sharply clawed, gilt bronze feet, surprisingly threatening for a decorative object.

"Do you like it?" Marina asked me. She stood by the bookshelves, leafing through a small, thick book and eyeing me.

"I do. I've never seen anything like it."

"That's because it is French," Marina explained, "made in Chantilly in imitation of real porcelain from the Orient."

How worldly she was. Even though she was the one wearing a dull, black wool habit, and I was dressed in rich silks, it felt like I was the peasant, and she was the queen.

"Here is something else from France," she said, coming toward me with the book in her hands. "It is a splendid treatise on wisdom by the French priest Pierre Charron." She sat close to me on the sofa and handed me the book. "I have my *conversa* Laura bring me all the banned books from Venice."

"Why is it banned?" I asked, as the illicit book seemed to come alive in my hands. "What could be wrong with the topic of wisdom?"

"Monsieur Charron is accused by his detractors of having been an atheist," she said. "But he is a freethinker more than anything else." She turned to a page she had marked with a thin silk ribbon. Her fingers brushed against mine as I held the book open for her.

"Listen," she said, leaning in to read. I could feel the warmth of her cheek near mine. She read the sentences first in French, then translated them effortlessly.

> "The most noble minds are the most liberal. Nothing does more deprave and enthrall the mind of man than to let him have and understand but one opinion, belief, and manner of life."

"You see," she explained, "he is only saying that we should not be slaves to one idea."

"He does not deny God?" I asked. I pretended to examine the book more closely, though, of course, I could not read it. As I did this, a few strands of our loose hair mingled together over the pages.

"No—he never denies God," Marina said gently. She took my finger and pointed it to follow the words of another line.

"*God has created man to know the Truth, but he cannot know it by any human means*," she read. I noticed she kept hold of my hand. "He is arguing for the possibility of different opinions—even different religions—to free ourselves from fanatical beliefs. Who can ever know the Truth for sure, Caterina?" She turned her face toward mine. Her dewy lips mesmerized me, as though they were created by God to be kissed.

My head was swimming. I think she was enjoying my confu-

sion. She held my gaze and gave me the hint of a smile. Before I
knew what was happening, she stole two kisses on my mouth.
Oh, but her lips were soft!

I pulled away from her. Giacomo! What had I done?

"I have to go," I said, jumping up and beginning to stammer.
"Concetta—Concetta will be back any minute with my letter
from Venice."

"Of course," she said coolly. "You await a love letter." She
closed the book, as if it held no more interest for her, either.

I ran back to my room. My face was burning. I buried my
head in my pillow. My God, forgive me! I vowed to forget
what had just happened. I had been filled with longing for my
husband, maybe, and the lonely love had somehow slipped out.

I lay tossing on my bed the rest of the day, too embarrassed
to show myself. Still, my heart would not settle down. I felt
filled with ecstatic excitement from head to toe, whether from
the unexpected kisses, or the expected letter from my husband,
I did not know.

I was hungry, and the room was beginning to fill with shadows when Concetta finally slipped in the door to see me. She
wore a big grin on her face, and from her pocket pulled out a
sealed letter. When I saw Giacomo's handwriting on the envelope, I kissed that old sea sponge right on the cheek. The kisses
made her happy, but not as much as the two extra coins I gave
her.

Later, pacing back and forth in my room, I read his letter a
thousand times.

> *My angel, beloved Caterina—*
> *The arrival of your letter this morning brought*
> *me from point of suicide to a soul overfilled with*
> *joy! It came while I was shaving and considering*
> *slitting my throat with the razor.*
> *I have been unwell, sleeping badly and waking*

*up not wanting to leave the blissful happiness I find
only in dreaming about you. I spend my waking
hours gambling, and I always lose. Stumbling home
at dawn, I pass our secret door and push on it like a
madman, cruelly forcing myself to remember all
over again that you are gone.*

　　*Caterina, when can I see you? I must see my
wife again or I will drown in despair!*

　　Your Giacomo, who kisses the page right here

I kissed the same spot. I wanted to taste and feel the warmth
of his kiss, laid there just hours ago. It was as if he was with me
in the room, making me smile and laugh and feel adored, as always. What had I been thinking, seduced for a few brief moments by the nun, Marina Morosini?

　　*Oh, Giacomo! Forgive weak Caterina! I love only you, with
all my heart.*

CHAPTER 40

Concetta went to Venice each Wednesday. This way, Giacomo knew to expect a letter from me on that day, and he always sent me one back. The week was spent writing to him, pages and pages, every detail of my days. I even told him about Marina, and—worriedly—that she had kissed me. He took it lightly, writing to reassure me, *Do not trouble yourself about a few kisses, my angel. Who could possibly resist your charms? I can only admire Sister Morosini for seeking to satisfy a nun's obvious longings.*

Still, I wanted some way to show him my constancy, and devotion. One day soon after, I had an idea.

> *Giacomo, my sweetheart, have a miniature likeness of yourself painted, and then have it set inside a ring. Only, ask the jeweler to hide the little portrait with a cover of some sort, so that no one suspects it is inside. This way, with my ring, I can admire you, tell you secret things, and cover you with kisses, wearing your longed-for face on the finger with the vein that feeds right to my heart.*

Two weeks later, Concetta brought me a flat, wrapped package from Venice. I took it—surprisingly light—from her hands.

"This is what he gave you?" I asked, disappointed. "It looks like a book."

"He gave me only this package," Concetta said. "He said, 'Tell her to pray to Saint Catherine and say a Pater Noster and an Ave Maria every day, just as I pray to my patron Saint Giacomo each day.'"

"He said this?" I sat down on the hard bed, feeling dizzy.

Concetta shrugged as if to say, *I don't understand him, either.* It wasn't a good sign when your lover told you to pray more. We both knew that.

Concetta left me and I held the wrapped package for a few minutes. I was in no mood for a book. Finally, I started to pull on the string and tear open the paper.

I saw an old leather cover with copper clasps. *Mary and Christ Enthroned* were stamped on the cover, rudely done. A Book of Hours. What could I possibly need less at a convent, Giacomo? I opened to the first page, expecting unwanted words.

But instead, there was the strangest sight: a square cut right through the center of all the pages. Inside the square sat a tiny octagonal box. And inside this box, I found a gold ring.

I turned it over and over, trying to figure out where the portrait hid. The ivory face of the ring was painted with a picture of my name saint, Santa Caterina. Her portrait was surrounded by a white enamel setting. I traced around it with my finger, feeling for some clue. I felt a small bump. I pushed it with my finger. Nothing.

I took the ring over to the window and inspected it more closely. Now I could see that on the bump was painted an almost invisible blue dot. I took a metal pin out of my hair and touched the dot with the pointed end. The face of the ring sprang open.

I squealed with happiness. Before me I saw Giacomo's face,

in profile. It was a very good likeness, and so finely painted, it must have been done by the artist with a single-hair brush.

In the back of the mutilated book, glued to the endpapers, I found a note. It read—

> *Giacomo is jealous of the portrait who gets to live on your finger each day. He is being talked to, he is being kissed, he is being touched by Caterina's dimpled hands . . . she is stroking him . . . oh! . . . come here and save me from forcing nature like a schoolboy!*

I slipped the book into a drawer of my desk. I still have it. It was the best prayer book I ever read.

"Why is it banned?" I asked, as the illicit book seemed to come alive in my hands. "What could be wrong with the topic of wisdom?"

"Monsieur Charron is accused by his detractors of having been an atheist," she said. "But he is a freethinker more than anything else." She turned to a page she had marked with a thin silk ribbon. Her fingers brushed against mine as I held the book open for her.

"Listen," she said, leaning in to read. I could feel the warmth of her cheek near mine. She read the sentences first in French, then translated them effortlessly.

> *"The most noble minds are the most liberal. Nothing does more deprave and enthrall the mind of man than to let him have and understand but one opinion, be- lief, and manner of life."*

"You see," she explained, "he is only saying that we should not be slaves to one idea."

"He does not deny God?" I asked. I pretended to examine the book more closely, though, of course, I could not read it. As I did this, a few strands of our loose hair mingled together over the pages.

"No—he never denies God," Marina said gently. She took my finger and pointed it to follow the words of another line.

"*God has created man to know the Truth, but he cannot know it by any human means,*" she read. I noticed she kept hold of my hand. "He is arguing for the possibility of different opinions—even different religions—to free ourselves from fa- natical beliefs. Who can ever know the Truth for sure, Cate- rina?" She turned her face toward mine. Her dewy lips mesmerized me, as though they were created by God to be kissed.

My head was swimming. I think she was enjoying my confu-

"A gift. From—your husband?"

"Yes," I said, my head down. I had a strange feeling to protect myself. I should not have invited her to discover more about him or the ring.

"Then, of course you cannot sell it." She moved a little farther away from me on the bench. "I never sell any of the gifts my lover gives me. My jewelry box overflows with trinkets!" She looked at me without blinking, measuring my reaction.

"You—have a lover?" I asked, startled. How did she manage a lover at the convent?

"Of course!" she said with a sudden sharpness. "He is French. An important man here in Venice, but—"

"But?"

"I can't say more. He is a foreigner, and I am noble-born. There could be trouble if anyone ever finds out about us. The Council of Ten might suspect I am leaking secrets to him about the Republic."

"As if out here we know anything!" I said, waving my arm at the whole dismal scene: the baking cloister with its crumbling columns; the lonely nuns, asleep in their rooms; the flat lagoon that kept us apart from all of society.

"True." She laughed. "But still—I must be careful. I am enjoying myself too much to ruin things with loose talk." She puffed herself up like a peacock. She was the most beautiful bird in this colorless place, and she knew it.

"But—how do you see him?" I ventured. "Do you leave here to meet him?"

"I told you, Caterina. Only the stupid ones follow the rules." She got up, wiped her forehead with her sleeve. "Are you coming?"

She expected me to follow her, as usual.

"I—I'm going to stay here a few more minutes," I said. "I'm not tired yet."

She arched her eyebrows, clearly displeased with me. I shifted on the bench. How ungainly I felt. She scowled and left.

Once alone, my mind started to race. Why had she wanted my little ring? Was she in love with me . . . the way I was with Giacomo? Was the story about her foreign lover even true? Or was it that she simply coveted anything of value? Wanted the precious things that belonged to others?

I went to the fountain, cupped my hands, and splashed water on my face. I knelt before the bowl and kissed my ring. From a distance, I might have looked like I was adoring Saint Catherine. And in a way, I was. For a few weeks now, I had started to believe that she had granted me a miracle. A miracle that was going to get me out of there.

CHAPTER 42

Venice, 1774

"Abbess Marina had a lover?" Leda's eyes were big with news of a scandal. "And—she once kissed you?"

Caterina nodded. She reached to drink a little more of the Turkish coffee Leda had made, but only cold dregs were left in the cup. Leda had finished every morsel of the orange cheese, and only a sad heel of crusty bread remained on the table.

"You must never let Marina guess that you know any of this," Caterina warned her. "It is our secret." She winked at Leda, trying to appear playful.

"How did she ever become abbess?" Leda asked. A reasonable question. Caterina had never understood it, either. It had happened long after she had left the convent.

"I suppose she always wanted power," Caterina said. Her voice had a note of bitterness she had not intended to let out.

Silence fell between them. Caterina prayed Leda would not pick up on her feelings about Marina. But she did.

"I take it you and the abbess are no longer friends?" Leda asked.

"That's something I don't wish to talk about." Caterina could feel her face becoming hot. She scooped a few crumbs from the table into her hand, which was trembling.

"Then why did Abbess Marina ask you to help me?" Leda persisted.

"Enough. *Finito!*" said Caterina, sharply.

Leda pulled back her head as if Caterina had bitten her nose.

Caterina began to clear the dishes, keeping her eyes down. She wished she had not flared her temper at Leda. But the girl was treading too close to dangerous secrets. And whose fault was that? Caterina vowed, once again, to keep the rest of her stories to herself.

CHAPTER 43

June came, with summer smells of jasmine in the night air. Leda was now six months with child. Her face had grown puffy, with a little extra chin. Her feet also swelled in the heat, pink flesh pushing at her flat leather slippers. She spent more time sitting, and Caterina had moved a low stool in front of Leda's favorite armchair by the water so that she could raise her legs and be more comfortable. Caterina also begged her cousin Zulietta to come visit again. Leda needed some distraction.

Zulietta came one Sunday and presented a special gift to Leda after the meal. Pastels. Caterina had never seen these sorts of colored sticks before: such promise laid out in a wood box.

"*Grazie, Zulietta—grazie!*" Leda thanked her, effusively. Caterina breathed a sigh of relief that Leda seemed to finally appreciate her cousin. "My drawing tutor always talked about pastels—said Leonardo da Vinci used them—but he made me stay with ink and chalks. He said pastels were too soft for me, that I would smear them on my clothes and make a mess of my drawings."

"I am happy you like them," said Zulietta. "Pastels are best used to imitate the look of hair and skin and such. And I brought you some paper, too." She unrolled a bundle of sheets on the table to show Leda. "Blue, like Rosalba Carriera used. Its texture is rough, to hold the colors."

"Who is Rosalba Carrara?" asked Leda.

"Carriera," corrected Zulietta. "She was an artist famous for her pastel portraits. All kinds of noblemen and women—foreigners here on their Grand Tour—sought her out for her skills capturing a flattering likeness. Rosalba lived—until about fifteen years ago—right here in this neighborhood of Dorsoduro. She can be an inspiration to you."

"Caterina!" Leda called out. Caterina turned from where she had been heading into the kitchen with a stack of pasta bowls. She smiled to see Leda running her fingers over the lineup of pastels. "Will you be my first model?"

"Me?" answered Caterina, blushing. Still, she was flattered Leda would want to capture her likeness on paper.

"Certainly, you," Leda said, beginning already to pluck out colors from the box. Pink. White. Black, for Caterina's eyes and hair.

"*Brava!*" Zulietta concurred enthusiastically. "I can tidy up while you sit, Caterina."

"*Grazie,*" said Caterina, grateful to her cousin. Since Leda had come to stay with her, she did spend much more time cooking and cleaning than ever before. Who knew this was such a big part of having a child in your home? But, worth it.

Caterina pulled over an armchair and sat down to pose in front of Leda. She watched, fascinated, as Leda stroked out her fair skin, her somewhat faded dark hair. As her face took form on the blue paper, Caterina noted how the moist, greasy pastels gave her skin the radiance of a considerably younger woman. She liked the effect very much. In fact, it made her melancholic, to see her old beauty hinted at in the portrait. But she was making an effort these days not to dwell on the past, not to get lost down painful paths of memory, and so she willed her melancholy away. Cheerfully, and somewhat impulsively, she glued the picture right on the wall when Leda was done. Zulietta and Leda came over to admire it mounted in the graying afternoon light.

After a few minutes, Zulietta turned to her cousin. "Truly, I hate to leave but I have to reach the mainland before dark."

"I understand," said Caterina, a touch of sadness coming over her again. She hated that Zulietta did not live in Venice anymore, as she had when they were girls. She missed her all the time.

"Farewell, beautiful Caterina," Zulietta teased, pretending to kiss the portrait good-bye. Leda giggled and pinkened, realizing Zulietta was complimenting her on how true to life the drawing appeared. *Does it?* Caterina wondered. *Even more than I realize?* Maybe more of her beauty was still visible, when she had imagined it was mostly gone.

"Zulietta," Leda said. "*Mille grazie*—again. I love my pastels." Leda hesitated a moment, then pecked Zulietta on the cheek.

Caterina watched Leda approvingly. How far she had come from the sullen, miserable girl she had taken home from the convent. On the other hand, Caterina noted, Leda did, in fact, have pastel smeared all over her clothes.

Some things did not change.

After Zulietta had gone and the sun had lowered into the lagoon, Bastiano drifted upstairs. Caterina and Leda were finishing a light omelet supper. It wasn't unusual for Bastiano to come and see Leda at the end of the day. He often brought her simple gifts for the baby from the mainland, like corn husk dolls, or pull-horses carved out of wood. Caterina thought most of the toys were ugly, but Leda seemed to like them. She always kissed Bastiano's cheeks in appreciation, and he would pat her, pleased but a little stiff, on the back. There was a tenderness between them.

This night, Leda drew Bastiano. She showed him in an armchair reading the *Gazzetta,* a cup of chamomile tea by his side. Caterina studied the portrait over Leda's shoulder. It captured the humility of his quiet habits, the surprising grace of his hands. *How is it,* Caterina asked herself, *that Leda sees so much more in my husband than I do?* She wondered if she was shallow, that this older, awkward, but nevertheless intelligent and gentle man, could not hold her interest. Instead, she always found herself wishing he were someone else.

That night in bed, Caterina tossed restlessly. Finally, unable to sleep, she lit the candle on her nightstand. She craved seeing her portrait once more. How truly beautiful she looked in the drawing. She could not get enough of seeing herself through Leda's eyes. These past years, she had rarely even looked in the mirror for more than a minute. She felt somewhat lost to herself. Now, she realized as she tiptoed down the hallway, candlestick in hand, she wanted to see herself again. But only in the dark, when no one could see what she was doing.

"Oh! Leda!" She was surprised to find Leda still awake and sitting at the table, sketching. Leda startled when she heard her voice, turning and stopping midair with what looked like a black pastel in her hand.

"I'm sorry I scared you," whispered Caterina, coming closer. Leda was working by lamplight. "What are you—"

Leda covered the drawing immediately with another sheet. But Caterina had already seen the portrait. A young, handsome face. A small mole.

"Is it . . . Filippo?" she asked. She sat down next to Leda.

"It is—but no matter," said Leda. "Goodness"—she yawned— "I am tired."

"Do you . . . still miss him?" Caterina asked.

"No," Leda said. "Only sometimes," she added. Caterina saw her lips were quivering just a little.

"Oh, sweetheart," she said, reaching to hug her. She realized she felt a mother's protectiveness for Leda. Still, there was not much more she could really say. She could not predict the future, and it felt wrong to make false promises. Besides, Leda would not believe any. She was no fool.

"It's alright," Leda said, struggling to get up.

Caterina tenderly slid the blank sheet off the portrait, exposing Filippo's unfinished face.

"It's a fine portrait," she told Leda. "Do not give up on it."

CHAPTER 44

"I have a surprise for you!" Leda greeted Zulietta and her children—the baby Ginevra, nine-year-old Giovanni, and Zulietta's eldest, fourteen-year-old Maria Maddalena—when they came to visit the next time.

The children mostly ignored her, running instead to see what dessert Caterina was making for them in the kitchen (*fritelle*—which she would let them shape into rings before she fried the dough in bubbling oil). Caterina coaxed them out of the sweet-smelling kitchen so she could greet her cousin.

"I want to do a portrait of the children!" Leda was exclaiming to Zulietta when Caterina came upon them in the entrance hall.

"She has been practicing with her pastels every day," said Caterina, proudly. She kissed Zulietta on the cheeks to welcome her.

The three of them paused at the table to admire Leda's piles of sketches, and then Zulietta and Leda took seats on the sofa. Caterina stayed standing, as she planned to finish preparing the meal. Little Ginevra climbed into her mother's lap.

"Perfect," said Leda. "Giovanni," she spoke to Zulietta's son, who was busy watching the boats out the window, "will you come over and pose for me with your sister?" Reluctantly, Giovanni came over, sat in an armchair, and took Ginevra onto his lap. But the little girl quickly squirmed off and ran back toward the kitchen. Maria Maddalena, who had been busy stealing glances at herself in the entrance hall mirror—she was lovely-looking, but a bit vain—went in pursuit of her.

"You can draw just Giovanni," suggested Zulietta. "Like Rosalba. We can pretend he is here to have his portrait done on his *Grand Tour!*" She used the English phrase, laughing, and squeezed Giovanni's skinny knee. He giggled and kicked his leg in the air. Leda grinned widely, which set Zulietta laughing more.

Caterina interrupted the fun to tell them she was going back to the kitchen. Maybe she was mumbling, but no one seemed to hear her. Or even notice when she left.

Leda continued working on the portrait of Giovanni for several hours. He came and went from the chair, returning whenever she needed to see his eyes, his chin better. Caterina watched the picture take form: Giovanni turned three-quarters, his gray-green eyes alive with a miraculous spot of white showing light in his pupils. Zulietta was thrilled.

"Leda, it is wonderful!" she cried. "I can't wait to show Giovanni's father! He is too modest to ask for one of himself—but we must get it done. And the girls—!"

"And you, Zulietta," Leda broke in. "You will be my Galatea." Zulietta did not seem to know the story, but recognized she had been complimented by some reference to a classical beauty from long ago. She blushed with pleasure.

Caterina watched it all and said nothing. She felt strangely alone at the sight of the two happy friends—the two happy mothers. A deep, heavy feeling settled inside. She realized she was as tired as the grave.

* * *

It felt like forever until they left. At times, the clouds over Caterina parted, and she managed to join the conversation with forced words. But a storm was brewing within. Jealousy spun into a great well of sadness. She longed for nothing so much as her own bed.

Once everyone had gone home and she was finally alone, she reached under her pillow for her letters. The ones she had already shared with Leda. But even more than the comfort of these, she felt a terrible longing to read the others still left in her ivory box. The next part of her story.

She had been aware of this desire growing inside her for a while now. Was this part of Marina's cruel game of cat and mouse with her? That she should feel this awful urge to revisit what had happened so many years ago?

The rest of the letters sat compressed at the bottom of the box. True—maybe she had stolen a kiss or two from the top of the pile over the years. For their memories of love. But these others? These, she had kept suffocated down below.

"Caterina?" Leda startled her now in the doorway of her bedroom. She stood with her hand still in a fist to show she had knocked.

Caterina slammed the box closed.

"Are you alright?" Leda asked.

"I am fine."

There was an awkward pause while Leda simply looked at her. Caterina felt trapped in her own bedroom.

"I prefer to be alone right now," she said. But as soon as the words came out, she realized how untrue they were.

Leda studied her a little longer. She looked confused, and a little sad. Then, obediently, she pulled the door closed and left Caterina alone.

* * *

"Caterina," Leda whispered to her much later in the night, "you have fallen asleep. Let me help you."

Caterina lay on her bed still wearing her clothes from the afternoon: a bad habit she had gotten from her mother. Not being able to say good-bye to the day in a final way, always thinking more might come of it.

Leda started to make a gentle pile of the scattered letters and pulled the shutters in the room closed. She sat down close to Caterina on the bed, and Caterina felt comforted by her warm weight.

"Tell me why Giacomo did not become your husband," Leda said, softly. "What happened to your lover?"

"No—sweetheart. It's a story you had best never hear." Caterina took the pile of letters from Leda's hands. She laid them on the nightstand, rather than back in the box.

"Please tell me. How is it you believed Saint Catherine was going to get you out of the convent?"

"I—I can't say."

"Why?"

"The story will frighten you." And that was only the beginning. Leda would be frightened—then horrified.

"I want to hear what happened," Leda insisted. "Not knowing things is worse. Not knowing where Filippo is. Not knowing where my father is. Or my mother. Where do we go after we die? Is my mother in the ground, or in the sky, with God?"

The shuttered room was entirely black around them. Leda's words floated in the dark air around them, seeming separated from the act of speaking.

"It is true," whispered Caterina. "Sometimes not knowing things is more frightening than anything else."

She sat up slowly. And she began to talk to the girl in the cover of night. But she vowed to hold on to some secrets too awful to tell.

CHAPTER 45

Murano, 1753

My father surprised me with a visit at the convent. The abbess sent hunchbacked Arcangela to fetch me in my room with the news. I had planned a long nap after *pranzo*—I was sleepy all the time in these late summer days—and not happy to be interrupted. Or to have to face my father.

"*Vieni, vieni!*" urged Arcangela, pulling on my hand. I lay on my bed in a loose linen chemise. Strange how comforting the bed felt, hard as it was. My little room had become my home.

"You mustn't keep your father waiting!" she warned me. She threw open the shutters I had closed and flooded the room with sharp sunlight. I put my hand over my eyes and did not move.

"Caterina, *vieni!*" Arcangela tried again. She seemed frantic, burrowing through the clothes chest for a dress, tossing one onto the bed at my feet, then grabbing a comb off the dressing table, and shuffling over to me as fast as she could.

"Stop!" I said, shielding myself. "What do you care? Leave me alone!" The cruel words just came out.

She looked stung, and stopped dead where she stood over me.

"I'm sorry," I mumbled, after a few moments. "The truth is, I don't want to see my father."

"You don't realize how lucky you are that he comes to see you at all," she said, unable to meet my eyes.

My mouth hung open in shame. I obediently put on the dress she had picked out and followed her mutely downstairs.

She led me into a small room where I sat down behind a window fitted with iron bars. I was lucky? I felt like an animal in a menagerie.

"Caterina, *figlia mia!*" My father came in and approached me with arms outstretched, reaching through the bars for my hands. I was revolted by the feel of his calloused fingers. He sat in the armchair in front of me. I noticed his hair had more gray in it than when I had left.

Silence.

"You look well," he said. "Well fed!" He winked at me. I gave him a weak smile.

"There is my happy girl. Now, Caterina, as you know, the abbess does not encourage visitors. But I am leaving for a long trip abroad at the end of the week. I may not be back before Christmas. I wanted to see you—and tell your mother that you are well—before I go."

At the mention of my mother, my heart softened. How I suddenly missed her! I had hardly realized it. The longing for Giacomo was so huge, it ate up everything else.

"How is she?" I asked. "Why did she not come with you today?"

He cast down his eyes, avoiding my anxious face.

"Your mother has been—sad. You hurt her very much by your irresponsible actions. She—needs rest. I let her rest." *Rest* was the word used when my mother was experiencing one of her collapses. I was being blamed for my mother's heartbreak?

It was my father who had sent me away, and probably nearly killed her doing so.

"And Pier Antonio?" I didn't ask about my brother because I truly cared, but because speaking about him always pained my father.

He sighed heavily. "I paid his debts. What else was there to do? I couldn't let him rot in prison. He has rented rooms on Via Maranzaria, near the fruit market. The place smells like fresh oranges all day." At this, he laughed. I almost did, too, but stopped myself.

"He assures me he is beginning a new life. We can only pray," he said, meeting my eyes.

Ha. Pier Antonio with a new life. "Yes, pray," I echoed with spite.

Another silence. I squirmed in my chair. I felt nauseous and must have looked green and miserable.

"Caterina—" he started. "I know you do not agree with my decision to send you here. But it is a good place. The abbess tells me you are thriving under her care—keeping to your prayers, and making friends with the nuns and other boarders."

I stared at him blankly, not interested in how the abbess drew me for him. My life as seen by her was a lie.

"You have to understand—" he went on with no encouragement from me, "my decision was made to protect you." I noticed his teeth were yellow. He never took good care of himself when my mother was ill. "Venice is full of evil vices. Fools who gamble day and night, frivolous lives made up of theatergoing and parties. Did you know, Caterina, there are more hairdressers in the city than merchants?"

I did not know this. I found it funny, and smirked a little. He missed it.

"And these vices are only spreading! Like a disease—a pox. Pier Antonio has already fallen prey. He is weak in spirit, like his mother. My Sebastiano—he was stronger, but the Lord took him from me—"

He stopped, wiped his eyes with the back of his hand. I started to feel a little pity for my father at the mention of my youngest brother. I saw his aching heart.

"Caterina, when you reach eighteen"—he changed course abruptly—"I will help you find a suitable husband. There is too much about the world you do not understand for this to be your own decision."

I froze. I stared in open challenge to his rule over me.

"Consider that I don't plan to abandon you here like so many of the other girls," he reminded me, his jaw tensing. "Consider the generous dowry I have set aside for you."

I rolled my eyes, knowing it would bring on the storm of his fury.

"That's right!" he said, beginning to shout. "Your dowry, which no doubt played a large part in attracting Signor Casanova's attention! Like a wolf to the chicken coop!"

He got up to go, cursing and sputtering. But he took a deep breath and gripped the wood sill between us. His nails turned white.

"I do not fault you for your foolishness, *figlia mia*," he said with forced calmness. "Wisdom comes only with time. I do not expect it to have ripened yet in so young a girl."

"Yes, Father." I seethed with loathing. I could feel my dress pulling tight across my chest and stomach. "Things ripen only with time."

I smiled with my secret as I left him.

CHAPTER 46

By this time, I knew I was pregnant. My bloody flow had not come for two months. My breasts felt tender to the touch, and I realized, looking back, that my occasional spells of dizziness and nausea were signs. Alone in my bed at night, I found it thrilling to hold a hand over my firming belly, already protecting my baby. How strange to love someone you cannot see! But I did. I was convinced it was a son.

Boy or girl, a scandal was my way out of the convent. I would not be allowed to stay. I knew Santa Maria degli Angeli was too old and prestigious a place to house a pregnant boarder. I would dishonor the whole convent, waddling through the hallways on my way to prayers. Being gaped at by flocks of curious virgins. No. The abbess would be forced to send me home.

Home. Not to my father. Not to some lesser convent on the mainland where he might try to hide me. But, as I dreamed it, to Giacomo. Oh, the hours spent in fantasies! Lying in my shuttered room, lost in a better world. A new home with Giacomo, filled with books and frescoed walls. A crib in the nursery, where the baby slept on sheets sewn by my mother. Zulietta holding the swaddled bundle over her shoulder, rubbing his little back. Giacomo's huge pride in his son—and love for me.

I wrote to Giacomo hinting at the news, that I believed I would be coming home in a few months' time. But I said no more. I kept my secret joy to myself, nursing it until I was further along.

"You seem changed," Marina said to me boldly one day. She closed the French grammar book we had been studying together on her sofa and eyed me head to toe.

"Changed?" I felt my face flush and pulled my hands onto my lap.

"Yes—you used to be more . . . jumpy. Always running off here and there. You seem more . . . settled now . . . is that it?" She regarded me longer, until I felt undressed down to my swelling belly.

"Oh—I suppose I am more content." If only she knew the truth! "How sleepy I am!" I yawned. "I should go."

"Yes—I've noticed you sleep more these days," she continued. "And you eat less, but you look . . . my dear, you are a little heavy."

"Am I?" By now I was panicked to get out of there. I did not trust Marina with my secret. I stood quickly and knocked over a crystal vase filled with porcelain flowers. A few of the glazed petals chipped off onto the table. The hard flowers were scented—just like Madame du Pompadour herself had in France, Marina had once told me—and the sweet smells floated around us.

"Oh Marina—forgive me!" I said, righting the vase. "See—I am still jumpy after all!"

Marina took my hand. She looked me in the eyes, and I was surprised to see some softness in her expression. "I know what you are hiding," she said. "You can tell me anything."

Tears sprang to my eyes. I needed a friend so much! Truthfully, I was frightened. I felt alone. I sat back down and let her hug me.

"There, there," she comforted me, rubbing my back. I felt her warm breath near my ear, her soft lips brush my neck. "What happy news!" she whispered closely. "But how will I ever stand it here without you?"

I melted in her arms. I was not ever able to keep myself away from her. But even then, I feared her more than I loved her.

CHAPTER 47

A few days later, waking up and using my chamber pot, I found a reddish-brown stain on my chemise. Fear seized me. My mother had had several miscarriages between Pier Antonio and myself, which was why he was so much older. But she had also told me she bled through all her pregnancies. I prayed I was not in danger. I had no pain in my womb. I lay back down on the bed, tried to stay calm and think of what to do.

I needed medicine. I remembered the smells of the mixture my mother used to soak into a rag and put on her belly when she bled with Sebastiano. Rosemary. Marjoram. Wine. And something else that smelled like the woods. Pine, was it? Cypress?

White cypress, that was it. And she used to hold a glassy stone about the size of an egg in her right hand. She called it an eagle's stone. It fascinated me because she said you could only find it by an eagle's nest. The stone was hollow, with a smaller stone inside. "*It is like my womb with the baby inside,*" she would say to me. "*I hold the stone to keep my baby safe.*"

I went to find Concetta in a storeroom near the refectory.

She often cleaned in there, sweeping up dustings of flour and sugar spilled by the younger girls baking. I told her I had a terrible headache and begged her to go to the pharmacy for me. I had to give her double the coins since it was not Wednesday, when she usually left the convent to do errands for the abbess.

"An eagle's stone?" she repeated when I told her what I wanted. She gave me a sharp look.

"Yes—an eagle's stone. My mother always used one for her headaches."

"For headaches, *vero?*"

"Yes." I was flushing wildly. This was not going well. Concetta was a loose-lipped gossip. She could ruin me.

"Is there anything else you need, *cara?*" she asked me with surprising kindness. Her eyes were full of pity. How I longed for my own mother! I felt suddenly like an uncorked bottle, and all the tears of missing her were about to spill out.

"Nothing else," I snapped. "Just the herbs and eagle's stone. Please hurry."

I felt a convulsion and something warm and thick run down my leg.

CHAPTER 48

I ran back to my room to clean up the blood with a sheet. I lay down on my bare mattress, afraid to move. I was afraid the baby might fall out. Still, I willed myself not to give in to despair. Maybe this was nothing. Normal bleeding, in the course of things.

Concetta returned in a few hours with the items I wanted from the pharmacy, and she brought some extra linens and rags. It was clear she knew my secret. Sweat beaded on her forehead. I noticed she smelled bad—like fear—as she leaned over to lay the rag she had soaked in the herbs and wine on my belly.

"There, *cara*," she soothed me. "Get some rest now. I told the abbess you have a headache. No one will bother you."

"*Grazie*, Concetta." I gave her my first smile of the day. The bleeding slowed. I began to feel calmer, swaddled in all my mother's cures. I rubbed the eagle's stone in my right hand over and over.

Concetta surprised me and moved a chair next to the bed. She settled herself comfortably, muscular legs stretched out, and looked ready to chat for the rest of the afternoon. Hadn't she just told me to get some rest? Instead, she started to jabber like the fishwoman she was.

"You're in good hands," she said, patting my forehead. "I will take care of you. I know a few things. Delivered my daughter Tonina by myself!"

She held up her strong, rough hands to show me. I wished she would leave, but at the same time, I did not really want to be alone.

"No midwife, no surgeon," she went on. "They think they know everything! More than the mothers! Well, I will tell you a story. It will fry the hairs on your arms."

I turned my head away and closed my eyes. I clutched at the pillow, longing for everyone in the world who loved me to come and lie beside me. Especially, Zulietta. I missed her most of all in these hours. Her steady kindness, her compassion. I wished I had had a way to write to her these past weeks. But she was out of reach, on the mainland.

"This peasant girl, she lived outside Padua." Concetta was talking on. "She was eight months along with child." I turned to face her, willing myself to be distracted.

"The girl was strong, healthy, out in the fields threshing grain. She brings down her flail, and each time the handle hits her in the belly." Concetta slapped her own big stomach to show me. "By sundown, the girl notices she can't feel the baby.

"She carried for another month. Her belly got swelled up to her chin. Got hard as wood to the touch. She stank from her body parts. Something is wrong, the girl knows. Her family calls a surgeon to deliver her. No midwife dared.

"This surgeon pulls out the baby's head. But it's rotted, no more solid than wet paper. The head comes off in his hands. Same with the foot—"

"Concetta!" I yelled out. "Stop!" I felt a grinding pain deep in my insides. This could not be right.

"Oh! I've frightened you!" she cried. "See—that surgeon

didn't help the girl at all! Died herself a few days later, poor thing. Black all over. *The Lord gives and the Lord takes away.*" She shook her head. "But don't worry, Concetta will look after you—"

I sat up now, hysterical with fear. "Go to Ca' Bragadin," I begged her through clenched teeth. "Find Giacomo Casanova. I need him!"

Concetta ran out. She did not even stop to ask for more coins.

I squatted over the chamber pot and let some heavy blood drip in. I broke down in sobs. The loss was crushing me like rocks. All I had wanted was a sweet, fat baby to hold in my arms like Mary.

CHAPTER 49

The bleeding got worse. The few rags I had were soaked with blood. I shredded my sheets when the rags ran out. Heavy shutters kept all the sun from my room. I felt like an animal in a cave, clutched in a ball of pain. Every so often there would be a light knock at my door. I held my breath, tears leaking down my face. I could not let anyone know my secret.

I wanted Giacomo! I wanted my husband to comfort me. I remembered our last night together, desperate against the wall in Campiello Barbaro. My legs open . . . his hot breath on my skin. Was this the night that had led me to where I was now? Or one of the nights in my brother's room? At some magical point, our baby had started to grow. But now, the baby was leaving me—why? When I wanted it so much, more than anything else in my life?

I heard Concetta slip into my room. "I am back, I am back," she reassured me, whispering. She balanced a pile of sheets in one arm and dragged in a big satchel behind her.

"We stopped in the *ghetto* and bought a Jew's whole stock of linens—oh, God!" she said when she saw me lying there in the dark. "You are covered in blood! It looks like a butcher's shop in here!"

I could see pieces of her sweaty hair stuck onto her ruddy skin. She was working herself like a mule. She was not a smart woman, but maybe this kept her loyal to me. She just did things that she saw needed to be done, acted simply.

"Is he here yet—Giacomo?" I asked weakly.

"Yes, *cara*. He is at my house. He is crazy with worry, waiting for news. He wrote you something in the boat—"

Concetta fumbled for her pocket, pulled out a folded sheet, and brought it to me. I grabbed it with a strength I didn't know I had. I forgot my pain for a breath or two.

The message was written in pencil with a shaking hand.

> *Be brave, my angel, I promise I will not leave*
> *until the bleeding stops. Promise me not to weaken*
> *yourself with thoughts of the child who is gone.*
> *There will be others. But there is only one*
> *Caterina, and you must be strong! I love you with*
> *all my heart, my innocent love.*

I kissed his words. Giacomo was just outside the convent walls. I was safe. I felt I would not die.

I howled as new waves of convulsions brought out more bloody lumps. After, Concetta stripped away the old sheets and remade the bed around me. It felt good, clean, but more blood ran right onto the new linens almost instantly. I lay in a warm pool of my insides and felt I might faint.

"Lord, help me!" I heard Concetta say. She lifted my arm off the sheets and felt for my pulse.

"Dear child," she said, still holding my hand, "you are the color of wax. You need a physician! Caterina—do you hear me? I don't know how to stop the flow of all this blood! I have to get the convent physician."

She started for the door, reaching to grab bloody rags as she went, and stuffing them under her skirts.

"No! No!" I screamed after her. "No one can know about this!"

"But the hemorrhage will kill you!" She paced around and spoke what looked like prayers to herself. She kept looking up to the ceiling as if someone up there might tell her what to do.

I was frightened for my life—yes. But I couldn't let anyone at the convent know what kind of hemorrhage this was. I would be ruined in the eyes of everyone, forever.

"Send Giacomo—" I said, reaching into my memories for what to do, "—send Giacomo to find Elia at the Vivante pawn-shop. Her uncle is a physician. He will know what to do."

"This girl is in the *ghetto?*"

"Yes. Elia is—a friend."

Concetta scowled her disapproval, but went to the door. When she opened it, Marina was standing there.

"What is going on?" I heard her say.

"Nothing—the *signorina* is sick."

"I smell blood. I need to see her. *Now.*" She reached over Concetta's head and started to push the door open.

"No—I am taking care of her! She doesn't want any visitors." Concetta pulled the door closed, pushing Marina back into the hallway with her strong body. I heard the door lock behind her. All became silent. The bells began to ring for Vespers.

Marina. I called for her, I think. But no one heard me and I found myself alone with my fears. My thoughts spiraled. Was Marina a friend? A friend like Zulietta? Or even like Elia? I did not trust her. She loved me because I was something new, like that shiny ring she had wanted to take from me.

I surrendered to tears. I cried for everyone I missed, one by one, in my old life. I cried for my mother. I cried for my cousin. I cried most of all for Giacomo. I curled myself into a ball, hugging the pillow against me as if my husband was there next to me.

Come to me, Giacomo! I cried into the dark air.

CHAPTER 50

I woke up to water being splashed on my face. Water and something else strong. It burned my nostrils. Concetta flicked liquid onto my hands, arms, and legs, then went to a basin and dipped a rag. She laid the dripping cloth across my belly.

"Dottore Vivante told us vinegar and water all over, child. Vinegar and water to stop the bleeding." She laid a rough hand on my thigh.

"And—I'm sorry—I have to put a plug in. . . ."

I had too little blood left to blush. I opened my legs. I could feel the crusted blood there, with fresh blood still crawling over. Anything to make this stop!

Concetta made a ball out of what looked like coarse yarn and dipped it in the basin. She pushed it inside me. After the first shock, I felt soothed.

"There, child," she said. She propped me up with a second pillow and poured watery-looking wine into a spoon. "This will thicken the blood and calm your spirits. Later, I will bring you some broth."

She yawned. The poor woman was exhausted.

"And—Giacomo?" I asked, feeling the sweet effects of the wine already. "Is he still here?"

"He is." She sat down with a great sigh in a chair in the corner. "He refuses to eat or sleep—he is in despair! What a pity! Tonina is doing her best to take care of him."

My ears pricked at the mention of Tonina.

"How old is your—?" I started to ask. But Concetta was already lightly snoring. I closed my eyes, too. Sleep washed over me.

When I woke up, the shutters were open and fresh morning light shone in the room. Concetta was gone.

Marina was there.

"*Buon giorno!*" she said, kissing my forehead. Her black habit swooped over me like a great bird's wings. "How relieved I am to see you awake!"

"What hour is it?" I asked, scrambling up.

"Just past Matins," said Marina. "You must have slept through the night."

She offered me a few spoonfuls of wine. My whole body relaxed. I felt bled out and empty. The hemorrhage had stopped, the crisis was over. But along with relief, I was also aware of a deep melancholy settling over me. The very skin on my face felt slack, as if it wanted to slide off my bones and lie in a sad little heap beside me.

"Is it—is it my fault this happened?" I spoke, barely audible, not so much to Marina, but more, to God. I turned to Marina, who eyed me with her brows creased in compassion, the first time I had ever seen so much feeling expressed on her face. "Did I exert myself too much? Or—or eat the wrong thing?"

"Caterina, stop." She laid a finger on my lips. "These losses happen all the time. There is nothing that you did to cause it."

I swallowed back tears. Still, I could not stop asking myself, what made this child not grow and thrive, when I wanted so much to bring it into the world?

"And—my husband—" I started again. I could not help myself. No one else except Marina knew my secrets. My dreams.

"Will my husband be revolted by me?" I went on, my voice

rising as the full force of my fear and disappointment came over me. "He expected a baby, and I gave him nothing but bloody rags!" I started to cry, losing control of myself. Tears and mucus ran down my face.

Marina moved onto the bed and scooped me into a tight hug. I clung to her.

"Shh, shh," she whispered. She released me and wiped my face with a rose-scented handkerchief. "It would be impossible not to love you."

CHAPTER 51

My Giacomo sent me a letter stained with tears and full of re-
pentance. He said he was beyond comforting. He was still on
Murano, holed up in Concetta's house. *I wait so close by,* he
wrote, *I can almost hear your beating heart behind the walls.*
Oh! That I could see him! It was sweet agony, to be filled with
so much longing, to try to conjure over and over the picture of
him painted by love in my mind.

Abbess Paulina came to visit me in my room, once the news
had spread that I was recovering. Until then, Concetta terrified
everyone, telling them the Evil Eye had fallen on me and would
fall on them, too, if they came close.

"I hear you are improving each day," the abbess said stiffly,
keeping herself well away from my bed. She held a bunch of
lavender to her nose to purify the air. "You gave us a scare."

I saw her glance uneasily at the doorway. Clearly, she could
not wait to get out of my room. Worried she might fall sick
being near me! Lord, she had no idea what went on in that convent right under her fat nose.

Arcangela came to see me the next morning. She had no idea

what had happened, either. She could never have imagined it. Hers was a little girl's world, locked away in the convent for life.

She tried to cheer me with an invitation.

"Come—come with me!" she begged from a chair pulled to the side of my bed. "Leonora Vendramin has turned sixteen and is making her profession today! The convent is upside down getting ready for so many visitors. The abbess has said we can all go to greet them at the water gate!"

"No, thank you," I said. "I'm not in the mood to join everyone coming to see that poor girl marry Jesus Christ." The only marriage I was interested in was my own.

Arcangela's face fell. After all, this would be her fate in a few years, too. I regretted my careless words.

"Do you think Leonora will wear a beautiful white robe?" I asked, pretending to be excited for her sake. I could feel my face warm with a little blood and a smile.

"Yes! She will! And at the best part of the ceremony, the patriarch will give her a special ring—just like a wedding ring!"

Arcangela's face glowed with the vision of it. Who was I to ruin her happiness? Ruin it by telling her Leonora was not so much a bride in my eyes, as a witness to her own funeral?

"Let's go together," I said to keep her happy. "I can lean on you if I feel too weak to reach the gate on my own."

"Oh!" Arcangela gave me a sloppy hug and kiss. "Thank you!"

I got up slowly and started to dress with her help. I felt dizzy at times, and moved like an old woman. I could see in the mirror my face was very white. What a picture we must have made limping together down the hallway, the figure of Death and her good friend, the Hunchback.

We reached the shaded arcade of the cloister. I kept my arm around Arcangela's waist. But when we stepped out from beneath the stone arches, I felt the blessed sun kiss my face. I looked up, grateful I had been spared dying. Grateful and sure of God's love. I felt a small pulse of vigor return, the spark of being alive.

I heard the sounds of fiddles and tambourines in the distance, and saw the flash of lagoon water down at the far edge of the lawn. I dropped my arm from Arcangela's stooped body.

"You go on," I said to her. "I am slowing you down."

"You don't mind?" She gave my hand an affectionate squeeze.

"No—I will catch up later." I kissed her cheeks, then pulled my hand away.

Arcangela ran awkwardly to join a group of nuns ahead of us. I felt relieved to be free. I did not need her as a crutch. She was trapped in her deformed body for life, but mine was healthy—born to be out of this place, to be a lover, be married, be a mother someday.

I went on alone and slowly down the wide brick path that ran across the lawn. The younger boarders skipped and sang beside me, and some nuns were even dancing in the grass. Eventually, I reached the gate to the convent. Waves of visitors were stepping out of gondolas and being greeted by the girls' high-pitched shouts and squeals. I watched the empty, bobbing boats left on the water: Oh, to jump in one—escape home! I leaned against a thick old tree, steadying myself in my fantasy. It scared me, it felt so real. I closed my eyes, dizzy and spinning as wildly as the white ribbons that blew in the branches above me.

I opened my eyes. The crowd was swarming. My gaze caught on a golden waistcoat sewn like a tapestry and gleaming in the sun. A pair of black, glittering eyes held me still.

Giacomo! Not four paces away from me!

I wanted to run to him, throw my arms around him, have him lift me and carry me home. But he put a finger to his mouth as if to say, *Be careful. Keep our secret. Do not come closer.* I obeyed, backing up against the tree.

He watched me with a lover's tormented longing for what he cannot have. His face looked pale. My heart melted with love for him—my husband. I loved him more than ever. For staying with me, for refusing to leave my side, until he had seen me and given me the happiness of seeing him.

Giacomo closed his eyes, kissed two fingers deeply, looked at me, and blew. The kiss floated in the air, carried on the bright beams and magic of the day. *I will wait for you,* he seemed to be saying.

The bells rang to call us back to prayers. And then he was gone.

CHAPTER 52

Venice, 1774

When Caterina had finished her story, Leda did not immediately get up from where they sat huddled together on the bed. There was no clock in the room, but it felt to Caterina as if several hours had passed. It was probably past midnight, she imagined.

"Can I sleep in here with you tonight?" whispered Leda. Caterina nodded, grateful not to be left alone. Leda snuggled into the feather pillow and closed her eyes. Soon, she was breathing lightly, the easy, sound sleep of the young.

Caterina herself did not sleep well. Dreams rushed in her head. Giacomo appeared to her—his golden waistcoat, his glittering eyes. She saw their son; he had been born after all. Giacomo was balancing him on his knee, kissing and nuzzling his ear. The boy was laughing. He was a beautiful, happy child. Caterina's heart swelled to see them together—everything she had ever wished for.

She awoke in the dark, her body still, but her world spinning. For an anguished moment she did not know what had happened. The baby, Giacomo—they were both gone. Then she realized she was back in her bedroom, with Leda asleep beside her. At some point in the night, Leda had taken her hand, or she had taken Leda's. The girl held it now, over her heart.

Caterina woke the next day to find Leda in the kitchen. This in itself was remarkable, as Leda was used to a life where servants—or, these days, Caterina—did everything for her. But there the girl was, mixing cornmeal dough and heating water for tea. The cups and saucers, small plates, and shining spoons were neatly laid out on the counter.

"*Buona mattina!*" Leda sang out.

"*Buona matt . . .*" Caterina mumbled. She was still in a daze from the night before. She had woken up empty, black inside.

"I am baking us *zaletti!*" Leda said with what sounded like determined good cheer. "Only we have no butter. I used oil instead."

"That strong olive oil we have?" Caterina found her voice surprisingly sharp. "For cookies?" The oil was bitter, made from early harvested green olives.

Leda's face fell. Caterina was immediately regretful. She reminded herself that Leda had no mother still living, no one to teach her what to do. How to run a household, how to take care of herself and a family one day.

"We will eat spicy *zaletti,* then," Caterina said, managing a smile. "That will be a new experience!" When your heart aches, it is hard to do your best for the young who count on you. But Caterina sensed that forcing herself to be cheerful was good for both of them.

Leda smiled with what seemed like relief and began to busily shape the dough. After a minute or so, she was humming to herself.

Caterina delighted in watching her. Whether breakfast turned out sweet or savory, she mused, what did it matter? The girl was sweet.

A few days later, Leda brought home a kitten. Its fur was white, or more, dirty gray, with patches of black and brown.

"Where did that come from?" Caterina asked when she saw it clinging to Leda's shoulder. She recoiled. It was probably diseased. How could Leda even touch it?

"I found her crying by the wellhead in the courtyard," said Leda, kissing the creature's nose. "Isn't she pretty? Do you see these black lines around her eyes, like long teardrops? I named her *Lacrima*. She can keep us company!"

Leda brought the kitten over to where Caterina sat and tried to coax it onto her lap. But the scared animal stiffened its legs and refused to leave Leda's arms.

"Clearly it likes you more than me," Caterina said. She felt a little rejected. Her mother's dog, Amor, had never liked her much, either. Still, it was good to see Leda caring for a living thing who needed her. Caterina touched its fur very lightly.

Leda placed the kitten back onto her shoulder and spoke soothingly into one of its mangled ears—something about anchovies. They went off toward the kitchen.

Caterina sat alone, wondering. *The baking . . . the kitten . . . why is Leda doing these things? Is it simply for herself, to feel more like a mother? Or*—a disturbing idea entered her head. *Does Leda feel sorry for me? Feel that she needs to take care of me, that she has to make up for losses she cannot possibly undo?* Caterina felt uneasy that maybe their roles were becoming reversed.

She got up to find Leda in the kitchen. She would show her where she kept the anchovies. And—Lord, how did she get herself into these crazy things?—how to wash a cat.

CHAPTER 53

The late July days grew hot. Who stayed in Venice now except the poor, the ones with no place else to go? All you could do was splash water on your face to stay cool, and sit wilting with your fan. Caterina usually got relief from summer at the farmhouse they owned near Asolo. It was a simple place inherited from Bastiano's family. But this year, she wanted to stay in the city with Leda, who was too far along in her pregnancy to bump over bad roads and get stuck in a remote place far from a midwife. They decided that Bastiano would go alone to the mainland for the month of August, and return just before the baby was due.

He came upstairs early to say good-bye, on the morning he was leaving. Leda was still asleep.

"What are your plans for Leda's delivery?" he asked Caterina in full voice from the entrance hall, as if they were alone. He did not really know how to whisper. Caterina came closer.

"Zulietta sent me the name of a good midwife in Venice," she said in a hushed tone. "The woman is her midwife's cousin." This was as far as Caterina had gotten in making any plans.

"I see." Bastiano took a handkerchief from his pocket and blew his beaked nose. Caterina winced, as the sounds disgusted her. "The best surgeons are in Padua, at the university," he said, wiping his nose again. It chronically dripped.

"Surgeon? Padua?" Caterina raised her voice in surprise. She felt instinctively she did not want Leda to leave Venice. "What is wrong with a midwife—here?" But at the same time, the memory of Concetta sweating over her own bed came back to her, the terrible fear, the bloody, stinking sheets.

"I was at the library consulting a legal book last week," Bastiano continued, "and I did some extra reading on the care of women during and after pregnancy."

"Truly?" said Caterina. The womanly reading was hard to imagine, and yet, not. Bastiano relished doing research. He could settle down with a large tome for hours.

"Guglielmo della Motte, on the faculty at the medical school, has written a book on the subject," Bastiano went on. "If you agree, I can write to him, and ask if he would attend Leda."

"But she can't travel. You know that." Caterina could feel her negativity, a mood that often crept up when she dealt with Bastiano.

"Yes. True," he said, patiently. "But maybe he would be willing to come to Venice and perform the delivery. For a price." He smiled. His teeth were a little twisted, but his eyes lit whenever he smiled.

Now Caterina smiled back. "You would do this for Leda?" She began to warm to the idea. It *would* be a relief to know Leda was in the best hands.

"Of course! It is our responsibility to keep her safe." Bastiano pocketed his handkerchief, now ready to go. "No one else is going to do it for us."

Caterina nodded. She appreciated this part of her husband's personality. He was careful about things, while she was not. In situations like this, it made her feel that he was looking out for her.

"*Grazie,* Bastiano." On an impulse, she hugged him. His face reddened with pleasure at the surprise.

"Caterina," Leda asked her one afternoon, "can I ask you a question?" Caterina noticed there was unusual tenderness in her voice. She suspected what might be coming next.

They sat in the main room of the house by the windows, shutters open to catch a water breeze. The air was salty and still. Even Lacrima the kitten could do nothing but stretch out on the *terrazzo* floor to keep her belly cool.

"Um—I've wondered since I met you why you had no children," Leda said. "I guessed you could not conceive. Now I understand that you once did . . . and lost the child. Did you— did you not want another child after what happened?"

Of course, Caterina thought. A woman with no children has to explain herself to society. She pondered how to answer Leda's question without dragging her further into the story of her past. She wanted to reassure Leda about her own future.

"Oh—I wanted a child even after Giacomo was gone," she said. "In some ways, more than ever."

"With Bastiano, do you mean?" Leda's brow furrowed. "Are you saying you wanted to have Bastiano's child even more than Giacomo's?"

Caterina opened the shutter a little farther and peered out to the sea. She felt trapped now, trapped into confessing difficult things.

"My feelings for Bastiano have always been different from what I felt for Giacomo." She turned to look at Leda directly, which felt hard to do. To face her confusion, her innocence to the ways that love could feel not entirely full.

"I didn't pick Bastiano to marry," she explained. "My father picked him for me. Maybe—when you don't feel strong desire for your husband, you dream even more of a child to fill your world. To create love. I had little else." She looked down at her hands and rubbed the flesh of her finger where Giacomo's ring had once been.

"Bastiano and I tried for years to have a child," she went on. She didn't blush too much saying this; Leda knew so much about her already. "Every month I waited for fertility signs to tell me it was the right time to try. And every month my bloody flow came to tell me we had not been successful. Eventually, I gave up hope. What good is a marriage such as ours—which was one of convenience—when you have no children? The disappointment, year after year, became too much for us. One day, Bastiano simply moved downstairs."

"Was he angry at you?" Leda asked. "Did he blame you? Because it might have been his fault—"

"No, he never blamed me. I think that for him, wanting a child was an abstract thing, something you're supposed to want. Something he would want when he was old—a son, or a daughter to take care of him. But for me, it felt like a need, a craving. To hold a baby against me . . . to kiss the top of its soft head . . ."

Caterina felt she was losing the path of what she had meant to say. Her voice had gotten shaky and she feared she might cry. But she got hold of herself for Leda.

"Sweet girl, when a pregnancy happens so young—as happened to you, and to me—you imagine your whole life stretched out in front of you. What is even the loss of it? '*There will be others*,' Giacomo had told me. He believed it, and so did I. But other blessings do not always come. This is why you must try to see yourself as lucky now."

Leda looked at her in disbelief. She clearly didn't see herself as lucky, and Caterina knew it. But she planted the seed for Leda all the same, and hoped one day it would grow.

"Did you ever see Giacomo again?" Leda asked her.

"Hmm?" Caterina said, looking out the window again and trying to seem distracted. Did she ever see Giacomo again? Oh, yes. The meeting at the water gate was only the beginning . . . but also, the beginning of the end.

"Did you see your husband—Giacomo—again?" Leda repeated, moving her head to be more in Caterina's line of sight.

This time, Caterina turned and allowed herself a smile at the memory.

"I did," she said to Leda. "Do you think, having seen each other at the convent that one day, we could resist trying again? Love knows no bounds, *carissima*."

CHAPTER 54

Murano, 1753

Three weeks had passed since my miscarriage. It was the feast day of the martyrdom of Saint John the Baptist, the twenty-ninth of August. We all filed into the convent church. The iron grating of the choir screen served to hide the nuns and boarders from the laity. This service was more full than usual, as Saint John is such a popular saint. Marina sat next to me, craning her neck to look out. We could hear coughing, crying babies, murmurs of *"scusi, scusi,"* as people slipped in late. The hour was None, the service after lunch.

I yawned, already bored.

I noticed Marina's body did not relax even when the priest began to speak. She kept looking out from behind the choir screen. I pitied her a bit, that she imagined in that crowd of Murano fishermen, glassblowers, and their wives and daughters, there was anyone for her to see. Still, when she finally sat back I could not resist stealing a peek myself.

A flash of shimmering turquoise silk caught my eye—as it must have caught hers. A moment of sweet recognition flooded my whole body. My heart melted. It was Giacomo.

I could tell he did not see me, nor was he trying. He looked earnestly into his prayerbook for the whole service. He stood, sat, and kneeled at all the right times. He knew, clearly, that to glance into the choir stalls would arouse suspicion: about who he was, why he was there. Instead, I realized, he had come only to be seen by me, and to give me pleasure.

How I longed to kiss him, every inch of him! He wore his hair *alla dolfina*, the top part combed high and the back tail tucked inside a black silk bag. I adored this style on him the best, because it showed off the strong angles of his face. He looked like a dark-skinned god among the island plainfolk at prayer.

I tried to model my behavior on his, and show some self-control. But my face had grown bright pink, I could feel it, and my heart was racing. I squirmed in my seat, I even pretended to adjust my shoes and stockings, all to get a better view of him.

Of course, Marina noticed.

"Are you sure you do not know him?" she interrogated me after, on our way back to the dormitory. She grasped my elbow, trying to slow me down.

"Who?" I asked, avoiding her eager eyes. "The man in the blue silk suit you can't stop talking about? No."

"Then why were you all but opening your legs for him during the service?"

I flushed and stopped walking. How ashamed I felt! But more, I was terrified that I had revealed my secret like a fool. If it was ever discovered who Giacomo was, and that he had come to see me, he risked prison or exile. It was a serious crime to try to seduce holy girls in a convent. I had to protect him—and myself.

"He was handsome, that is all." I took her arm and we continued walking together. "Do you think he will be back?" I asked innocently.

"Oh—I think so," said Marina. She gave me a knowing smile like a cat who had just caught her mouse.

CHAPTER 55

Giacomo returned for every major feast day, five or six times in the month of September. Oh, how the nuns and boarders all waited for him! As soon as one of them spotted him dipping his hand in the font of holy water by the entrance to the church, she ran to get the others.

"He is back! Come—hurry!"

Our mysterious visitor was the talk of the convent. Young girls and old nuns, no one could stop gossiping about him.

"Maybe his wife has died, poor thing. He comes here to pray for her. He is alone!"

"No—he suffers from melancholy. He deliberately shuns the world."

"Maybe he comes here looking for a new lover?" Squeals and clapping from everyone.

Except Marina. She kept apart from all the excitement, all the speculation.

It was tempting to tell the others who he was, but for once, I restrained myself. Privately, I swelled with pride. My husband came only to be seen by me. There was no hope of more. No gratification possible for himself. How lucky I was, to be so generously loved!

The last days of September came. The stone benches in the cloister sat empty most days. The lagoon smelled less bad, the church at Matins felt cold again. A new season was blowing in.

Concetta returned one Wednesday with no letter from Giacomo. That had never happened before. He always knew to wait for my letter on Wednesdays.

"What do you mean, *he was not home?*"

"I went by to deliver your letter; he was not home. I went back two hours later; he was still not home. I couldn't wait there like an idiot!"

"Was his manservant there?"

"No. Ca' Bragadin was empty."

I sat on my bed, words failing me. Concetta made a few nervous efforts to puff my pillows and straighten my sheets and blanket. I handed her two coins. She left.

Giacomo did not appear in church over the next few days. I began to be sick with panic. I wrote him the following Wednesday.

> *My Giacomo,*
> *I have been worried all week! Has something happened? Are you angry at me? I beg you to write and reassure me in my desperation that you are well, that all is as it was between us.*
> *I love you from the bottom of my heart!*
>
> *Your C.*

I pounced on the letter that Concetta brought back from Venice.

> *Rest easy, my angel. You risk your health with worries. I am not angry with you. Still, I regret to*

tell you some news that will disappoint you. I can-
not visit you anymore on Murano. Serious matters
keep me away.
    Adieu, *my beloved Caterina. I kiss you a thou-*
sand times.

    Your Giacomo

What was this? I paid Concetta four coins to deliver my letter back the very next day.

    My Giacomo,
    You deny me the greatest happiness I have
here—that of secretly seeing you. What are these
serious matters that take you away from me? Write
me everything, I will accept anything, only love me
still—come see me again—I pray you!

    Your C.

He did not write back.

The girls all pined for him. Rumors started that he had been
spotted at the convent. Had it been him in one of the private
visiting rooms with an old woman? Kneeling and crying at an
altar in the church?

I did not know what to believe.

All I knew for sure was that I had been abandoned.

CHAPTER 56

I surprised Marina in her room. She sat at her desk writing by candlelight, a stack of crinkled sheets beside her and a stick of red sealing wax waiting to be used. I had never seen her write so many pages to anyone before.

"Are you writing to your lover?" I asked her.

She jolted as if awakened from a dream and covered the sheet she was working on with her hand.

"Yes—I am. I miss him, you see. He has gone to Paris."

"A long visit? He will not—not forget you while he is there?"

"Oh, no." She gave me what I felt was a condescending smile. "He is very attached to me."

She went back to her writing. I took an uninvited seat on her sofa. My eyes wandered to all the luxurious things in her room. Large gilt mirrors shining in the flickering candlelight; a small glass that looked like it was made of exotic polished stone, with swirls of amber, blue, and white; a hanging basket of flowers made of bronze and porcelain. The basket, now I knew, was French—probably a gift from her foreign lover.

"How do you—" I started to ask, desperate to learn from her, "how do you *attach* your lover to you?"

She put down her pen and studied me amusedly for a while, as if considering how much to say. What did she know that I did not? I wondered. I needed her to tell me.

"It is not easy to name any one thing," she finally offered. "I always meet him wearing my habit. Nothing excites him more."

"But it is ugly!" I blurted out. "Why does he like it?"

"Because, like all men, he enjoys taking what is forbidden. A nun. Every man has this fantasy. Am I the first one to tell you this fact?" She offered me one of her devilish smiles. "They all dream of plucking a woman right out of God's hands."

"But I am not a nun," I said, sorry about this for the first time in my life. "What else do you do to please him?"

"Oh—" she said, beginning to seem uneasy, "I wear... maybe some perfume, a mask during Carnival time, anything that is out of the ordinary. Men grow easily bored—and you have to—"

She stopped herself. She seemed more flustered than I had seen her before. She pulled strands of her hair loose from her chignon.

"Caterina," she began again. Her face was pink and burning. "I am sure Giacomo is still very attached to you. But he has to keep himself alive, preserve himself for you. Chastity is not a virtue in a man. It makes him dull."

She reached for her pen and avoided my startled eyes. Now my own face was burning. My breath was gone. I stumbled out of the room and crumpled against a cold wall in the hallway.

I had never told her his name.

CHAPTER 57

Carnival season started again the first Sunday in October. This meant that for the next few months—until Christmas—rules loosened at the convent. We were allowed occasional family visits and some modest amusements. Singers, musicians, and puppeteers came out to entertain us. The nuns showed off behind the window bars with powdered hair, rouged lips and cheeks, high-heeled clogs, and silk veils edged in gold and silver needlework. The *converse* set skillets over fires right in the visiting parlor, and fried doughnuts glistening with oil and sugar.

My mother and Zulietta came to see me that first day. I had not seen them in almost three months.

"My God, you look gray!" said my mother as soon as I came down and took my seat behind the grating. She reached for my hands through the bars and her eyes filled with instant tears. Zulietta gave my chilled fingers a loving squeeze. How happy she looked, ripe from her time on the mainland. Her auburn hair was more copper, and her large brown eyes glowed warmly in the dim afternoon light.

"I am tired, that is all." I gave them a weak smile. "I am very glad you came to see me."

Which was partly a lie. Certainly, I was happy and greatly re-lieved to see Zulietta after so much time spent away from her. But less so, my mother. Is there anything more disappointing, when you long for your lover—you are hungry for any word from him—and instead you receive news that your mother has arrived? Your mother always loves you; it is the other kind of love you crave desperately with your whole being.

My mother tried to talk to me about light things—gossip in the neighborhood, letters she got from my father, cute things the dog had done. But she could not hide her worry.

"Is your room cold?" she asked abruptly. "Have you been ill?"

"No—I mean, yes—my room is cold in the mornings," I said, not able to concentrate well. "And the church is cold."

Only mothers are interested in this kind of whining.

"The stone floor is so cold it seeps right through my slippers, so that my feet are blocks of ice by the end of each service."

"Oh, *poverina!*" she said. Of course, she suggested no solu-tion to my problem, not able to solve anything for herself or any of us. She still held my hand. But I didn't resent it. In fact, I was beginning to melt into the comfort of her. I wanted to lay my head on her heart and cry about what—I was fairly cer-tain—that whore, Marina Morosini, had done to me. And where was she, by the way? It was odd to see her absent on this social occasion.

"*Zia,*" said Zulietta, giving my mother a gentle tap on the arm, "I see the abbess just came in. Perhaps you can ask her to allow Caterina to bring a foot warmer into church on cold mornings? Tell her we think she does not look well."

"Yes—Zulietta, you are right—a very good idea—"

She finally let go of my hand and got up to cross the room.

"At last!" said Zulietta, jumping to take her seat. "What has happened to you? You look so sad, Caterina. How can I cheer my favorite cousin?"

"Oh—" I said, avoiding her worried eyes, "there is nothing much. I—I have not received a letter from Giacomo in a while."

"He is able to write you here?" Zulietta asked, clearly surprised and leaning in closer.

"Yes," I said softly, "but then he stopped." I did not offer more. I did not feel ready to say, you were right. *You never trusted him, and you were right.*

"Tell me about your time away!" I said instead, trying to muster my old enthusiasm. "Are you now the proud owner of an old horse?"

"Oh! Caterina!" said Zulietta, blushing. Or more, blooming. "There is so much to tell you." She leaned in even closer and gestured for me to do the same. I pressed my ear to the grating. A few of my loose curls went through the bars, as if daring to be free.

"Giorgio—he did something awful—truly heinous—and I had to flee the villa in a hurry. I went to take Farfalle and—oh, Caterina, there will never be enough time to tell you everything!" she despaired. My mother was heading back toward us.

"Write me," I urged Zulietta, under my breath.

"How long have you been writing and receiving letters?" she whispered back.

"Almost since I got here. Concetta—an older servant woman—delivers and picks them up for me on Wednesdays. I will ask her to stop by your house."

"Wednesday. Three more days," Zulietta said, rushing to complete our plan. "I will write you everything!" My mother was back and took her seat.

"The abbess said she could not give you any special privileges," she reported, "but on Sundays during winter she will let you . . ."

I wasn't listening. Neither was Zulietta. We exchanged conspiring looks. How I had missed her! And I sensed what she was soon to write me would make me see her in a whole new light.

CHAPTER 58

My mother and Zulietta stayed for a short concert given by the soprano Anna Medici from Modena. The autumn sun had gone down early, and candles were lit in sconces all around the parlor. We sat spellbound, the nuns, boarders, and all our guests as her high notes filled the vaulted room. She sang a selection of only religious music. But after she had finished, someone called out from the audience, "*Intorno all'idol mio!*" She smiled in recognition of the old love song, and started to sing again before the abbess even knew what was happening.

It is a song full of longing, of love being awakened. The singer asks the spirits of love to show her secret feelings to her beloved, who is sleeping: "*. . . and my hidden passion, reveal it to him for me, O spirits of love!*" I pictured her in a grove, maybe hiding behind a tree, asking the winds to kiss her lover's cheeks. I closed my eyes and floated on the sweet currents of her voice. How I wanted the winds to carry my own kisses to Giacomo! Bring him back to me!

After many promises to visit again as soon as they could, my mother and Zulietta left me and I started back toward my room. I walked the wide hallway that ran above the visiting parlor and the several smaller rooms that opened off of it. Some of these were also used for visits—as when my father had come—because they offered more privacy. My heels echoed on the *terrazzo* floor as I headed to the dormitory. There was no one else around.

I heard a trill of laughter rise up. A voice I knew. A voice I wanted to find.

I paced all around, inspecting this corner and that one, in a fever. The voice seemed to grow louder at one place. I bent down, and discovered an almost invisible crack where the floor met the wall.

I looked around anxiously, afraid I might be caught spying. I took a toothpick from my pocket and placed it behind a nearby stool set against the wall. This way, if anyone saw me, I could say it had dropped from my mouth and I had crouched down to retrieve it. I slid down on the floor like a snake and pressed my eye against the rough line of the crack at the base of the wall.

Below me, I saw Marina from the back. She wore her habit, and looked the part of any nun. But when she moved her head, I could see she had a tiny black circle pasted near the corner of her mouth. There is a whole language to these pieces of gummed silk, I later learned. At the mouth like this, it is known as *assassina*. Love's assassin.

Her visitor sat on the other side of the grated window, partially obstructed from my view. He wore a beaked white mask, black hood and cloak, and gold-edged tricorn hat.

By God, I pray he is a stranger! I squeezed my eyes shut, willing away my worst fears. My heart pounded against the cold floor beneath me. *Santa Caterina, protect me! Do not let me know his voice.*

The low ceiling and echoing stone floor of the small room into which I was looking meant I could hear almost everything.

"When can I convince you of my feelings outside these walls?" the man with the mask asked.

My prayer died on my lips.

"Whenever you can join me for supper at my *casino,* on this island," said Marina. "I need only two days' notice."

"Two days, then! May I ask—does your lover know about us?"

"He does. I do not leave him in ignorance of anything."

"How did he take it? He is not upset that you will have another lover besides him?"

"He is delighted to see me happy. He is dedicated to my pleasure." She inclined her black silk *assassina* toward him. "I presume you also have a lover?" She said it easily, like a piece of music that was her delight to play.

I held my breath for his answer.

"Alas, she has been taken from me! For six months I have been living the life of a monk."

"But do you still love her?" she pressed.

"I loved her so much I risked everything to possess her. I lost everything. But—I realize now that I am a man meant to be in love, not to pine after a woman who is gone."

"You are inconstant, then," she said, approvingly. She slipped one white hand through the grating and he bathed it in kisses.

"Perhaps I am. But still—give me a pledge."

"What sort of pledge?"

"Open the small window for me."

What small window was he talking about? I scanned the room from above. All I saw were bars. No one had ever told me about any visiting room window that could be opened to the world.

Marina rose and pressed a spring along the edge of the grated window. Four sections of bars at the center popped open, making a secret square about eighteen inches on a side. It was large enough for a man to squeeze through.

Giacomo slid aside his mask. He leaned in and hungrily kissed Marina. His new nun.

CHAPTER 59

I reached my room carried on a tide of despair. At first, the feelings that rose up in me were so strong, I could not move. I remember sitting on my bed in the dark with my fist in a pillow, unable even to cry.

Tormented memories of the night Giacomo and I had exchanged our marriage vows came back to me: *I promise God and you that from this moment until death I will be your faithful husband . . .* he had said. Had his words meant nothing? Mine had meant everything to me. I pictured Marina, like some evil sorceress who had enticed Giacomo away. Hot, stinging tears ran down my face. I punched the pillow. I twisted it and screamed into it and wanted to suffocate myself inside it.

Finally, I fell into a desperate sleep of escape. But my nightmares tortured me even more.

I dreamed I was in a tall house in Venice, a place I did not know. I was on the top floor, looking out a window. Suddenly, the lagoon below me rose up in a great green wave as high as the house itself. The wave was smooth like a thick wall, and at its height, white foam played like menacing, bony fingers. I panicked and ran to the other side of the building.

I realized then I had left behind someone I loved—a child. I ran back, but the house heaved with the impact of the wave. I wondered if the bricks and crumbling mortar could absorb all the force, or if the walls and windows were going to crash in and crush me. The whole building tilted at an awful slant and I was spinning . . . still spinning, I awoke, sweating and full of dread.

By now it was deep night in my room, and I noticed a strange, orange glow coming from my window. I got up to look out. A full harvest moon was in the sky, shining over wind-blown black water. This meant winter was coming. I shivered.

I went over to my writing desk. I pulled a wool blanket over my shoulders and lit a candle. A poem poured out. I say it like this because I did not intend to write it, and I've rarely written a poem since. It just came to me that night—

> *Where was it that I wrote my dream?*
> *I thought it was in the garden,*
> *Then I thought it was in the sea.*
> *Is it in my letters?*
> *Why did I need to search for it*
> *As if I can't remember it?*
> *Just to check*
> *Is it still there.*

I wasn't ready to give up on my dream. I wasn't ready for Giacomo to forget me. Marina was no powerful sorceress; she simply stole from me because it entertained her to do so. And what a fool she must have thought I was: banished by my father, miscarrying my child, now losing my husband. Unable to control what happened to me, or hold on to anything that was mine.

Well, those days were over. I could play her manipulative games just as skillfully as she did. Maybe, even better.

I dipped my pen.

CHAPTER 60

I wrote Giacomo a sweet letter. I had to play the part of an angel or I knew I would lose him. I paid Concetta double her usual coins to take it to him the very next morning.

> Giacomo—
> I must tell you that just hours ago, on my way back to my room and bending down to pick up a toothpick I had dropped in the hallway, I came upon a large crack where the floor met the wall. I could not help but look into the visiting room below, and I saw you with my dear friend, Sister Morosini. I quickly stood up and left.
> My husband—I deserve to know how you made her acquaintance. Do you love her? I assure you, I am not jealous! I understand that you cannot be expected to live a life of deprivation while you wait for me.

His message back to me that same day was full of even sweeter lies.

My adorable little spy—
You misunderstand what you saw. Sister
Morosini is a friend of my friend, the Countess
Seguro. I had her called to a visiting room to give
her a message from the old woman. There is noth-
ing between us. I do not love her. I am all yours,
my angel.

I knew this account of things was not what I had heard with my own ears. Could love continue to live on layers of lies? To keep myself sane, I told myself, yes, it could.

I wanted to know everything about their upcoming tryst. Maybe Giacomo would not go through with it, knowing now I had seen him? Maybe my words would act as water on his flames.

The next day, I waited alone in my room for the Evening Star to show bright. Then, I grabbed one of the French books Marina had lent me and headed toward her room. I found her, together with her *conversa*, Laura, just outside her doorway. She was wearing her habit and a wool cloak. She clutched a black velvet mask, its ribbons loose and ready to be tied on once she slipped away from the convent.

The color rose in Laura's cheeks when she saw me, but Marina's face remained white and hard as porcelain.

"How correct you are!" she said, noticing the book in my hand. "We are behind in your French." Her words fluttered out, but I noticed a little catch in her breath.

"Are you going somewhere?" I asked, trying to sound innocent.

"Yes—I am leaving for a while." She offered no explanation. With a quick lift of her finger she gestured to Laura to move along. They left me standing in the hallway, the book slack in my hand.

I walked, then ran back to my room. I was burning with rage

and disappointment. I shredded every page of that stupid French book. And threw to the floor every other book she had ever given me. Philosophy books. Plays. Novels. I hated her, I hated her whole mind, and I hated anything that fed it.

I ran to the window to watch her go. The full moon lit a clear sky. I saw a gondola pass by, its cabin a block of black against the shining sea. I realized I was never going to learn enough this way, skulking around the convent looking for clues, waiting to see what crumbs Marina might toss me.

No. I had to find another way. I would have to take matters into my own hands.

CHAPTER 61

The next day, now Wednesday, Concetta brought me my awaited letter from Zulietta. It had the weight of a pamphlet— as promised, she had written at length—and I ripped open the envelope eagerly, alone in my room. I needed comfort from my own agonies, but, at least at first, the letter was more horrifying than comforting. It told of recent events at the villa belonging to the Contarini family, where Zulietta and her family had been staying to become better acquainted with her proposed match, Giorgio Contarini. Now that Zulietta was once again home, I could finally learn everything.

> *Caterina, where do I start? If I wish and wish, will you appear here in Venice, be sitting in your loggia where I can find you? Walk with me in the garden, have a water fight by the well, like when we were girls?*
> *But no! I will never forgive your father for send- ing you away to that convent. Or, my mother. It was her meddling that started it all, I'm sure. And*

now, look where we are. Me in Venice, and you,
alone in the lagoon.

   Cousin, shall I tell you first about Giorgio? To
understand it, you have to know that before any-
thing that happened—what he did—I had been
visiting the stables regularly to see the old mare,
Farfalle. Stefano—you remember him, the hand-
some farrier—taught me how to brush and comb
her, how to fold a cotton cloth around her body,
even how to girt on a saddle. Whenever we sensed
everyone was asleep for the afternoon, I would ride
her around a back paddock. She was no great gal-
loper, and I no great rider. It was a perfect match.

   One time even, Stefano accompanied me as far
as a fishing pond fed by a spring. While Farfalle
drank her fill, we soaked our bare feet in the icy
water . . . oh, Caterina, I have never been happier
than I was on that day. I learned Stefano lives near
the villa on a small farm with his grandmother and
mother. His father died two years ago—an event
very sad for him still. He is an only child, as I am:
an adored, only son. No wonder so much joy shines
on his face. I think it comes from being so sure you
are loved, each day of your life.

   But we both knew fall was coming. The air grew
chill, the green leaves were turning brown. Soon, I
would be returning home to Venice. My father was
busy maneuvering to finalize the marriage agree-
ment with Signor Contarini: how much dowry I
would bring, when it would be delivered.

   "I do not like Giorgio Contarini," I dared one
time to tell him. He sat at the writing desk in his
bedroom at the villa, drafting the official request to
the Avogari to approve the marriage between our

families. "Please—let us find someone else for me to marry. I am in no hurry."

"It will get better," he assured me. "You are focusing on what is now, not what will be, Zulietta."

"What will be?" I echoed, incredulous. "What will be is what is. Giorgio is an overgrown child. And worse, he is cruel."

My father kept writing and waved me out. He was blinded by the prestige the marriage offered, and would not hear me. I suppose I should be grateful he is not a hothead like your father, did not lose his temper or threaten me, but the result was the same: My fate was sealed.

All through the summer, the Contarini entertained lavishly and new guests were always arriving at the villa. The last week of September, four Greek spice merchants, on their way from Venice to Crete, came to stay. Finding themselves with little to do—the weather was poor, days of rain—they began a game of practical jokes. They stole spectacles and canes from the old people, or had the cook prepare food that caused whoever ate it to fart constantly. The leader was Signor Demitrio. He was amusing, but I thought from the beginning he had the glimmer of the devil in his eyes.

When the weather cleared one afternoon, Signor Demitrio invited us—Giorgio and me—for a walk in the wilder part of the villa grounds.

"There is an unusual bridge I have found there," he said to Giorgio. "But I am afraid to go over. Can you—noble, and brave—lead us to the other side?"

Giorgio gulped at this bait.

We set out on soggy paths through the wild, wooded grounds. Within the hour we reached the bridge, which was no more than a plank spanning a muddy ditch. Giorgio ran ahead, eager to cross it. But when he reached the middle, it snapped. He was thrown into the mud almost up to his neck. Even his blond hair was caked with mud. It was awful, but I admit it was funny. Screaming, he looked like an enraged tomato. The farmhands, including Stefano, had to be fetched to pull him out of the slop.

That night, Giorgio refused to come down and eat, which was surprising. You see, it was part of the game that no one was expected to stay angry. The point is to show you are a gentleman, and laugh it all off.

The next morning, Giorgio appeared at breakfast looking pale and mumbling and giggling to himself. Signor Demitrio did not come down, and also did not appear later at pranzo. *Giorgio's mother went upstairs to check on him. When there was no response at his door, she peered in and saw that Signor Demitrio was still in bed. He was shaking with spasms and unable to speak. She immediately sent for a physician to bleed him.*

When the physician arrived, I accompanied him upstairs. As soon as we entered the room, I gagged at the smell—like metal, and putrid. The physician pulled the sheets down from around the sick man. And there, lying next to him in the bed, was the sawed off arm of a man. Caterina! Such a sight I hope you never see. A blackened, bloody limb, jaggedly cut at the edge. I turned away to vomit,

though miraculously, I held steady. Signora
Contarini fainted and had to be revived.

   This is what we learned: Giorgio had gone to the
church graveyard during the night, and dug up a
recently buried corpse. He sliced off the arm, and
put it into Signor Demitrio's bed in revenge for the
prank that had been played on him. Signor
Demitrio must have gone into a state of shock
when he found it, and did not even have the pres-
ence of mind to remove it. Who knows when the
poor man will regain his sanity after such a fright?
A priest had to be fetched to re-bury the arm.

   "Do you see now?" I asked my father. "Do you
see now who Giorgio Contarini really is?"

   "I do," he conceded, stricken. "I thought—
Zulietta—I had thought it was a good match for
you, the very best . . ."

   "I know you did," I comforted him, sensing my
time had come. "But now . . . ?"

   "Now we are done," he announced. "We will
leave today."

   Deliverance! But I panicked—Farfalle? What to
do. Would she be safe in this place where a
madman lived? Should I take her with me, as I had
been ordered to do by Giorgio, after all?

   I ran to the stables. I found Stefano in the lower
barn. He had heard the commotion, had seen the
physician and priest arrive, but did not know what
had happened.

   "Giorgio—in revenge—he put a severed arm in
the bed of Signor Demitrio," I explained. "Because
of this, I must go."

   "Of course," Stefano said, his jaw tightening. He
lifted an empty bucket off the floor, and when he

*spoke again, his voice was quiet. "Do you think . . .
you will ever be back?"*

*"Well . . . no," I said. "My reason to be here was
Giorgio, and now I wish never to see him again."*

*We stared at each other sadly. In that moment I
realized that while I had come to the villa to get to
know Giorgio, in meeting Stefano I had found a
true friend. I reached out my hand to touch his. He
took it and brought it to his lips. Before I knew
what I was doing, I moved in and kissed him on
the mouth. His sweet, now smiling, delicious
mouth.*

By God! What had I done? I pulled away.

*"My father will be looking for me," I
stammered. "Do you—shall I take Farfalle? Do
you think she will be safe here?"*

*Stefano—who by this point was blushing from ear
to ear—turned to pat Farfalle's muscled neck. She
nuzzled him. These two were clearly inseparable.*

*"Do not worry," he assured me. "I will ride her
to my own farm tonight. With everything that has
happened, the Contarini will not notice she is
gone."*

*"Grazie, Stefano," I said. I kissed Farfalle on her
forelock just above her eyes, so trusting and bright.
"I love you, old girl," I told her, my eyes beginning
to fill with tears.*

*I turned to Stefano, standing very near me. I
leaned to whisper in his ear. "And I think I may
love you, too."*

I folded the thick letter, pages and pages of Zulietta's neat,
small handwriting. I had read and reread it right through supper—but I had little appetite these days, anyway.

At first, I was mostly stunned by the news it contained. Stunned at Giorgio's crime—it surely was a crime against God and the Church, to defile a corpse like that—and stunned, too, that my rule-following cousin had broken so many rules. Had spoken up to her father. Had kissed a low-born man.

Then, I began to smile and laugh, feeling a crazy sense of elation. Because I was so happy Giorgio Contarini was gone from her life. And happy for Zulietta—happy even in my own imprisonment—she was free.

CHAPTER 62

Venice, 1774

The day faded around Caterina and Leda with soft light. The shutters in the main room were now fully opened, and the last slanted rays settled on an interior door painted pale blue with gold shell-shaped designs.

"So—" said Leda with a marveling smile, "the father of Zulietta's children is not Giorgio Contarini, after all!"

"No," said Caterina. Her throat was dry from talking for the last several hours.

"She didn't—she couldn't marry Stefano, the farrier—did she?" Leda asked, beginning to giggle. "That would mean she started off with a nobleman and ended up in the stable!"

"Another time," said Caterina, standing and stretching. She felt stiff from sitting for so long. "Shall we take a walk and get some sorbet?"

"Certainly," said Leda, always eager to eat. But for Caterina, the sorbet was mostly an excuse to end her story. She felt uncomfortably close to the next part. She wanted to forget.

Leda pulled her big body upright using the arms of the chair.

Caterina grabbed a shawl for her in case it had gotten cool. She neglected to bring one for herself.

The late afternoon streets were chilly with shadows. Caterina soon regretted forgetting her own shawl. She wrapped her arms around herself and felt her body tensing as the minutes passed. Leda cast a glance at her, and draped the one shawl over both of their shoulders.

Caterina relaxed into the warmth of their two bodies together. Leda pulled her in close.

They decided to walk all the way to Campo dei Frari, where the best sorbet was sold in paper cones from a cart. The walk had the rhythm of Venice: Narrow, dark streets led into bright open courtyards, then back down narrow streets. The last, late pools of light in the courtyards felt to Caterina like God's love—warm, then somehow, gone.

They bought their sorbet—blood orange for Caterina, lemon for Leda—and headed back along a different route, slurping contentedly. Leda fell behind a few steps as she drank the last of her melted ice from the bottom of the cone.

"Come here, *cara*," Caterina called back. She turned to face the wall of a yellow ochre–painted building. "I want to show you a shrine."

"I've seen enough shrines," Leda said. "There must be a thousand in this city."

"Come see this one," Caterina persisted. "It is different."

Leda approached reluctantly.

Caterina pointed out a small fresco of the Virgin, set inside a rectangular stone frame. Flowers and messages had been left on the shelf below the faded picture. There was nothing like it anywhere in the city. Christ's mother was painted almost naked, except for a simple cloth over her shoulders. She sat directly on an uneven bank by a brook. Trees and shrubs behind her looked windblown, as if a storm was coming. In the midst of this scene, she nursed her baby. Most strangely, she looked directly at her viewers, as if just interrupted.

"My God," said Leda. "She is—so exposed!"

"I know," said Caterina. "Just a mother and her baby. It is the most revered shrine in Venice for this reason. Every expectant mother comes here to make her offerings."

"Who painted it?" asked Leda, studying it again.

"It is a mystery. Every few years someone repaints it, so at this point no one knows when the painting was born or if it will ever die."

"You say that as if the painting is alive," Leda noted.

"True." Caterina laughed. She admired Leda's perceptiveness—the girl was smarter than she had seemed months ago when they had first met. "In some ways the painting *is* alive. It is as if the Virgin looks up at each visitor and asks, *Who are you and why have you come?*"

"And your answer would be . . . ?"

"Oh—I don't know," Caterina said, beginning to feel uneasy. Who was she, after all? All her schemes. Her lies. Her desperation.

Leda regarded her closely, until Caterina felt considered to her soul. "*Bene,*" the girl finally said. "Maybe one day, we'll know."

"Perhaps . . . one day." Caterina turned away from the mysterious picture. "Come—" she said, holding out a hand to Leda. "It's getting dark and my whole body is cold from that sorbet!"

Caterina and Leda grasped chilled hands. The wind picked up. Leda draped the shawl around them again, tight as a cocoon.

"I want to know what you meant," Leda whispered, "when you said *you would have to take matters into your own hands.*"

Caterina shivered. Then she began to speak again, quiet as a secret.

CHAPTER 63

Murano, 1753

Where else did I have to turn, when I wanted to seem like an angel but act as clever as the devil? Do the lowest thing I'd ever contemplated in my life?

I sent word to my brother to come see me at the convent.

"There she is!" he called out with mock cheerfulness when, a few days later, I greeted him in the visiting parlor. I let him kiss my cheeks through the iron bars. "*Mama* was right. You look awful, Caterina."

"Thank you. You do, too," I retorted. It was true. Though it was midafternoon, Pier Antonio's face was unshaven and his eyes were bloodshot. He smelled like bad wine and long nights spent praying for his luck to change. But the nuns and other boarders didn't seem to mind. He was a man under fifty at the convent, and that was good enough. They cast glances at him and giggled inside the nearby caged windows. Pier Antonio started immediately winking and blowing kisses at his admirers.

"Stop it!" I snapped at him. "The abbess will be over here in no time, and that will be the end of this visit or any other!" The abbess was actually nowhere around, but the sight of my brother flirting filled me with fury. I had called him out to the convent to help me, not suffer the humiliation of watching him make the place his hunting ground.

He reluctantly brought his gaze back to me.

"Your message said you needed some help?"

"Yes, I do. You see—"

"You admit that when I needed help in prison you were hardly my angel of mercy. You sent a few of my things, but otherwise—"

"What else could I have done?" I cried in a high voice. A few other visitors turned to look at me. I caught myself.

"Let's not revisit the past, Pier Antonio," I said, more softly. "There is no point. I asked you to come out here because I need a favor. Something . . . only you can do for me."

"A favor?" He raised a brow and smirked at me. "Let me guess. You want me to deliver a letter to Venice. No—wait. You have a servant to do that. You want me to bring Giacomo Casanova to you? Shall I dress him as a priest? Have him meet you by the altar?"

He laughed. "Come on—that is funny. Have you forgotten how to enjoy yourself in this place? Love is all a game, Caterina."

"Exactly. That is why I need your help." I brought my mouth close to the bars. "I need you to hire a spy for me."

"What?" His bloodshot eyes sprang awake.

"Yes. A spy. To follow Giacomo. I think—I—I know for sure he is having an affair."

"If you know for sure, what more is there to learn from a spy?" He chewed on his fingernail. The skin around it was raw from the habit.

Actually, his point was a good one. Smarter than I usually gave him credit for.

"I know the fact of the affair, but not much else about it," I explained. "Is he consumed by her, or is it just a distraction? You see"—it felt hard to confess, knowing Pier Antonio might laugh at me—"Giacomo and I are secretly married."

Pier Antonio grinned at the news. Yes, it was all a good joke to him. But he managed to stop when he saw I was not smiling. His eyes softened, and I felt a tiny wave of his love for me.

"*Bene,*" he said. "I will help you." He gestured for me to lean in more. "I know the perfect spy. He is a Grimani, but his family has no money. He will want the job."

I felt some panic rise at the mention of a real man, a real spy. Not just a fantasy anymore, living in my fevered mind.

"Is he the sort of person who can keep a secret?" I asked, needing reassurance from—of all people—my brother. "Giacomo must never know what I am doing!" I put my head in my hands and closed my eyes. Did I have the stomach for this?

My brother reached through the bars and pulled my hands from my eyes.

"Trust me," he said, gripping my wrists. "Casanova will never suspect a thing."

CHAPTER 64

"Did you bring the spy's report?" I asked my brother when, just a week later, I met him in the visiting parlor. I knew he had not come out to the convent so soon simply because he missed me.

"I did." He patted the pocket of his breeches. "But it will cost you."

"Of course." I reached a hand into my own pocket beneath my skirts. "How much?"

"Ten *zecchini*."

"What?" That was going to take just about all of the money I had left. Money that Giacomo had given me. My mind went again to that last night in Campiello Barbaro. My body hoisted against our garden wall. Our hearts beating against each other, our love and our desperation. A wave of desire stirred in me right there in the convent visiting parlor. I would do anything—pay anything—to feel that way again.

"Keep in mind," my brother went on, "Signor Grimani has to pay for the information he gets for you. Do you think servants who know secrets simply talk for nothing?"

"And he has to pay you, too, I'm sure." It was all adding up for me. I noticed my brother's chin and cheeks bristled with stubble, and his eyes shone. He was probably drunk.

"I take a small fee, yes, as his—agent." Pier Antonio flushed deeply. I had never seen that before. The embarrassment of profiting off his sister showed on his face. Who knew he was capable of any shame?

"You will read for yourself what a fine job Signor Grimani has done for you," he went on. "He was able to get the nun's servant, Laura, to tell everything."

"Oh! So you read the report?" I wanted to strangle him. Every fresh word out of his mouth lit me on fire.

"No!" He pulled the report out and pushed it through the bars. "See—it is sealed. He just gave me . . . a few details." He looked like he was stifling a laugh.

I grabbed it and slid it into my pocket. Whatever was written on those sheets felt like it was burning a hole of humiliation in me. When I saw no one was looking, I plucked out ten *zecchini* and pushed the coins through the bars. Pier Antonio scooped them up so quickly that they were gone in an instant.

I knew he would probably spend them that fast, too. And if I wanted help from him again, he would demand even more.

I walked as quickly as I could back to my room and shut my door. I sat on the floor to read. I don't know why. Perhaps, to be hidden by the bed in case someone came in. Or because the floor felt natural to me then. Low, base. I ripped open the seal.

My eyes scanned the first sentences. The handwriting was slanted, spidery.

> *I do not do this for the money . . . no, I desire only to help Pier Antonio's sister—who is innocent, honorable, and shut away—keep an eye on her wandering husband.*

I jumped farther down the page. I was only interested in what news Signor Grimani had managed to find out. At last, I found the heart of his account.

> *Signorina Capreta, I have copied out these words exactly as I heard them. They are all true—at least, as I was told. What changes could I ever make? I am no writer, nor lover, either.*
> *Here follows an account by Laura, servant to Sister Morosini at the convent of Santa Maria degli Angeli on Murano:*
> *"Sister Morosini and Giacomo Casanova meet as lovers in a* casino *in the garden of the old Villa da Mula. The* casino *belongs to this nun's other lover— I cannot name him—who is a Frenchman. He is rich, but ugly. Signor Casanova is not rich, but he is handsome.*
> *"How does Sister Morosini manage to escape from the convent? She is from a noble family, she can do as she likes. She pays the abbess to turn a blind eye. Sister Morosini and I leave by the back door of the kitchen garden, which opens onto a side canal. There, the Frenchman's gondolier waits to take us away. Why does he help his lover meet with a second lover? I have never dared to ask!*
> *"Often we are late leaving the convent, held up by Sister Morosini's excessive vanity: She has very long nails, which she insists I polish with a special stick covered in suede. Her hair, I might have to change the style three or four different times before she is satisfied. I sponge and rouge her face. She wears a rose perfume she keeps in a rock crystal flask. It was created by the French king, she tells me, and only a few people in the world are rich enough*

to own it. It was a gift from her lover.

"I think she also takes her time to draw out Signor Casanova's desire for her. His anticipation. The casino is decorated like a temple of love. There are candlelit mirrors along every wall. And the tables are piled high with books of engravings showing lovers in various acts of coupling. To excite the senses.

"They dine upstairs on French food, wine, and champagne, and then spend the night together. Sister Morosini always leaves before sunrise, to get back to the convent in the dark. Signor Casanova sleeps on until noon. He must be tired from his exertions! I sleep on the ground floor, and I am often awakened by the sounds of their lovemaking. He has astounding vitality. Every woman should be so lucky!"

Oh! To read these words—this poisonous proof written in a stranger's ink. I crumpled the report in my hands and clutched it like a ball of pain against my stomach. I gnashed my teeth, wanting to wail out loud but knowing I could not. Instead, I went down on all fours like a dog, crying to the silent boards, clawing at them until I had splinters under my nails and my fingers bled.

I vowed to kill them both in the night. Kill Giacomo and Marina.

But in the light of day, I thought better of it.

CHAPTER 65

Zulietta came out to visit about a week later, surprising me that she was alone. This was not typical of women in our social class: It was not considered acceptable behavior to be out on your own.

"Pier Antonio was supposed to accompany me," she explained, glancing around uneasily, "but at the last minute he sent a message that something else had come up."

Had Pier Antonio not wanted to face me? Did he not have the spy's report I had paid for earlier in the week—pawning the gold crescent-shaped earrings my father had brought me from Crete? Anything, for news.

I swallowed my fears and slid my hands outside the bars toward Zulietta. She clasped them warmly. "Tell me," I asked her, "have you been writing to Stefano? Has he written you?"

"Oh, no, Caterina," she said, pulling her hands away and blushing. "I can't let that happen."

"Why not? Didn't you write me that you thought you—"

"Shh, Caterina—please!" she quieted me. Her honey-brown eyes looked panicked. "I cannot give in to that temptation. You know—and I know—that Stefano is no match for me. Our

families are too . . . different . . . and I see that clearly now that
I am home."

"But, Zulietta," I urged her, feeling disappointed at what I
had to admit were not unreasonable words. "He obviously
loves you, and you love him—"

"No." She shook her head, as if banishing demons. "It cannot be." She forced a smile. "Oh!" she burst out. "I almost forgot! Pier Antonio gave me a letter for you." She cast her eyes
around furtively, then slipped an envelope out of her pocket.

I saw the familiar spidery handwriting. My spy's report. Relief. But my blood also burned at my brother. What a fool he
was—risking Zulietta finding out what I was doing. Or maybe,
that was precisely why he had given it to her. To stir up trouble.
Love is all a game.

Zulietta slid the letter under the bars. I snatched it. Then, not
seeing the abbess anywhere around and unable to resist my terrible curiosity, I broke the seal to read.

> *Here follow the words of Signor Baumanière, chef*
> *and owner of a casino near San Moisè:*
> "Signor Casanova has rented my casino until
> Easter. Fool that he is, he told his lover he owned a
> casino in Venice. Now he has to quickly rent one to
> make his story appear true.
>
> "My casino makes a fine impression. I have deco-
> rated it to delight the senses: The walls are adorned
> with painted porcelain tiles showing the sixteen
> pleasures of love, and the walls and ceiling are mir-
> rored, to reflect back to lovers the happiness found
> in each other's arms.
>
> "The first night he stayed, Signor Casanova asked
> me to prepare a supper for two with eight dishes. He
> likes everything highly seasoned and exciting to the
> senses—game on the very edge, sticky salted cod,
> cheeses when the little creatures are visible. But the

next day, I learned he had dined alone. You see, all the food is sent up on a dumbwaiter concealed in one of the walls. I never intrude on what is happening in the upstairs rooms. I realized he was testing me— which is ridiculous, since I have cooked for many finer men than he is!

"The next night, he asked me to prepare another elaborate meal with game, fish, truffles, oysters, fruit, sorbet, and Burgundy wines. This one, I'm sure he ate together with his lover. I saw her myself. But I never saw her face, because she arrived masked, and more—disguised as a man. It is clear she cannot let anyone know who she is.

"She left the casino *before sunrise. I watched her gondola head toward the Grand Canal, but that is all I know about her. Signor Casanova bragged to me she is very beautiful. And he showed me a pair of slippers and a nightcap trimmed with French lace he had bought for her."*

"Caterina!" cried Zulietta. A few visitors' heads turned. She quickly lowered her voice and moved her chair closer to the bars. "What is it you are reading? I would not have given it to you if I knew it would upset you!"

"It's alright," I said, wiping away tears with shaking fingers. "You have done nothing wrong."

"What is it?" she asked. "You must tell me."

"Giacomo—Giacomo has taken another lover," I confessed to her. Her eyes widened and she looked aghast.

"How do you know for sure? Is that what this letter is saying?"

"Yes. I asked Pier Antonio to—to keep an eye on him."

Zulietta smiled with relief, thinking the letter really was from him. "Caterina. You know you cannot believe anything Pier Antonio says."

"No—I'm sure it is true." I lowered my voice to a whisper. "It is someone I know. A nun. Here."

"Here?" Zulietta was too surprised to keep her voice low. The abbess, who had appeared across the room, turned sharply and gave us the Evil Eye.

"Shh." I signaled for Zulietta to lean in closer. "She escapes from here and meets him in secret. She is a noble, and very rich, and buys her way out whenever she wants." More silent tears started down my face. My situation was so miserable, and unfair!

Zulietta gave me her handkerchief. She knew I rarely carried my own. She always carried four: one to peel fruit; another for sorbet, chocolate, or coffee; and two more for her nose.

"How—why did he choose a nun?" she asked. I dried my face and held on to her handkerchief.

"He used to come to see me in church on feast days. He hid in the crowd. She spotted him and snatched him. At least—that is what I think happened."

Zulietta sat thinking for a while. She was not one to babble. She always waited until she was sure what she wanted to say.

"Maybe," she offered, "he chooses to chase a nun because she can never be his wife. Think about it, Caterina. Think of all the beautiful women in Venice. Why trouble himself with someone who is shut away for life? This way, he can have his fun—as—as I hear men like to do—but it will not be a lasting thing. That is the beauty of it."

She looked very satisfied with her explanation. Clearly, she believed her little love affair over the summer made her wise in the ways of the world.

"Do you honestly think so?" I asked, desperate.

"I do," she assured me. "*Stai calma.* It will all work out in the end."

I breathed a sigh of relief. This is what dear friends can do in our lives: make us feel so much better.

Even when they are wrong.

CHAPTER 66

Only two nights later, as I listened to rain strike the glass of my convent room window, I was startled by a knock at the door. It was the abbess, holding a small lamp to my face.

"Caterina—good, you are still awake." She was wearing only a chemise and a coarse wool robe, which considerably undermined her authority. Her drab brown hair, usually hidden by a wimple and veil, was cut short and thinning.

"Your cousin—Zulietta, is it?" she went on.

"Is she alright?" I asked, my heart beginning to pound.

"She is, child. She is downstairs. She says she has an urgent message for you. Someone is sick—not your parents, thank God. A friend on the mainland. Frederica?"

Frederica. On the mainland. My mind raced. *Farfalle*. Zulietta meant the horse, Farfalle.

"Yes, Abbess," I said, sweetly. "Frederica is quite old. Could you maybe allow Zulietta to come upstairs to my room and see me? It will be cold and dark downstairs. I—I have some coins for your trouble." Oh yes, I had learned a few things from Marina about how to handle our abbess.

"Certainly," she said, smiling. She waited in the doorway while I got the coins out from my pocket. Then she slipped away.

In less than five minutes, I heard the sound of leather slippers coming quickly up the stairs. My cousin stood at the end of the hallway, shrouded in a heavy cloak and carrying a lamp.

"Zulietta!" I whispered loudly from my doorway. She ran toward me.

"Oh! Caterina," she exclaimed as she collapsed in my arms. She came in, set the lamp on the floor, and did not even take off her cloak. "You must help me. I did not know where else I could turn."

"What has happened? Farfalle—?"

"Yes—Stefano wrote me—"

"He wrote you?" I couldn't help a surprised smile, as only two days before she had firmly told me they were not writing each other.

"He sent me a message through Father Ludovico," she explained. She rubbed her hands together over the candlestick I had burning near my bed.

"Our priest—at San Gregorio?" I exclaimed, now very surprised. We both adored Father Ludovico. He was fat, with terrible bumps all over his face—some the size of chestnuts—but a nicer, more caring man there never was.

"Stefano did not know my address," Zulietta explained. "At some point I must have mentioned the name of the parish where I lived. After Mass today, Father Ludovico gave me the letter while my mother wasn't looking."

"Did you bring it with you?" I asked.

Zulietta nodded, pulling it out of her pocket. As she handed it to me, I noticed her hands were still wet and cold. She had come all this way in the freezing rain. I read the soft and slightly soggy sheet.

Zulietta,
Forgive me for writing you, when I understand

*it is not what you may want. Of course, I have not
forgotten you. And neither has Farfalle. She has not
been herself since I took her away from the villa.
Recently, worms have bred on the gross humors in
her body: She is lean and tired, her eyes are dull,
her breath is hot, and she constantly lies down and
gets up, or rolls on the ground in violent pain. I fear
she may be far gone. Can I ask you, as a friend, to
come see her? I think your presence will comfort
her, even if it cannot save her.*

    Yours,

    Stefano

"What should I do?" Zulietta cried as I handed her back the letter. She folded it tenderly back into her pocket. "Stefano needs me—Farfalle needs me—but how can I leave Venice without my parents knowing? Even to come here tonight I had to sneak out after they had gone to sleep. How would I ever travel all the way to the mainland?"

"Shh, shh," I comforted her, taking hold of her hands. I suspected Stefano wanted Zulietta to come for more than the old horse, and I was determined to help. I went to sit on my bed and think. Zulietta remained standing by the window.

"It will not work to sneak away," I said, "because you would be gone too long. Instead, you need a reason why you have to go."

"A reason," she echoed. But scheming was not Zulietta's strength. She looked back to me.

"A reason . . ." I continued, "that cannot be denied. Something high-minded. Something . . ." I paused, my mind going to places I had heard about on the mainland. "What about the Basilica di San Antonio, in Padua?"

"What about it?" asked Zulietta. "It is a church."

"It is a great pilgrimage church, for healing," I went on, my ideas beginning to churn. "The faithful come from all over to lay prayers at San Antonio's head. Or feet. Or somewhere on his body." We both giggled. "Tell your parents you need to go there, for healing."

"Healing from what?" she asked. "And why wouldn't my mother or father come with me, if I were sick?"

"True," I said, thinking more. "Maybe not *your* healing. Someone else's." I stood up and started pacing.

Pier Antonio.

It was more than perfect. San Antonio was even his name saint. Or at least, one of them.

"What if . . ." I said, "we offer Pier Antonio money—believe me, he will take it—to say *he* needs to go to Padua. For . . . spiritual healing. God knows—he could use it!" Zulietta smiled, which encouraged me further. "He asks your parents, *Can my sweet cousin Zulietta come with me? To keep me out of trouble. To inspire me to stay on a better path.* You know everyone is desperate for a change in him. With luck, they agree to let you go."

"*With luck they agree to let me go?*" Zulietta echoed worriedly.

"Well—you will have to make your parents feel bad for you," I encouraged her, "how you suffered at the hands of Giorgio Contarini, how very wrong they were about him . . . and how right this trip is for you. Tell them also you want to see those paintings you are always talking about—who are they by—?"

"Giotto!" said Zulietta, giving me her first genuine smile of the night. "The frescoes by Giotto in the Arena Chapel in Padua, showing the lives of Christ and Mary. They say those paintings begin the whole Renaissance in art." She sighed happily.

"Religion. Art. However you choose to do it, Zulietta," I said, trying to give her confidence. "You must convince your parents that this trip, *right now,* is what you need."

Zulietta nodded her assent, but she still looked terrified. Her face, usually rosy and shining with good health—as if her humors were in perpetual perfect balance—had gone pale.

"I believe in you, Zulietta," I said, echoing the words of strength she had given me in the days just before my banishment. I went over to hug her close.

"I believe in you," I whispered again against her soft hair, which smelled like thousands of days spent together in Venice. "And I believe in your Stefano, too."

CHAPTER 67

I sent Zulietta away with my clever plan, knowing I would not hear from her—successful or not—for several weeks. I planned to send Concetta to her house each Wednesday, hoping eventually for news.

November came to the convent, the worst month in the Venetian year. It rained all the time. This day, as we sat in the choir of the church at Matins, we could see our breath. The sun was just rising, greeting us through the eastern apse windows.

I huddled next to Arcangela. The priest was late, as usual. I think he drank too much. Typically, he would ramble on from the lectern, until by Vespers he was simply scolding us. I rarely listened.

Arcangela started to sing to herself while we waited, a melody I had heard my father hum before. I leaned in to hear her better. She had a sweet singing voice, as if God had given her this one gift to make up for her hunchback.

Ah, Robin, gentle Robin,
Tell me how thy lady does . . .

The song was in English. I did not recognize many words. But it had a melancholic refrain, so that I guessed it was about lost love. Eventually, one row of us, and then the next, grew silent, until her song filled the church. I imagined even the souls buried under the floor turned in their tombs to listen.

A gust of cold air rushed in and broke off the song. We all turned. Marina stood at the far door with her head high and chest thrust out, a look of unmistakably proud pleasure. I noticed something flash around her neck. A heavy gold chain.

She approached the choir. I could smell rose perfume floating out of the folds of her habit as she took a seat opposite me. She did not meet my eyes.

A large oval medallion hung off the gold chain, with a picture of the Annunciation painted on it. I gaped at her, speechless. Even from where I sat, I could recognize the fine, precise style of the miniaturist who had painted my ring—my gift from Giacomo. And his portrait? Was it hidden under the thick cover of this medallion, too?

"Venite exsultemus Domino . . ."

The priest had arrived and was chanting the opening psalm. Marina was singing, but I had turned to stone.

I needed no more spies. No more eavesdropping on the floor. With that piece of jewelry, she—they?—were sending a message to me. A message as bold as the black notes in a choir book.

I thought I would vomit on the floor. My legs shook uncontrollably beneath my skirt. Arcangela put a hand on my knee and huddled in closer to warm me. But I felt hot, burning with shame and rage. I broke away and ran out of the church. I felt God had left me anyway.

CHAPTER 68

I ran to the cloister and threw my ring into the rain-filled fountain. Let some pipe eat it. I did not care.

"Caterina!" Marina's voice echoed from under the stone arcades. I kept running.

"Caterina! Stop!"

I turned. Oh, there were things I was bursting to say to that whore.

"Why did you run out?" she called, hand to her heart as she approached me. She was shivering from the cold, and looked surprisingly human, and vulnerable.

"You know why!" I spat.

"Are you jealous over Giacomo?" she asked, softly. "Because you shouldn't be."

"Why not?" I cried, sure she was lying. But still, I wanted to hear her answer.

"Love is only a game, Caterina."

Where had I heard that before? Oh yes—my brother. The two of them were snakes in a pit.

"It's not a game to me," I wailed. "You knew—you knew I—"

"—considered yourself to be married to Giacomo? True. But at the same time, false. A man like that cannot be held captive by one woman. I did you a favor."

"A—favor?!" I was dumbfounded.

"Certainly. He was going to be tempted away from you by somebody. Did you think he would wait panting at the convent doors for you for four years? Of course not. This way, you can be assured he will not marry me—or anybody else."

"Oh—then I must thank you!" I had a wild urge to attack her. But I also yearned to get my ring back. I imagined it sitting in the cold water, alone and freezing. I vowed to rescue it as soon as she was gone.

"I feared you would take it this way," she said with a sigh. "That is why I hid things from you. But now that you under-stand—"

I started to walk away.

"Caterina!" she called after me. "I can help you! I can help you see Giacomo again!"

I stopped dead. I made her speak to my back.

"He told me he cannot bear to think about his old love. He still loves you, you see," she coaxed me. "I'm sure he wants to show you his feelings. I have an idea how this could happen."

I turned to face her again. I noticed that her black silk slip-pers—Marina rarely wore ugly nun clogs—were wet with morning dew. Her face looked drained from the chill. Or was it from something else? A fear of losing the game? She desired me; she desired my Giacomo. Yes, love was all a game to her, and she required all the pieces in her hands.

"This Saturday is the Carnival ball," she said, as if I needed reminding. The ball was the biggest event of the season. True, the nuns and boarders had to remain behind the window bars and only watch all the other dancers, but we had been waiting many weeks for this night.

"Giacomo plans to come in disguise and meet me at my *casino* afterward," she explained. "But—what if we dress you as a nun and send you instead of me? Make a switch and surprise him? He will be delighted!"

"Why would you do this for me?" My head was spinning. It made no sense. Steal my lover, then give him back? Still, I could not resist the prize she offered.

"To please Giacomo," she said. "To please you. I've told you before, men require novelty. We will please him, and at the same time, we will both get what we want."

"Which is?"

"To enslave him."

CHAPTER 69

For the Carnival ball I disguised myself as Colombine. She is the clever and cunning lover of Harlequin. Her costume is simple: a servant's dress made of cotton, lace collar and apron, and curled ribbon and lace cap. The dress was easy to find at the convent, and Concetta brought me the other items I was missing from Venice. Colombine wears no mask. Instead, I powdered my face with flour.

"Here," said Marina, who was helping me with the final touches of my costume in her room. "Let me glue this on." She showed me a tiny circle of black silk balanced on her finger. I immediately remembered the one I had seen glued near her mouth when she was with Giacomo—*Love's assassin*. Of course, I wanted one, too.

"Near the eye it means *irresistibile*," she explained, pressing it high on my cheek. She pulled a ringlet of my hair aside and showed me my reflection in a mirror. I was surprised that my spine tingled with the brush of her fingers on my skin. I was hungry to be touched, and loved.

"What will you wear?" I asked her.

"My habit," she said. "Giacomo must expect a nun tonight." She laid a long-nailed finger on my forehead and gave me one of her devilish smiles.

We joined the other nuns and boarders behind the bars in the visiting parlor to wait for our guests to arrive. I could hardly wait to see Giacomo. In my mind, he came only for me. He was my precious gift for the night. And I would be a gift for him, as well. A surprise that I hoped fervently he would welcome with open arms.

I pressed my nose outside the bars to breathe in the sweet smell of frying dough. Candles flamed in every sconce along the walls and danced off the polished silver. A group of musicians tuned their strings in a corner, making awful sounds. I put my hands over my ears and giggled. Marina smiled at me, taking me in keenly. I had a strange feeling that I was an actor in some play, and she was my audience.

Boatloads of masked revelers began to arrive, and soon the room came alive with calls and laughter. I saw Harlequins in boldly colored jackets and trousers, Punchinellos with bulging stomachs and hunchbacks, Scaramouches in black Spanish dress. One costume in particular caught my eye: the Plague Doctor. He was dressed in a long black robe and wore a wax mask shaped like a bird's head. The long beak was meant to keep out unhealthy vapors. I noticed everyone stepped away from this character wherever he went, as if just being near the costume of plague might sicken them.

I tried to spot Giacomo in the crowd, but could not find him. I began to grow impatient. Oh, it was cruel entertainment, watching everyone dance from inside our cages.

Marina touched my arm. I felt the hairs on my skin stand up— part pleasure, part fear of the unknown that lay ahead of me.

"There he is," she said, signaling with her eyes.

I saw the crowd part for the strangest disguise of all. A tall man wore an oversized white linen tunic with wide sleeves, and wide trousers that came down over his heels. A white cap covered his hair, ears, and neck, and a white mask covered his face. A piece of gauze hung in front of his eyes.

"Are you sure it's him?" I asked.

"Yes," she said. "He is Pierrot. A French character."

Giacomo glanced over to the windows where we sat, but did not let himself linger on us. Instead, he grabbed the hand of a pretty girl dressed in a checkered Harlequin costume and danced a minuet with her. He moved about in perfect character as the clownish fool, pretending to veer and fall, but then catching himself before he hit the floor. I stood up to see him better. I felt he was putting on a show for me. Or was it for Marina?

"Watch out!" I called to him. The pretty girl's lover, also dressed as Harlequin, had approached from behind and started spanking Giacomo with a wooden sword. Giacomo quickly grabbed him by the leather belt and lifted him right off the floor. How strong he was! He slung Harlequin over his shoulders and ran around the room, the Harlequin's checkered legs kicking wildly in the air. We screamed and squealed at the scene from behind our windows.

Mayhem broke out. A Punchinello dashed out in front and tripped Giacomo. He fell over, and Harlequin toppled off. All three men started to wrestle on the floor. Giacomo ripped open Punchinello's coat, and when that happened, his false stomach and hunchback fell out. I was laughing so hard my belly hurt.

The abbess marched toward them with a scowl on her face. Giacomo stood, handed Punchinello back his stuffings, and offered the crowd a last, theatrical bow. Just as the abbess was about to reach him, he turned on his heel and ran out.

"Now," said Marina, briskly.

"Now?" I was still in a childlike state of mind from all the laughter. I had to make a switch to become a woman, a lover.

"Follow me."

CHAPTER 70

Marina led me from the visiting parlor back to her room. She lit a single candle near the bed and took a folded habit from a chest of drawers.

"Why can't I stay dressed as Colombine?" I asked, retying my lace apron tighter around my waist. I did not want to face Giacomo in a shapeless black habit.

"I explained my plan to you already," she said, smoothing out the rough wool with her hand. "Be sure to turn away from him when he first walks in. Otherwise, he will instantly know it is you. We want him to fall happily into our trap."

"Are you sure he will be happy?" I asked, filled with last-minute doubt. I sat down on the bed.

Marina got behind me and began to unbutton my dress. "What man would not be happy to see a wife as adorable as you are?" She kissed my bare shoulder and I shivered with undeniable pleasure.

When she had finished helping pull the habit over my head and tied it loosely with a coarse leather belt, I took the candlestick and went to the mirror.

"You have never looked uglier!" I said to my reflection. Still, I was laughing at myself. I felt ready for my adventure.

"On the contrary—you are beautiful," said Marina in the dark, her voice soft and admiring. "An angel in black. Come, the gondolier is waiting for us by the shed." She blew out the candle and threw a heavy black cloak over me.

We slipped down the stairs and ran through the empty cloister. There were no stars that night. The sky was thick with clouds, and a cold wind blew my habit and cloak like sails. As we passed through the garden, the silvery leaves of the olive trees were shaking and whispering. A storm was coming.

I saw an empty gondola thrashing in the turbulent water. As soon as we reached the edge of the canal, the gondolier, dressed in red cap and sash, appeared from behind the shed. He jumped in the boat and reached around my waist to lift me in. I paused outside the door of the cabin to wait for Marina's parting words for me.

"Be careful," she said.

I looked at her, confused. Was I in danger?

"Signorina, inside," the gondolier ordered, opening the cabin door for me.

I made my way onto the soft velvet seat and wrapped my cloak around me. The cold night had already seeped into my skin. I tried to warm myself with my excitement, a little fire inside.

"*Al casino*," I heard Marina say.

The mooring rope made a *thump* as it was thrown back into the boat. I heard the oar slide into its lock. The boat turned and rocked violently. I was on my way.

CHAPTER 71

I arrived in minutes at what I guessed was the Villa da Mula. Icy rain pelted me as the gondolier lifted me from the boat. Before me I saw a high brick wall and, at its center, a stone entryway carved with strange animals and plants: curled serpents, tangled vines, monkey-like creatures with wings. I felt I was about to enter another world—maybe something like the exotic East, full of deception, and desire. I took out the key that Marina had given me, and unlocked the door.

The garden inside was a ruin. It looked as if someone long ago had planned it, loved it: There was an abandoned fountain now filling with rain, jagged brick paths, plants left to die over winter. I approached a small building, I presumed the *casino*. Its columns were made of thick coils like twisted snakes, all inset with gold glass and lapis lazuli. I could see lights burning upstairs, and hoped for a fire. My leather slippers and the hem of my habit were soaked.

I flew up the stairs, wondering if Giacomo was already waiting. He had left the ball before me. But when I opened the door to the upstairs room, it was empty. My heart sank. The fireplace was cold. I found a tinderbox and wood splints on the mantel, and after struggling a minute with my wet hands, I created a spark. To be warm again! Nothing must be as freezing as watery Venice in winter.

I kept my back to the door as Marina had told me to do, but it was hard to resist peeking around. The walls were covered with deep rose paper painted with knotted trees and flowering plants. The blossoms were bigger and softer than anything I knew, light pink and white. All kinds of exotic birds perched in the branches. The furniture was glossy and painted bright red, green, and gold. I presumed this was *lacquer*, made from what I had heard was a tree in China called a lacquer tree. In an alcove was the gilded bed, covered in luxurious red silk damask.

The wait for Giacomo was an eternity. I could feel prickles of sweat starting under my arms. To be reunited after four months apart! I pushed any thoughts of Marina out of my head. When he saw me again, Giacomo would be all mine.

After maybe half an hour, I heard the downstairs door open and slam shut with the wind. Eager footsteps climbed the stairs. I held on to the mantel to steady myself and turned to face the wall. My heart was beating light and fast.

"Forgive me." I heard his voice as he approached me across the room. "Fortune was with me at cards tonight." He reached for my waist to turn me around. "As it still is, my dear."

I turned to face him, smiling at the surprise I was giving him. He jumped back.

"Giacomo?" Of course I knew exactly who he was, but he was still wearing his white Pierrot mask over his face.

He did not answer me, and I saw he was shaking.

"Giacomo?" I reached to take his hand, but he pulled it away. He dropped into a chair by the fireplace and seemed turned to stone.

"You—you must be startled to see me," I stammered, mortified. I realized immediately I had been set up to fail. Marina had foreseen he would reject me, and her victory over me would be complete. "I—I am surprised, too. I had no idea who—that I would be meeting you here tonight."

He continued to stare ahead in a cold gloom. It was agonizing. I took a seat across from him and bowed my head. A penitent nun.

Eventually, he untied the handkerchief that held on his mask. I felt I could breathe again, seeing his real face. I smiled, but his face expressed only disappointment. His skin beneath the mask had also been whitened by flour, so that he looked sickly, and his teeth yellow.

Finally, he broke the silence. "Forgive me, my angel. I am only very astonished by the switch you have made."

"If you are displeased," I cried, "I am in despair!"

"I could never be displeased to see you. How could you think that? But—I have been tricked. How is it you were persuaded to put on this disguise?"

"My friend—Sister Morosini—told me that her happiness depended on my doing this for her." Lies came pouring out. "How could I refuse her? She dressed me in her habit, and said nothing about what would happen here. It was just an innocent game—meant to please you, I'm sure!"

I sprang from my chair and fell at his feet. I laid my head on his knees, but I felt that every muscle in his body was taut, and unforgiving.

He lifted my chin to see my eyes.

"Did you tell her about me? Did you betray our secret? Because I have never told her about you."

"No! No! Of course not. Maybe Concetta told her. I don't know how she found out."

He said nothing, caught in a labyrinth of lies.

"Do you love her?" I asked after a minute, searching his face. "Do you love—Marina?"

He looked down at me, stricken. I could feel his knees begin to tremble beneath my hands. "My innocent, when I found

myself unable to live with you, I could not resist her charms."
The final guillotine came down. "I have fallen madly in love
with her."

I jerked my head away. I felt the room pressing and spinning
all around. I heard his next words as if I were floating outside
my own body.

"But Marina plays tricks and scorns me in return. If she
loved me as I love her, she could never have done me the excruciating favor of sending you here in her place."

"Oh my God, oh my God," I cried, clutching my stomach. I
closed my eyes, afraid I might vomit. I heard Giacomo get up
and walk over to the fireplace. When I looked up, blood was
streaming from his nose.

"Giacomo!" I screamed, as he hurriedly fished for a handkerchief from his pocket. "What is happening?"

"A leftover from my childhood disease, my angel. It happens
when the blood rushes to my head. Do not worry."

He came and sat back down, still with the handkerchief to
his face. The nosebleed—cruel remnant of his youth—seemed
to make him even more wretched. But at the same time, it softened him toward me.

"Caterina," he pleaded, "try to understand me. I am weak. I
have fallen in love with Marina—yes. But you know I can never
marry her—she is a nun. You, on the contrary, will be freed one
day from the convent. Our love has time enough to be rekindled."

I sat at his feet and tried to make sense of what he was saying.
Was I still his wife—and in *time enough* he would rediscover he
loved me? Did love work like this: a fire you light, extinguish,
then relight?

He sighed deeply, then stood to go. "Tell Marina she has
made me unhappy for a long time to come." He took a key out
of his pocket and dropped it ringing onto the table. Tying on
his Pierrot mask again, he turned toward the door.

"Giacomo! Don't go!" I burst out, running after him. I
pulled on his arms, grabbed his thin linen tunic. "I love you!"

"Caterina, I am sick with grief. I love you with all my soul, but now I am in a situation to be pitied." He slid aside his mask and kissed me on the cheek. Its plaster edge brushed my skin roughly.

He left me standing there—ridiculous in my habit, loved like a sister. The wind howled and banged the shutters against the outside of the building. I did not even know how I would get back to the convent. I had not made any plans. Too busy running after the illusion of the night's happiness, and carelessly not thinking a minute beyond it.

CHAPTER 72

Venice, 1774

So that was the end of Caterina's love affair. Or, what she intended to tell about it. She would no longer discuss it with Leda or anyone else. She preferred to focus on the future. And especially on Leda's baby, due to arrive in about a month now.

Who knew where this baby was going, once it was born? Most likely, a foundling hospital near Venice or Florence. Marina would figure something out. That was the secret job of any abbess. But before this happened, Caterina wanted the baby to have a few beautiful items. A set of fine sheets for the cradle. Lace-trimmed gowns. Some lace caps. Burano was the destination for these kinds of things, as every Venetian knew. So Caterina hired a boatman one early August morning, and told Leda they were going on a special expedition.

Burano lay about three or four miles beyond Murano, and there was no way to reach it without passing the convent of Santa Maria degli Angeli along the way. About a mile out from the northern shore of Venice, they spied its high brick and crenellated walls. Caterina winced. The sight filled her with violent memories, but at the same time, their vividness made her feel alive. Nothing since had ever felt as real, as fully lived, except perhaps when Leda had come to stay with her.

"Would you like some cheese, Leda?" she said abruptly, to distract herself. She got busy unpacking a picnic from her satchel and tore off some bread with anxious fingers. She felt a little nauseous, and hot, as if she had dressed too warmly.

"No—*grazie*, I'm not hungry," said Leda.

"Water? Wine?"

"No." Leda watched the convent walls slowly recede behind the boat.

"Caterina..." she asked—as Caterina had suspected she might—"was that night at the *casino* the end of your affair with Giacomo? Were you ever able to forgive him after he said that Marina had—"

"—done him an excruciating favor?" Caterina broke in sharply. It felt less humiliating to say it herself, than to hear someone else repeat it. It had unburdened her—yes—to tell Leda her story, but certain pieces still cut like glass.

"It was never the same after that night," said Caterina, simply.

The cabin smelled like soft cheese and her own sweat. She dropped the piece of bread she had torn off back into the satchel. No appetite, after all.

The sound of Leda laughing awoke Caterina from a rocking sleep in the boat. The shutters were wide open, and Leda was pointing out to the green sea.

"Look! Look at that bell tower!" she cried. "It is tipping!"

Caterina peered out the boat window and saw the island of Burano rising from the shallow water. Rows of simple cottages were all painted bright colors, each different so that the fishermen could find their way home in haze and fog. The leaning bell tower of San Martino did not make a good first impression.

"That poor tower began to slide very soon after it was built," Caterina explained.

"I suppose Venetians don't build as well as Florentines do," Leda teased her. "Brunelleschi, Alberti, Michelangelo . . ."

"It is harder to build on shifting sands than solid ground," said Caterina, putting the haughty Florentine in her place. "You try building a church with water all around it!" They were giggling together when the boat bumped to a stop. Children on the dock flocked to help knot the mooring rope around a gaily striped pole.

The children led them into the main square, where dozens of market stalls were set up under canvas umbrellas. Women of all ages sat hunched over small pillows held in their laps. Their fingers danced in the air, guiding almost invisibly threaded needles over lace patterns. Caterina inspected the piles of finished work laid out on tables. She didn't dare touch anything—so delicate and white—but Leda could not resist and picked up a baby's cap.

"Isn't it sweet?" she said, placing it on top of her head. Caterina was about to scold her, but the old woman at the stall saw a likely sale.

"Ah—Venetian *punta in aria*. The very best kind."

"*Stitch in the air!*" sang Leda, taking it off to run her finger over the swirling lace trim. "What a perfect name!"

"Do you know the legend, Signorina?" the old woman asked her. "The legend of making the first lace?"

"No." Leda smiled. "Tell me."

The old woman was mostly toothless and so shrunken she hardly had breasts anymore. But she had large, magnificent blue eyes, much like Leda herself.

"There was once—oh, many hundreds of years ago," the old woman said dreamily, "a young woman in Venice. Young, beautiful, and in love." She nodded to Caterina, as if convinced Leda's story was similar. "This young woman's betrothed gave her a piece of seaweed as a love token. But seaweed . . . it does not last, Signorina. A love token should last forever, just like love. So this young woman, she set herself to imitating the patterns of the seaweed, using only needle and thread."

"So—" said Leda, fingering the lace cap with new wonder, "the designs are meant to be like the forms of the sea?"

"Exactly, child."

Caterina felt now she could not resist buying the cap. It would remind Leda of Venice, and of their happy months together. She bought the matching gown, too, and a set of lace-edged sheets and pillowcases. At another stall, she also bought a set of six bibs.

"*Grazie!*" exclaimed Leda as the women wrapped the last of her linens in clean paper. Caterina was fairly sure that Leda had no sense of the cost of all these things. No matter. She yearned to spoil the girl this day, to delight her. They were both smiling as they left the stalls.

Yes—sometimes money can buy magic. She and Leda sat down in a square of shade they found on a small bridge, slid off their slippers, and dangled their hot feet over the water. Leda took out her pastels and a sketchbook and drew a bit. The yellow, red, green, and blue houses along the canals begged you to try to capture their colors. Caterina leaned back and closed her eyes. It had been a near-perfect morning.

The trip home brought them again beneath the looming walls of Santa Maria degli Angeli. Caterina pretended to count their packages sitting at her feet, but Leda stared out the cabin window as they rowed by it. Her questions for Caterina began anew.

"After you were tricked by Marina—Caterina, did you give up? Let her win?"

"Well, no—" Caterina reluctantly answered. "It wasn't simple like that."

"Because it seems—no offense—the more I learn, that she controls you something like a puppet." A flush spread across

Leda's face. "Isn't that why I am here? She forced you to take me in?"

"No—no!" Caterina struggled to keep calm in the face of this accusation. "Marina asked me for a favor, and I granted it. I'm glad I did." She said it with finality, hoping she might end this unfortunate conversation.

"A favor?" Leda asked, her voice rising. "What could you possibly owe that evil woman who set out to hurt you again and again?"

"Oh—it is complicated, Leda. There are parts you do not know—could not understand." Caterina's stomach was turning over.

"I think I *am* beginning to understand," Leda said, shaking her head at her previous blindness. "I think I am Marina's latest pawn. A way to still control you—for whatever reason—years later."

"No—no, Leda, it's not like that!" Caterina was beginning to panic. Where was this leading? Was Leda thinking she might try to beat Marina at her own games? Keep her baby? That would be insanity. "Marina simply asked me to take care of you until"—*until the thing is done*—"until the baby is born, and then she expects you back."

"Marina expects this—Marina asked me for that—" Leda's voice was full of a sixteen-year-old's outrage. "What could you possibly owe her? Nothing! Why not simply stand up for yourself?"

"*Basta!* Enough, Leda!" Caterina felt herself snap and break away from whatever rope had been holding her. "Do you want to hear what happened when I tried to fight back? Is that what you want?"

Caterina's mind seethed. She felt the waves of the lagoon as if they were inside her head. *Oh—I fought back. I fought back until I nearly killed her.*

CHAPTER 73

Murano, 1753

I had been left alone by Giacomo in the *casino*. His words echoed in my head—*madly in love with her . . . excruciating favor . . . I love you with all my soul*—and bits of my heart felt like they were cracking off. I went to sit on the bed and recoiled at the sight of its red silk cover, mocking me with false promises. Marina, too, I knew now for sure, was false to the core, pretending to give me things but all the time stripping me bare. I groaned and clutched my stomach. I felt a sob living inside me, getting ready to be born.

"Caterina?"

I swung around. Marina stood across the room in front of a large green cupboard. She was nowhere near any door.

"What are you doing here!" I screamed in fright. I jumped up and cowered behind the bed. She was like a ghost that had floated in. "How—?"

"Never mind that—are you alright?" She started to cross the room toward me. I could not make sense of how she had appeared, but I knew she was my enemy. My boiling blood told me that.

"Leave me alone!" I screamed. Rather than let myself be cornered against a wall, I ran toward her and started beating her chest with my fists.

"Get out of here! Get out!" I screamed, as if she were seeing something open—my heart, and all my dreams—and I had to close it, close it before she took more away.

"Caterina!" she cried, trying to grab my wrists. "*Calma ti, calma ti.*"

I fell against her and she tightened her arms to hold me. I longed for my mother, for any hug. But I quickly pulled away.

"How did you get in here?" I demanded to know.

She looked pale. Her eyes had dark half-moons under them. Whatever she had been planning for this night, it had evidently gone wrong.

"Come—" she said, "I will show you." The hand she reached out to me was shaking.

I trailed behind her in the direction of the green cupboard. She opened its doors, and I saw it was empty inside, with no back. Instead, there was a miniature door in the wall. The door handle was formed of a mask, some leering animal with a bronze ring in its mouth. Marina put her hand in the ring and pushed the door open. She crouched to go inside, and I followed her.

I found myself in a dark closet with no windows and another door on the opposite wall. Marina lit a candle on a small table. I could see a sofa was set facing the wall of the main room we had just left. There was an armchair and a desk. Enough furniture to be comfortable for a few hours. But why?

"I don't understand," I said to Marina. The flame of the candle lit up her clear, pale skin to a frightening glow. I did not like being in this small place with her, no matter how curious I felt. I turned to escape out the little door.

"I was watching you," she said.

I turned back to face her, my eyes full of fury.

"Watching me? Why? How?"

"I will show you." Her voice was steady, like someone intent on confessing all. Or maybe, intent on pretending to confess all. I couldn't believe anything she said anymore. I was like a snake that had been roused, ready to strike and protect myself.

She stepped in front of the sofa and unhooked a board that hung low on the wall. Behind it, I saw many small holes. Light shone in from the other room. I looked at her, confused.

"Look through," she said.

I sat on the sofa and leaned forward. Through the holes I had a perfect view into the main room. I saw clearly the bed in the alcove, with its red silk cover. The single candle still burning on the mantel.

"So—you came for a show!" I cried. I felt as if I had no clothes on. "Did you like what you saw?"

"No! No, I did not! Caterina—you must believe me." She took a seat at the far edge of the sofa. "I had the gondolier return for me after he dropped you off, so that I could come enjoy what I was sure would be a happy scene. I hid in this room. When we saw it was going badly—that Giacomo felt tricked, and scorned by me—I kept thinking I would make an appearance to right things. I waited, believing in my heart that two people who loved each other would reconcile as the night went on. But—it did not happen."

I felt crazed with outrage. "You wanted him to reject me—don't lie to me!"

Her face slackened as if I had punched her. Oh, I wanted to. I wanted to kill her right there, take that candle and burn it into that perfect white skin of hers. I thought of Giacomo touching her, adoring her, preferring her, and I felt I would vomit.

"If I ever did hold power over him, it is gone now," she said flatly. She picked up the board and placed it back over the secret holes. Her hands moved clumsily, but I wondered if it was an act. "He will come to despise me, the more he considers what I have done."

Could she be right . . . ? I felt my rage curdle into something else. Revenge, mixed with hope. Would Giacomo finally see her for what she was?

I couldn't know what would unfold from this night. But I realized then I had nothing to gain by making an enemy of Marina. Better to play my best part: the innocent angel.

"I'm sorry," I said. I looked right into her eyes and struggled to steady my voice. "If Giacomo loved me more, we would not have both lost everything."

"Don't blame yourself." She slid nearer to me. "It is not your fault things turned out badly." She took hold of my hand and laid her head against my shoulder. My spine stiffened.

Her words from before came back to me.

Had she said, *when* we *saw it was going badly?* Who else had been watching me?

CHAPTER 74

I spent the next several days hiding in my room at the convent. I dreaded seeing anybody, especially Marina. Finally, on Wednesday, Concetta returned from Venice with a letter from Zulietta. I broke the seal immediately, hungry for news. I needed to be lifted away to another place, anywhere other than the miserable convent. A place where friendship, and perhaps even love, was still possible.

> Caterina, darling cousin,
> Forgive the bad handwriting. I am actually riding in the carriage home. I bought a small folding desk today in Vicenza, just to be able to write you. I could not wait.
> Where to start? By the time you read this, it will be just over two weeks since I saw you in your room at the convent, yet it feels as though a lifetime has passed since then.
> First, you will be very proud: I managed to deceive my parents. I paid Pier Antonio twenty zec-

chini *for help with my plan, which we set in motion
two Sundays ago, when my father and mother, and
yours, were together for* pranzo *after Mass.*

*"I have been thinking," Pier Antonio began,
speaking earnestly, hand to his heart, "how much I
want to start my life anew. To ask San Antonio for
healing, and guidance, etcetera, etcetera."*

*Then, he fed them the part about me: "Zulietta
and I are like sister and brother. And what is family for, but to help in times of need? I beg you to
allow her to come with me to Padua. I promise to
protect her, just as I would Caterina." (Ha!—that
one made me laugh.) "She, too, will be healed by
the saint."*

My God, it was beautiful!

*My father was the first one to be convinced. Are
you surprised? He has been so terribly remorseful
about what happened with Giorgio Contarini, I
knew he would be willing to grant me almost anything. It was my mother who proved more difficult.*

*"What if—" she started. "Pier Antonio, of course
we trust you, but Zulietta would be there alone . . .
and with only you to watch over her . . ."*

*Here, your father, without knowing it, came to
our rescue.*

*"Sister, are you implying Pier Antonio would not
fulfill his promise to protect Zulietta?" He bristled.
"That he has so little honor?"*

*"Oh, no, brother," she assured him. "Of course
not. These are just worries a mother has—for her
only daughter—"*

*"Have her bring her maid then," he snapped, "if
you are so concerned."*

"Elisabetta?" I offered. "I could use her anyway,

to help dress me and do my hair." Of course, you
know as well as I do—Elisabetta has designs on
your brother. I knew she would not be watching
me. In fact, she would be thrilled if I were to disappear.

"Elisabetta it is, then," my father said, smoothing the way. "A trip to Padua will be good for you,
sweetheart. And don't forget, take advantage and
go see—"

"The frescoes by Giotto!" I smiled at him, and
he glowed with pleasure. "I will bring you back my
sketches," I promised.

Voilà. It was done. We left two days later, the
delay killing me but I could not exactly run out of
Venice like a lunatic. Then, they would suspect
something was amiss.

Pier Antonio accompanied me on the journey to
Stefano's farm, which is in a small town north of
Vicenza, called Thiene.

"All this for an old horse, hmm?" he teased and
poked my stomach as we pulled up to the modest
farmhouse.

I waved him away and stuck out my tongue.
Yes—after ten hours together in a carriage, we were
now truly like brother and sister.

Stefano was pacing around the small courtyard
in front of the house, waiting for me in the noonday
cold. (I had dispatched a messenger to him as soon
as we reached the mainland, to let him know when
he could expect us.) He greeted me with friendly
kisses on both cheeks. Then, his very unfriendly
mother, Agnesina, came out to see me.

"You have come here to see the horse,
Signorina?" A glance over to Stefano, with

eyebrows raised in disapproval. He raised his brows
back at her, as if saying, "No—I am not going to
send her away."

"Yes, Signora, to see Farfalle," I answered, trying
to be as sweet as possible.

"You don't prefer to stay with your cousin at an
inn, in Vicenza?" True to form, Pier Antonio had
already turned the carriage around and left with
Elisabetta.

"Oh, no, Signora. I prefer to be here in the fresh
air—and, near Farfalle."

"For how long, may I ask, Signorina?"

I blushed at my unwelcome. "Oh—not too
long," I stammered. "You will hardly notice I am
here."

Another long glance to Stefano, whose face by
now had turned bright red.

"Oh, I think we will all notice you are here,
Signorina."

She clearly distrusted me. Not liking our differ-
ences in social rank, and probably fearing I was
toying with her son.

But enough about her.

The farm is a simple place, well-kept. The house
has only two rooms on the main floor. One is large,
with a great stone hearth, where they do all of their
cooking and relaxing together. And on the other
side of this room, they keep the pigs and sheep!
Stefano tells me the closeness of the animals keeps
the family warm in winter. A bit disgusting—yes?

Upstairs is a large bedroom for Stefano's
mother, and on the other side of the stairway, two
smaller bedrooms for his grandmother and him-
self. Thank God, the grandmother moved into the

*mother's bedroom when I arrived, to give me my
own room.*

As soon as I had revived from the trip with some
bread, salted farm butter, and tea, I insisted on visiting Farfalle. Stefano led me to where she was
staying, in a barn behind the house. (The family
also owns one heavy draft horse, Orso.) The
ground was frozen beneath our feet, the mud like
rocks under my slippers. We could see our breath,
and I wrapped my wool cloak tightly to try to stay
warm.

Farfalle smelled me enter—she immediately
raised her head and started looking around. Then,
she whinnied. I ran over to her. She looked wobbly
on her feet but was standing, a good sign. She
stretched out her neck to get as close as possible to
me, and even tried to hug me by curling her head
around my neck. In the end, though, it was too
much effort for her, so I just scratched her between
her ears. She gave a long, deep sigh.

I saw a dent about the size of a man in the straw
on the floor of the stall.

"Have you been sleeping in here with her?" I
asked Stefano.

"Yes," he confessed. "I find I sleep better if I am
near her, instead of worrying all night."

"She seems better than when you wrote me," I
noted. "Have you tried more remedies?"

"Oh yes," he said, opening the door to her stall, I
presumed to offer her food—though her oats were
barely touched. Farfalle followed his every move
with her eyes. "Remedies of milk and honey. White
wine and black soap. Turmeric, anise seeds,
brimstone, and spirits. She is better, but nothing has

completely worked. I still find the worms infesting her dung each day."

"Are there no remedies left to try?" I asked.

Farfalle had closed her eyes, and Stefano was stroking her eyelids, which she seemed to adore.

"Only one—I hesitated to do it. Bleeding her at the neck."

"Then let's do it," I said.

"In that dress?" he asked. It was one of my less fancy wool ones, with only a little lace at the neck and sleeves, but still one thousand times finer than the coarse cotton clothes his mother wore.

"Yes, in this dress," I said. "This is all I have to wear." I cast down my eyes, feeling criticized for my wealth—which I cannot change.

"No, no, Zulietta," he said, putting a hand on my arm as I stroked Farfalle's soon-to-be-cut neck. "You misunderstand me. I am very grateful you are here with me—to help us."

Stefano went to a nearby cupboard and took out a large, glazed clay bowl and a small silver box. Inside the box was a lancet. He lit a candle and held the blade in the flame for about a minute. Then, while I kept the bowl under Farfalle's head and tried to distract her with nonsense talk, he made a nick in the large vein of her neck. The blood came running out fast, soaking her brown hair in an instant. We collected about three cups into the bowl. And, I'm proud to say, I never turned away from the sight.

After we were done, I pressed a clean cloth on the cut to stop the bleeding. Stefano went to get her some linseed oil stored in another part of the barn.

"The idea," he explained when he returned, and

Farfalle was lapping the oil from a small cup, "is to cleanse her body of gross humors with the bleeding, then kill the last worms with the oil. Let's hope it works."

Well—whether it was the remedies he tried before, or this last one we performed together . . . Farfalle's health did start to improve. The next day, she ate more of her oats and remained standing for longer. Each morning, I rubbed her face, head, and neck clean with a cloth, and in the evenings, Stefano tossed up the straw to make a soft place for her to rest. After about a week, her eyes started to shine and look bright, and we knew she was getting well again. Stefano returned to sleeping in his own room.

All this time, we worked together as two companions, saying nothing about what had happened between us over the summer. But as I watched Stefano care for Farfalle, I found myself falling in love with him all over again. His kindness, his gentleness, his steady love and faith. On his part, Stefano showed me nothing of his feelings, if any remained. With no future for us, I was sure he knew he had to keep a distance. Only sometimes, I would catch him staring at me—in the barn, or across the table while the family ate together. His mother did not like seeing that, let me tell you! "Pass me the salt," she would say with irritation, to break the spell between us.

Late the last night, I was packing my clothes in my room. I felt hugely relieved my trip had been a success—that Farfalle was well again—but I also felt some melancholy. Stefano and I had not rekindled our affection, as only now I admitted to myself, I had hoped would happen.

*I heard a soft knock. I prayed it was not his
mother, nosing in on me.*

Stefano stood at the door.

*"Come in," I said. "The hallway is cold." He
came in and sat on the bed. There was no chair, so I
sat next to him, keeping myself about half a pace
away.*

*"I'm sorry you have to go so soon," he said. "I
wanted you to have more to remember from your
trip than bleeding a horse." He smiled at me, but
his eyes were sad.*

*"Oh—Stefano." I put my hand in his, without
thinking. It felt natural to comfort him. "Taking
care of Farfalle—healing her together—has made
me truly happy."*

*He smiled again, but not his usual, confident
smile, full of life and boyish joy. He seemed
serious—and nervous. His hands were trembling.*

*"Zulietta," he began, "I realize all this"—he
gestured to the plain, cramped room we were in—
"is not what you would ever want, and that I do
not deserve you—"*

*I put a finger to his mouth. "Shh," I said. "Stop.
I told you how I feel about you." Hearing this, he
kissed my finger, then my wrist, and, seeing no
doubt the invitation in my eyes, leaned in to kiss
me on the lips.*

*"I love you, Zulietta," he said. "More than you
could ever know."*

*After those sweetest words, we kissed and
caressed each other in new ways that felt so good,
and right. Though I assure you, Caterina, I did not
carry on like a sailor all night! "In time," I assured
him, leading his very eager hand away. "In time."*

The next morning, I cried as I said farewell to him by the carriage.

"Will you come back to me?" he whispered in my ear, clasping my arms tightly. "Promise me you will."

"I promise," I said, kissing his neck and laying my head on his shoulder a last, long minute. "I will always come back to you."

Oh, goodness! I realize writing this letter I never did do any sketches for my father. I will have nothing to show him. Perhaps it is for the best—the time for truth has finally come.

The time for truth has finally come. I folded Zulietta's letter, about ten pages of elated, carriage-written script. Well—maybe the time for truth had come for her, since she had gotten what she wanted. I swear, I was honestly happy for my cousin, and the small part I'd played in her success.

Now, if only I could get what *I* wanted.

CHAPTER 75

Late the next night, as I was about to go to bed, I heard the tapping of fingernails on my door. It could only be Marina.

I almost didn't let her in. But curiosity quickly got the better of me. Had she reconciled with Giacomo? Did she maybe have a message from him for me?

I tiptoed to the door and opened it a few inches. I was wearing only my nightgown and a deep pink damask robe.

There she was in the doorway, so close I could sense her warm skin, her pulse beating in the dark. Marina was still wearing her habit, no doubt back from some tryst with one—or both—of her lovers.

She held out a single sheet of paper to me, folded and unsealed. "It is from Giacomo," she explained.

I snatched the note from her hand. I went over to my desk and lit the lamp to read.

> *Caterina—*
> *I owe you an apology for the miserable night we spent together. Now I understand that Marina only*

wished to bring me happiness, and I was too much
of a fool to see her gift in the spirit of generosity
with which it was given. I believed I was not loved
enough, when in fact I was loved in excess of what
I deserved. I am a weak and imperfect creature,
beneath you both in everything. Can you forgive
me, my angel incarnate?

    Giacomo

I laid the sheet down, realizing this meant he had forgiven Marina. He was blind to what she really was, and I suppose he was blind to me, as well. He didn't want to see what burned down deep.

"He begs you to let him make it up to you," said Marina, who had followed me into the room, uninvited. "Come dine with us at the *casino* the day after tomorrow."

"No, thank you," I said. To sit there with the two of them, while they ran circles of love around me? No.

Marina pressed.

"He has begged me to bring you. And . . . there is someone else who wants to meet you."

Ah. There it was.

"Someone else?"

"I told you about him once before. My friend. The Frenchman."

"Your lover?"

"Yes."

"Why does he want to meet me? How does he know who I am?"

"He was with me that night, watching you from the secret room. He admired your beauty. Your intelligence. He has asked to meet you."

I felt angry, but also, oddly excited. My heart started to beat rapidly. I was vain, and hungry for admiration. "Why are you willing to share him?"

Marina considered. "His pleasure is my duty, and his pleasure now is to meet you. You will find him . . . witty and refined, in the way of the French."

I already knew the Frenchman was ugly from my spy's report. I knew Marina was lying to me about him, or at least, only telling me half truths. But an idea was quickly forming in my head.

> For love is strong as death,
> jealousy as hard as hell,
> its lamps are fire and flames.

It was something I remembered from the Bible. I decided to take those words now as my guide, like the boys who carried lighted lamps down the dark streets of Venice at night. I would go to the *casino* and enchant this Frenchman. Flirt with him. I would do it right in front of Giacomo.

He would burn with jealous love for me.

And just maybe . . . I would get him back.

CHAPTER 76

Marina dressed the salad. She tossed the leaves in vinegar and oil, salt and pepper, maneuvering the silver servers to show off her beautiful, dimpled hands. I sat at a small round table next to the French ambassador to Venice, Francois-Joachim de Bernis. Giacomo sat across from me. He had begged me to come to the *casino*—or so I had been told two nights before—but had seemed uneasy all through the meal. He kept jumping up to fetch the servant to complain about this or that. *The oysters are sandy . . . the* polenta *is lumpy . . .* he couldn't be pleased. Now he sat sulking. I wanted to draw him out of his foul mood, and at the same time, have him notice my charms working on the ambassador.

"Monsieur de Bernis," I asked in my most cheerful voice, "what is the most exciting experience you have had in all your travels?"

The ambassador considered my question while taking forkfuls of salad into his soft mouth. He was an unappetizing creature. No wonder Marina was more than willing to share him. He had a weak chin and several of them. He was bald and wore a wig to disguise it. Emerald and ruby rings squeezed the flesh of his fingers, so that puffy folds swallowed up the thick gold bands. Still—he was rich, and he bought Marina her freedom now and then from the convent. She clearly saw the trade as worth it.

"Signorina," he said, his eyes resting too long on my bare arms, "the most exciting moment I ever had was watching a woman experience *la petite mort* without ever being touched by me."

Marina broke into a mischievous smile. Giacomo winked at her. I blushed.

"What is *la petite mort?*" I asked. "A small death?"

"It is what the French call an orgasm," Marina explained to me. "A man's weapon wounds a woman to death without taking her life."

"Oh!" I giggled. "Go on, Monsieur de Bernis."

"Yes—one evening in London about fifteen years ago, I went to see Farinelli, the *castrato* singer, at the Opera of the Nobility. When this gelding opened his mouth, his voice was so melodious, neither man's nor woman's, I thought I was in paradise. At one point, he sang a single note that rose in strength until my heart flooded, and my whole body experienced a new kind of excruciating pleasure. I looked over to my beautiful companion at my side, and her eyes had sprouted tears. She took my hand and said, "*Merci*. I have experienced *the little death* with you."

"But, Monsieur," said Giacomo, "was it that she experienced *la petite mort* with you, or with Farinelli? It was he who brought her to the climax of pleasure. You were merely the *voyeur*."

De Bernis scowled. Marina shot a reprimanding look at Giacomo. He risked alienating her lover, who controlled their access to the *casino*, as well as her ability to escape the convent at all.

"Signor Casanova," de Bernis addressed him in a luxuriously condescending tone, "I find there is almost as much pleasure in watching other lovers, as in making love oneself. Unless the unfortunate situation should arise, that a lover is too pitiful or selfish to make love to a woman who loves him." His small black eyes flashed.

Giacomo's face turned dark red. I had not felt this embarrassed since the night my brother had made love to his mistress right in front of me. De Bernis was clearly referring to the night he had watched Giacomo and me from the secret room in the *casino*.

"Signorina"—de Bernis turned away now from Giacomo and spoke to me—"my friend Sister Morosini has pleased me immensely by bringing you here tonight." He dotted his oily mouth with a napkin. "I have rarely enjoyed a supper more. I am eager to see you again. Tomorrow night, perhaps—with Sister Morosini?"

"Tomorrow night is too soon for Caterina to leave the convent again," Giacomo broke in. "She cannot risk it."

"Yes, I can!" I sensed Giacomo was becoming jealous of de Bernis's claims on me. Just my plan. I intended to keep it going.

"Caterina—"

"Good," de Bernis interrupted Giacomo. "Then it is settled. Tomorrow night. I have a French book I want to share with you two beauties." He flicked his tongue. There was something obscene about him that left little to the imagination. "It is called *The Academy of Women*. I think you will find it . . . entertaining."

I started to panic inside. Was he expecting me and Marina to make love in front of him? Or . . . to both make love to him? I had no intention of letting his fat fingers touch me. I told myself Giacomo would step in well before that ever happened—step in and keep me from ruining myself. I was his angel incarnate.

"And what about Giacomo?" I asked, sweetly. "This has been—such a pleasure tonight, and it would be a shame not to include all of our merry group."

"Signor Casanova, please do join us," said de Bernis, with a sneer in Giacomo's direction. Then he stood and gazed right down my dress. "The best pleasures are shared—*oui*, Signorina?"

I blushed and smiled gratefully, believing I had maneuvered the situation perfectly. I had kept a very unappealing ménage à trois from taking shape, and in doing so, made sure I would see Giacomo again the very next night.

But after, when I caught Giacomo's glance, I was surprised to see his eyes looked sad. I think he realized I was being corrupted, and that he had led me to this point.

CHAPTER 77

"I am sure Monsieur de Bernis will be here soon." I saw Marina steal a glance at the green cupboard set against the wall.

It was the next night at the *casino*. My stomach felt hollow. We had been waiting for the ambassador for close to an hour. Supper was late.

"I will not be disappointed if he does not come," said Giacomo, who joined us by the warmth of the fireplace. I noticed he seemed to grow more at ease as the minutes passed. He had taken off his silk jacket, and unbuttoned his linen shirt at the cuffs. One long arm was draped over the back of the sofa. He had the forearms of a musician—lean and muscular. I watched him hungrily, then offered a coy smile. *I adore your dimples when you smile,* he had said. He answered me now with an appreciative flame in his eye.

As the hands on the table clock inched along and Monsieur de Bernis still did not show, I began to wonder if my real dream was going to come true this night. If the ambassador was not coming, did this not mean Giacomo was all ours—mine—for the night? My heart raced along deliciously. I dreamed only about myself, excluding Marina from my fantasy.

"Shall we eat?" I suggested. "Maybe Monsieur de Bernis will join us later." I said it to the far wall. I felt sure he was hiding behind it, in the secret room.

"Yes—let's," said Marina. "The food will all get cold." Her clipped tone told me that Monsieur de Bernis had surprised her, too, with whatever game he was playing. She liked to be the one in control of all the games. She stood to get a handbell to call the servant.

Giacomo leaned forward as soon as she left us.

"I am almost beside myself, my little charmer," he whispered. His eyes traveled over my décolletage. "It is like I am seeing you again for the first time. You have reached the perfection of your beauty."

I squeezed my thighs together at his words and felt a wave of pleasure overtake me.

Marina sat back down in her chair. Giacomo sat back. She adjusted the folds of her habit and shifted around uneasily. I hoped I looked calm and my most beautiful beside her. I had worn a flattering dress with just this intention: She was covered in black wool, while my cream-colored dress was cut deep with wide, pink silk bows sewn down the bodice. The tight sleeves exploded in flounces of lace and more silk bows. I wore a lace and ribbon collar at my neck—most fetching.

There was a light knock at the door and the servant entered with a simple supper of eggs, cold meats, bread, and wine. We ate and drank like wolves. Eventually, Marina, too, started to relax. She pulled out the silver pins that held her veil and let loose her chestnut hair.

"Doesn't our Caterina look beautiful tonight?" she asked Giacomo. She rose and tucked herself next to me in the wide chair. "She is irresistible." She had drunk too much, her words falling loosely from her wine-stained mouth. My own head was spinning.

"She is," said Giacomo, regarding us both with a gleam in his eye. "Why don't you show me how irresistible she is to you, Marina?"

"Would you like that, Caterina?" Marina asked, beginning to kiss my ear softly.

My first instinct was to stop her—did I not hate her? I longed only for my husband . . . for Giacomo. That was why I had come this night. But some part of me must have loved Marina, too. I could not resist her. I surrendered to misguided desire.

Oh! How tender is a woman! Her lips, her skin, her breath, her tongue—I dissolved at what I was feeling as she made love to me. The next thing I knew, Giacomo had sprung up from his chair and gone down on his knees. He lifted my skirts and buried his head between my legs. He kissed me where the body knows no reason, and together they brought me to the most intense climax of pleasure I have ever felt. The exquisiteness of it made me cry and never want it to stop at the same time.

When it was over, I begged for more.

We went over to the bed. Marina and I undressed Giacomo, all the time giggling and covering him with kisses. We held him down to make him ecstatic with desire. When it was clear he could stand it no longer, we released him and he flung himself on top of me. I was thrilled I was the one chosen to receive him. I opened my arms and in less than a minute he gave up his soul to me. I experienced my second *little death* of the night. Marina pleasured herself after. She seemed to have no jealousy in the bedroom—it was all love to her, all just a game.

We three finally gave in to Morpheus and slept.

The chime of the clock sounded to wake us an hour before sunrise. I was the only one who heard it: Giacomo and Marina slept on. I was no longer intoxicated by drink and desire. My mind was clear. What had I done? I wanted Giacomo for myself. I wanted Marina gone.

I rolled over and kissed Giacomo in my favorite spot, at the fine angle of his cheekbone.

"I long for your child again," I whispered to him, surprising myself how deeply I felt these words. I dreamed he would wake, would pull gently on one of the ringlets hanging near my face. I dreamed he would beg my forgiveness, we would leave Marina alone and cold in the bed. We would run away and—

But Giacomo did not wake. I lay near him and wept silent tears.

CHAPTER 78

When you make a pact with the devil, he expects to be paid. It was clear, the more I reflected on what had happened at the *casino*, that Monsieur de Bernis had given Giacomo a night with me and Marina to enjoy by himself. Whether the ambassador had been watching from the secret room or simply not shown up, it had been a gift. And a gift demanded to be returned. I realized that Giacomo would have to absent himself the next time.

Only I had no intention of playing along.

"Monsieur de Bernis expects you to come," said Marina. She stood over the desk where I sat in my room and prodded me with sharp words.

It had been about a week since our unexpected ménage à trois. I had returned at dawn regretful, exhausted, and at the end of my strength. Pleasure had conquered reason that night.

"I—I can't," I said, lowering my eyes back to the Bible I was reading. I couldn't stand the thought of Monsieur de Bernis being anywhere near me. In my mind, I had set myself aside for Giacomo. My husband.

"You must come tonight," Marina insisted. She knew where I was weak. "For Giacomo."

"For Giacomo? Why?" I felt the opposite. For Giacomo, I had to remain pure. Be a good wife.

"If you do not go, Monsieur de Bernis will be convinced Giacomo made you stay away. He will appear jealous, ungrateful, and ridiculous. Is that what you want?"

"No."

I got up with a sigh and started to dress.

I pulled on an old chemise that had a grease stain down the front. I paired it with my ugliest skirt, a mustard colored one that made my skin look sallow. I didn't comb my hair or wear any perfume. I hoped Monsieur de Bernis would be repelled by me: I counted on it.

"Ah—my two beauties!" He greeted us at the *casino,* where he sat on the sofa cracking open pistachios. He popped the little morsels in his mouth and licked the salt from his hands. There were piles of shells on the table.

"I'm afraid I have some unhappy news," he said. "Come sit." He opened a few more nuts.

My heart jumped and I felt dizzy. Had something happened to Giacomo? Had he insisted he come tonight—and Monsieur de Bernis harmed him in some way? Giacomo was an ant compared to this fat, powerful ambassador.

"What is it, my dear?" Marina joined him on the sofa. She took his hand. He spoke his next words to her, as if I were invisible.

"I've learned I have to spend some months in Vienna on a matter of great importance to France. I cannot say more at this time—soon, it will set all of Europe talking."

"But you will be back?" asked Marina. Her concern sounded genuine. Was she worried she would lose all her privileges? Her secret comings and goings, her jewels and gifts, the *casino?*

"I may not be able to come back," he said. "I am not my own master in these affairs."

Marina's mouth tightened to a line. I saw her mind was working to calculate what this news meant to her. I wondered what it meant for me, too. If Monsieur de Bernis took away his money, his gondolier, his *casino,* Marina would be just another trapped nun. Giacomo might lose all interest in her. My heart soared at this possibility. Then, went cold. Might he forget about both of us trapped on Murano?

"Do not look sad, my pet," de Bernis said to Marina, kissing both her hands. "There is no reason to be sad tonight, when we are all three together." He turned to acknowledge me, finally.

"Shall we enjoy a little fun, Caterina?"

I was startled.

"Oh—Monsieur de Bernis—I could not think of trying to have fun at a time like this. We are both in despair at your news."

"Nonsense, little one," he said. "Nothing would cheer me more than to spend a last night together with my two beauties." He began to unbutton his jacket and rose to move over to the bed. He picked up a book from a table on his way. *The Academy of Women,* I presumed.

"No—Monsieur de Bernis—" I called after him, "I—I—it is my monthly time. I cannot possibly join you tonight." He turned to face me, and I willed myself into a fiery blush.

"I see." His mouth twisted in disgust. I saw his desire for me die right then on his face. "Marina, please escort Caterina downstairs and tell the gondolier to take her back to the convent. I will wait for you in our alcove."

"Of course," she said, picking me up by the elbow like a smelly rag that needed to go out.

"I'm sorry—I couldn't—" I said to her as she pulled me down the stairs. We reached the front door. I had a sudden strange feeling that I was leaving the *casino* for the last time.

"The next time—when Giacomo comes—of course I want to join you—" I flailed about, trying to keep my place with them. Stupid. The winds were shifting on me, but I continued to fight back.

She opened the door out to the garden. I imagined I could hear the trees whispering about me.

"I don't need you anymore, Caterina," she hissed. "Monsieur de Bernis is leaving—and I've decided I want Giacomo all to myself."

She put her long nails on my shoulders and pushed me out into the night.

CHAPTER 79

After that night I became ... unhinged. *I've decided I want Giacomo all to myself.* My mind would grind so ceaselessly on these words, that only at dawn, when I heard the early calls of the birds over the lagoon, would I realize I had hardly slept. Exhausted, I spent hours looking out my dormitory window, staring at the flat, iron-gray water, and crying. I knew I risked ruining my health if I kept on like this, but I didn't care. I was broken.

One early morning as I sat there, I saw a single black gondola in the distance against the pink-tinged sky. The gondolier, wearing a windblown shirt and sash, was not in full control of the boat. It was moving from side to side in the water, and he struggled to keep on course. The boat drew closer to the convent. Now I could see that the gondolier was quite tall. He tied up the boat. Could it be? I squinted in the low light. Marina stepped out of the cabin. The gondolier gave her a last, parting kiss. It was Giacomo.

So—there it was. Monsieur de Bernis had left Venice, and they were continuing to use his empty *casino.* And Giacomo himself had turned gondolier for his whore.

I succumbed to rage such as I had never felt before. I paced my room in a frenzy. I wrote notes to myself like a madwoman. Finally, after several hours—the sun was well up, and I could hear clattering dishes downstairs from the refectory, for breakfast—a measure of calm returned to me. I wrote to my brother and asked him for help.

He hurried out the next afternoon, and brought Zulietta with him. I hadn't counted on her showing up, too.

"Caterina!" she said in alarm when she saw me at the visiting parlor window. "Pier Antonio told me you did not sound like yourself in your letter—and you look . . . terrible!" She reached a hand through the bars to comfort me. "Are you sick? Do you need a surgeon to bleed you?"

"No—no. I am fine," I answered. I took her hand. How good it felt to see her, even if it made what I planned to do more difficult. She was an angel before me with her auburn curls and worried brown eyes, but I felt she lived in another world from me these days. A world where no one ever told you they didn't need you anymore.

"I'm—I'm not sleeping well, that is all." I saw Pier Antonio at the other end of the room, strutting past all the nuns. I guess he figured by bringing Zulietta out to take care of me, he was done.

"What can I do to help you?" she asked. "My God, your hand is so cold." She pressed it, together with hers, to her cheek. "You know I will do anything for you. You have helped me so much, cousin." She smiled and blushed, and I felt her cheek grow even warmer beneath my hand.

"Oh—I hardly need anything," I said, taking away my hand, as it only felt right to do, before my lies began. "I am embarrassed to tell you . . . that I have rats in my room."

"Rats?" Her eyes widened. I felt terrible. I had never lied outright to Zulietta before. Omitted things, maybe. But never set out to deceive her.

"Yes—rats," I continued. "I've been stealing sweets from the kitchen. Doughnuts, *biscotti,* marzipan—I wanted to keep some in my room just for myself."

Zulietta nodded compassionately. This was going well. I got more animated in my telling.

"And then these *rats* came. Right from the walls. Huge. Each one as big as half my leg. I hear them all night, scratching and scurrying across my floor."

"How awful! Poor you!" I imagined Zulietta's skin was crawling. She hated anything dirty: pigeons and garbage and rats.

"What can I do to help you?" she asked again. Before I could answer, she turned and motioned furiously for Pier Antonio to come over. He put up a finger to tell her to wait, bowed in front of one of the barred windows, and made his way over to us. Slowly.

"*Buon giorno,* little sister! Is Zulietta taking care of everything?" He dropped into a chair and pulled out his watch to check the time.

"Pier Antonio!" Zulietta chided him. She was clearly intent on getting him to focus on my problem. My plan was working.

"Caterina has an infestation of rats in her room. It doesn't matter how they got there. We have to help her."

"Rats?" My brother cocked a brow at me. I saw now he would be the obstacle, not Zulietta.

"Yes—" I said, "I am ashamed to tell the abbess—she will only yell at me, and tell me I have brought them on myself. I was thinking—you could bring me some arsenic—I hear it is a very good rat poison—"

"Rat poison, eh?" I didn't like the way Pier Antonio was looking at me. Studying me. I felt my color rise as I tried to hold his gaze.

"In the *ghetto,*" I suggested, "Casa degli Speziali is a well-stocked pharmacy." Elia's uncle's pharmacy, where no one would know who had purchased the arsenic. "I don't need much—enough for a few rats, maybe ten—"

"Ten?" I noticed Pier Antonio's mouth tighten, and his jaw tense.

"She said ten," said Zulietta. "She needs poison to kill ten rats. Of course we will help you, Caterina." She took Pier Antonio's watch and studied the time.

"Come—" She put her hand on his shoulder. "Let's get going now. We can stop in the *ghetto* on the way home."

She stood and leaned through the bars and kissed both my cheeks. Pier Antonio just sat, watching me.

CHAPTER 80

Venice, 1774

"But—" said Leda to Caterina, "surely—you didn't intend to take the arsenic yourself? Or give it to someone else? To Marina?"

They had gotten home from Burano at dusk and Caterina had finished her story—more than she had meant to reveal—seated in their favorite armchairs overlooking the sea. Night had descended around them.

Caterina reached to light a lamp, but on second thought, laid the tinderbox down on the table. She decided she didn't need any light on her right now. She had been testing Leda, maybe, when she had talked about the arsenic.

"Oh—I meant no real harm," Caterina reassured her. She managed a shaky smile. "I knew Pier Antonio saw right through me. I was acting crazed from no sleep, and from despair."

Leda breathed a sigh of relief. She leaned back in her chair and rested a hand on her big belly.

"Sometimes I feel crazy, too," she said. "You feel, when you are forgotten, suddenly all alone in the world."

"You feel forgotten by Filippo, do you mean?" Caterina asked her, gently.

"By Filippo," said Leda, "and by my father. Cast off and forgotten." She did not cry, as Caterina expected her to do. It was as if these were such constant thoughts for her, they came into the world already worn.

They sat for a while in close silence. Something they had learned to do, the more comfortable they became with each other.

"I half-believed," Leda went on, "that one day Filippo would come find me here. He knew I was being sent to a convent in Venice."

"There are over fifty convents in Venice!" Caterina reminded her. "It would be nearly impossible for him to find you." But even as she said it, she was thinking, would it? Did Filippo ever love Leda, or was it a quick affair that meant nothing to him?

It was as if Leda read her mind.

"You once told me—*love knows no bounds.*"

"Did I?" Caterina was disturbed to hear her own words repeated back to her. Yes, her love had known no bounds. At some point, it had crossed into a kind of madness. "I don't remember," she said, wanting desperately to change the subject. She pretended to yawn, though in reality, she felt hideously awake.

"Do you know," Caterina said with forced cheerfulness, "that a letter from Bastiano arrived this morning, addressed to both of us? I waited to open it, since we were on our way out to Burano." She got up to fetch the letter from the entrance hall. Returning, she lit the lamp, broke the seal of the letter, and read out loud to Leda.

> *Dearest Caterina and Leda,*
> *I had a chance to speak to the surgeon*
> *Guglielmo de la Motte at the University of Padua*
> *Medical School, and he has agreed to perform your*

*delivery, Leda, when the time comes. He will come
to Venice on 15 September and lodge at the best
inn, Queen of the Sea. If anything should arise before that date and we need his help, he has
instructed us to send a message to him immediately.*

You are in good hands, my girl.

*I miss you both. The farmhouse is not the same
without you, Caterina.*

*I will be home to Venice shortly, by the end of
the month.*

Yours affectionately,

Bastiano

"Oh, goodness," said Leda, flushing with pleasure at the
news, "how well taken care of I am!"

"Naturally," said Caterina, smiling at her. "You are very important to us."

"God only knows where I would be without you," said
Leda. "What a saint you are."

A saint. That was a word Caterina had never considered for
herself. Leda's image of her was in many ways an illusion. Caterina knew the truth about herself.

"Well, then, bless you, child," she joked, though at some
level, she meant it. Blessings to Leda, who had changed her life
for the better.

"It is time for bed, *carissima*," she said, rising and leaning
over to kiss Leda on her forehead.

"Yes . . ." said Leda. "Good night, Caterina." But she lingered a little longer in the comfortable chair. Leda did not move
anywhere too quickly these days.

Caterina made her way down the dark hall to her bedroom.
Behind her closed door, she stared at the ivory box on her
nightstand, with the letters inside. Moonlight slivered in from

the window and illuminated the box eerily. Its deep, shadowed carvings looked like eyes to Caterina, all leering at her. She picked up the box and buried it in her clothes chest, under a wool cloak. Maybe, she told herself as she dropped the heavy lid down on it, that would smother the secrets inside.

CHAPTER 81

Caterina woke the next morning to the ringing of the Marangona, the deep bell from San Marco that summoned workers to start the day. Had she really slept so late? She scrambled up to make breakfast for Leda, but found that her door was closed. Leda was still sleeping. Caterina made herself a cup of sweet Turkish coffee, which caused her to sweat in the rising heat. Her heart fluttered.

Washing the few dishes, a swirl of memories came into her head as if they had been simmering there all night. The arsenic. The Casa degli Speziali pharmacy, where she had told them to go. And, Elia Vivante. She became consumed by the idea that she wanted—no, she needed—to go to the *ghetto*. Today. She needed to know if Elia was still there at the pawnshop. Elia, this person at the margins of her life who had played such a key—and mostly unknowing—role in events that happened long ago. There were things Caterina realized she ached to say.

The day promised to be hot. Caterina put on a pastel blue linen dress with silver lace trim at the edge of the bodice. She tucked a lace *fischu* at her neck for modesty, and to protect her from the sun. On her way out, she set out a plate for Leda in the kitchen, with two boiled eggs and a few slices of cured ham. She reminded herself to buy bread later in the day, and some fresh milk. Milk was important for the baby.

Caterina hailed a gondola nearby, and settled herself inside with the cabin shutters closed against the sun. Years collapsed in her mind as she traveled north toward the old Jewish neighborhood. She had not been back in all this time. The place was full of mixed memories: escaping there to pawn her silk fan . . . discovering the truth about the *cabbala* . . . Elia's uncle, who had stopped her hemorrhage . . . and Elia. She saw the girl in her mind's eye, fresh as a cream-colored rose. Her small body, her wavy brown hair. Her almond-shaped eyes, their intelligence, and kindness.

The boat bumped to a stop about a half hour later, and Caterina climbed out. The sun was blazing in the sky. She shielded her face, and ducked with relief into the tunnel that led from the outer walls into the main square.

Caterina looked around to get her bearings, and noticed for the first time that the buildings around the square were taller than any others in Venice. She shuddered—how terrible to live like these Jews, crowded in tilting towers. She spied the Vivante pawnshop at the edge of the square, its gold-lettered sign glinting in the sunlight. It looked like the same wood sign that had been hanging there twenty years before, maybe repainted a few times. With relief, she saw that the pharmacy next door was gone.

Still, at the sight of the old pawnshop, Caterina was seized with panic at her decision to come. She needed to sit down and calm herself. She made her way to the stone wellhead at the center of the square. It was a simple one, with no carved flowers or vines to decorate it, but it reminded her of her favorite well near her childhood home, in Campo San Gregorio. This soothed her. She sat down on its marble platform, next to a sleeping orange cat. Her face started to burn in the sun.

"May I bother you for a drink?" she asked an old woman who approached to draw some water. The woman eyed her suspiciously, then filled her bucket, untied a cup strung onto her apron, dipped it, and handed Caterina some cold water.

"*Grazie, Signora,*" said Caterina with an appreciative smile.

The old woman wiped off the drained cup on her apron, and continued to eye her. Caterina hoped she didn't look too out of place, seated at the base of the well in her silver-lace gown, frying like a fish.

"Are you lost?" the old woman asked her.

"Oh—no," said Caterina. She rose quickly, to show the old woman—and herself—that she was not lost at all. But as she left the cool well and headed toward the pawnshop, she noticed she felt unsteady.

Caterina pushed open the door of the shop. Inside smelled just as it had many years before—like old books, and dust. A small, brown-haired woman sat cleaning a pearl and diamond ring behind the counter. She looked up when Caterina walked in.

"*Buon giorno, Signora.*" She smiled and her eyes lingered for a confused moment on Caterina's face.

"Do you remember me—Elia?" Caterina offered. Elia startled hearing her name, and set down the ring and rag on the counter.

"I am Caterina—Caterina Capreta. You helped me—well, in many ways—long ago—" She did not know where to start her story. With the jeweled fan? The *cabbala?* Her miscarriage? The arsenic?

"Caterina!" Elia sprang up to kiss her on each cheek. "How good it is to see you again!" Caterina noticed that Elia had faint lines on her forehead, and her hair had thinned. Her looks were not ruined by any means, but Caterina had known her as a blooming girl. Nothing after could ever be as lovely.

"You are healthy?" Elia asked. "And happy? You were able to leave the convent? Such sad days for you there . . ."

"I left when I turned eighteen," Caterina said. It was hard to know what more to say. After my father forced me to marry someone I did not love? I have been unable to have children?

"Thank God you got to leave that place!" blurted out Elia. Caterina had to laugh. She was fairly sure Elia was not supposed to say God's name in vain, whereas Christians said it all the time. She suspected that Elia had grown up to be a rule-breaker.

"I have to say," Elia went on, "I have never understood the practice of sending young girls away from home to live in convents."

It had never occurred to Caterina that Jewish girls were not sent away like this. "Do you think your religion treats girls better?" she asked.

"Oh—no!" Elia gave a small laugh and touched Caterina's hand affectionately. "They separate us from the men in the temples because we are too distracting, then keep us in the kitchens all day plucking feathers out of chickens!"

Caterina laughed. She had always felt a spark of friendship with Elia, even though she did not know her well. That had been part of the problem. She felt she could trust Elia, but Elia was also in many ways a stranger. It had tempted Caterina to involve her in her affairs, knowing she would not have to face Elia in everyday life.

The door of the shop burst open. Two young boys, about five years old, ran in. Elia's face lit up—these were her sons, clearly. They stopped suddenly when they saw Caterina.

"Giacobbe—Samuele—I want you to meet an old friend of mine." The boys approached them. Caterina saw they were twins, with curly dark hair and melting brown eyes. She felt raw jealousy at the sight of them, but she swallowed it down.

"Caterina—what brings you to the *ghetto* today?" Elia

asked her, finally. The boys had run behind the counter and were both sitting on her lap, hanging on her shoulders. She looked weighed down by them in every way a woman can be, and happy.

"Oh—" said Caterina, realizing that with the boys there she could not say what she most wanted to say to Elia: *You saved my life long ago—and I never even thanked you.*

"I have been thinking over the past," she said instead, "and I wondered what had become of you."

"Ah," said Elia. She gave each restless boy a kiss on the cheek to settle them. "I often wondered, too . . . whether you ever got free."

"You mean—from the convent?" Caterina asked. She knew it was time to go, but Elia's comment confused her. Intrigued her.

"I meant more—" Elia went on. "It always struck me . . . that you deserved some happiness in your life."

"Thank you," Caterina said simply. And bowed her head to this old friend.

CHAPTER 82

In the gondola on the way home, Caterina opened the shutters and eyed the busy canals and walkways with a strangely unburdened heart. It had been good for her to see Elia, to see that time had in some ways stood still—enough for her to be able to revisit her past—but in other ways, the years inevitably marched ahead. The old Jewish pharmacy was gone, and with it, another trace of her actions had disappeared.

She leaned back into the velvet seat of the cabin and closed her eyes. Her tired mind traveled home now, only a few more minutes away. Leda would have been awake several hours, and was probably waiting for her in her favorite chair by the windows. Caterina had bought eggs, bread, and milk in the *ghetto*, as well as almond *biscotti*, a Jewish delicacy. She felt sure Leda would adore the special treats.

Leda.

An uneasy feeling washed over Caterina. She should not have left Leda for so long. What if the baby had started coming, early? Leda was all alone.

The gondola slowed as it attempted to snake past a vegetable barge that hogged half the canal. Caterina rubbed her forehead with anxious hands. Peering ahead, she saw that the last narrow canal toward home was also crowded with boats.

"*Signor!*" She opened the door of the cabin and called to the gondolier, "Please stop! I will get out here!"

He looked at her as if she were a bit crazy, but rowed the boat to the water's edge. Climbing out, she stepped on the hem of her blue linen dress and heard it rip.

Caterina walked briskly the rest of the way home, arriving probably no faster than the boat would have gotten her there. She bounded up the steps and fumbled with her key.

"Leda? Leda?" she called, bursting inside the door.

Silence.

Glancing down the hallway, where her bedroom door was ajar, Caterina had a terrifying thought. Sweat started to prick under her arms.

Had Leda gone in search of the box of letters while she was out? Perhaps not set out to do that—but gone to find Caterina in the small room and wondered, *Where is the ivory box that usually sits on the nightstand? Why has it been moved?* And worse—*What is written on those pages that I have not seen?*

Caterina rushed to her bedroom and threw open the lid of her clothes chest. Yet there it was, the ivory box, sitting innocently where she had left it buried under a wool cloak. Hugely relieved, she lowered the lid back down.

Still—where was Leda? Caterina went into the girl's bedroom and opened a drawer or two. All her dresses were still there, undisturbed. Feeling bad for being nosy, she decided Leda had probably gone out for a short walk. She realized then how sunburned and worn out she felt. More than anything, she craved respite from the turmoil of the day: the simmering dreams, the blazing sun, the journey to the *ghetto*. She lay on top of the cool sheets on Leda's bed and fell asleep.

At some point in her dreams, Leda called out for her. Caterina snapped awake, heart pounding, and went running out of the room. But the house was empty. Shadows had started to climb on the walls.

A beam of golden afternoon light fell on the small table in the main room where they usually shared their meals. Now Caterina's eyes fell on several sheets of yellowed paper she had not noticed before.

She saw her own thick, cramped handwriting on the pages. She could not make out any words from where she stood. But she already knew which letter it was. The last one to her brother; the last one kept in the ivory box.

The letter had no seal. It had never been sent. But it told everything—and Leda had found it.

CHAPTER 83

Venice, 1753

Pier Antonio—

It seems whenever I feel lowest, I reach out to you. This is when I feel our blood bond, know sadly we are one kind. Maybe Sebastiano was the good child among us, and when he died, he left behind we two with blackened hearts. I hide it better than you; no one knows what I am inside. Instead, I am called an angel.

I saw you suspected I was up to something when I asked you for the arsenic at the convent. Zulietta—she couldn't let herself see the truth. But you knew. Did you not care enough to stop me? Or . . . is it that you understood and accepted my course of action?

Pier Antonio, brother—this is my confession, which I can tell no priest.

I know you read all of the spy's reports. I never believed for an instant you did not. You know,

*then, what Marina Morosini has done to me. How
she stole from me. She is no nun, but a whore
wrapped in God's clothing.*

*I wish I could say I lost my mind. That I went
truly mad. But I planned it all out. I played to win
the last game of love.*

*"What are you doing here?" Marina asked me in
surprise yesterday morning. I arrived at her room
carrying a tray with a pot of chocolate and two
warmed cups. It was morning right after Matins,
and cold rain dripped outside.*

*"Marina—let's not allow words said in anger to
come between us. We need each other here." I set
down the tray on the table and took a seat on her
sofa. I poured hot chocolate over the small amount
of white powder I had hidden at the bottom of
her cup.*

*"We cannot remain friends after what has hap-
pened between us—can we?" she asked me with
searching eyes. I felt almost sorry for her, that she
still craved my love. She never deserved it.*

*"Of course we can," I reassured her. "Come sit."
I took a spoonful of chocolate and slid her cup
temptingly toward her.*

*Marina gave me a relieved smile and took a seat
close to me on the sofa.*

*"I am glad to hear it, Caterina." She reached for
her cup of chocolate and blew to cool it. She winked
at me over the rim. "We will find you another
lover—a better one. It will be fun."*

*"Oh yes," I said. "That does sound like fun." I
watched as she took a sip, then another, and a third.
Voracious as she was in everything, she drained
the cup.*

We kept talking. The minutes crawled by on the table clock. Before an hour had passed, I saw a shadow begin to work its way across her beautiful face. She was transformed before my eyes. Her mouth twisted in pain, her blue-green eyes became fixed and shone like glass. I smelled loose bowels from beneath her habit. She tried to stand; she clutched her cup and began to say something. But she fainted dead to the floor.

Panic! I ran to her; I shook her to bring her back. I cried and wiped her drooling mouth with my skirt. Her eyes seemed to be staring up at nothing; her face was gray as stone. I grabbed the shards of the broken cup, threw them in my pocket—and ran for help.

Yes, I ran for help! You must believe me—I did not intend to kill her! I only wanted . . . to sicken her. Sicken her terribly, so that Giacomo would forget her. He is adoring at the first instance of suffering—I know this. But later, he loses all interest. Let him forget her as he once forgot me.

But I am wretched! A murderer! They say a dose the size of a pea kills a man, and I gave her what I thought was . . . a small pea? Impulsive, foolish— or, dare I face it about myself?—filled with rage I did not know I could feel, I gave her too much. She is dying! She may not survive even one more day, dawning now bright and frightening before me.

No one suspects what I have done. I play the part of an innocent angel in front of them all. Changing her urine-soaked sheets. Sponging diarrhea off her body. Laying my own body over hers, to keep down the convulsions.

But the agonizing regret! It is real and too much to bear! Does God not see me nursing her, trying to bring her back to life?

I pray now, until my lips are as parched and cracked as those of the one I have harmed—I beg God to lighten His judgment on this fallen angel!

Pier Antonio—sinner as I am—pray for me.

CHAPTER 84

Venice, 1774

Leda did not come home for supper that night. Caterina sat over cold spaghetti with anchovies, chewing her nails into soft shreds. She found herself wishing Bastiano was home. He would have helped her figure out a plan, asking question after question until he pieced together where to search, what to do. The very plodding, logical qualities that usually annoyed Caterina, she needed now. But, of course, he would also ask difficult questions about what might have driven Leda away.

She got up, looked anxiously out the window. She could hear the gates closing on the last shops for the night. She pictured Leda wandering the maze of streets in the city, pregnant and alone. The prey of gypsies and thieves. She shuddered, went back to the table, and stared at the noodles and crusted brown sauce. She had no appetite. In fact, the smell made her sick.

She slept only a few hours that night, with fast-moving dreams. She would startle awake, wishing, wanting everything to be better in reality than it was in her head. But instead, the truths of her life came crashing down on her all over again:

Why had she ever mentioned the rat poison to Leda? Why had she left the girl alone with the unlocked box of letters, tempting her?

Caterina even had to wonder if she had *wanted* Leda to know the worst about her. Wanted to be forgiven, and loved by her completely. At this realization—that perhaps she had done this to herself, willfully—she cried and punched her pillow fiercely. She felt scared to be in her own skin.

The arrival of daylight brought new hope. Caterina looked out to the cheerful boats bobbing on green, sunlit water, and decided she would go in search of Leda. She revived her strength with some Turkish coffee, and put on the same dress she had worn to the *ghetto*. The hem rip was not too noticeable. Had that trip been only yesterday? Time had seemed to stop, then fold over on itself since she had gotten home and discovered that Leda had read her letter to Pier Antonio.

She hailed a gondola outside her house and headed north, to the edge of the city. Yes, Leda could be anywhere. But the convent of Santa Maria degli Angeli seemed most likely. That she would run back to the place that was most familiar—even if she hated it. Where else in Venice did Leda even know?

The boat rocked on the choppy water and Caterina's stomach turned over. She had neglected to eat, and black coffee bit at her insides. By the time she switched boats for the final trip out to Murano, her panic had started to rise.

She would have to face Marina.

Would Leda tell Marina all that she knew? About Marina's betrayal of Caterina for Giacomo, and Caterina's final revenge? Maybe Leda would even feel new compassion for Marina, knowing now what Caterina had done. Caterina accepted it. She accepted that some sins could never be forgiven. But she needed to know that Leda was safe. If Leda was not at the convent . . . she would ask Marina for help.

A new wave of dizziness washed over her as she spied the

walls of Santa Maria degli Angeli from the cabin window. When she stepped out of the boat, the pavement moved like water. She grabbed the gondolier's forearm for a moment—how warm and strong he felt! Then she steadied herself, and walked alone to the great shut door.

CHAPTER 85

"Caterina Capreta."

"Eh? *Ancora?*" The old *conversa* who had opened the door leaned in to hear her better.

"Caterina. Capreta." She said her name with more confidence. "I am here to see the abbess."

The old woman nodded and admitted her, walking her down shining *terrazzo* hallways to a far corner of the building. The convent was quiet except for the occasional sounds of chattering girls from behind shut doors. Caterina could smell freshly baked bread coming from the refectory. A couple of boarders scampered by, arm in arm and giggling. How young they seemed!

The old woman told Caterina to sit on a bench in the vestibule outside Marina's chamber. She knocked and went in to see Marina, then came back out with no word for Caterina as to when she might go in. The bench was hard and had no back. Of course, Marina would make her wait. To make her feel small. To make her suffer—just a little. Her palms began to sweat.

Where was Leda?

Caterina wiped her hands on her skirts and bit her thumbnail. She imagined Marina finishing up some unimportant task simply to stretch out time and torture her. Finally, and for no reason that Caterina could figure out, the old woman told her it was time to go in.

Marina sat at her imposing red wood desk, head bent over some writing. Caterina approached and took a seat in the chair opposite. Marina raised her head, and Caterina felt any resolve she had pour out like water.

"Why have you come?" she asked. Marina's eyes were icy gray in the crisp morning light.

"Leda and I—we had a small quarrel," Caterina stammered, "and she went out for a walk—it's been a while, and I got worried—and just to be safe, I thought I might check whether she had come back here—"

"She has not." Marina dipped her pen and started to write again. It looked like a list of names.

"She has not?" The full weight of the situation fell on Caterina now. Her chest tightened, and without being able to stifle it, a sob rose up.

"I—I don't know where Leda is!" she cried. "She did not come home last night!"

Marina's temple twitched beneath her thin, waxy skin. "Let me understand this," she said, looking up. "I asked you to help me with Leda. To take care of her for a short while. Instead, you have lost track of her."

"Where—where else do you think she could have gone?" Caterina asked, ignoring Marina's taunt. Outside the window she watched a few yellow leaves fall in the air. She felt like them—falling, falling into oblivion.

"I have no idea where Leda has gone!" Marina's sharp voice rattled the room. "And honestly—I don't care anymore. I run a convent, not a prison. Leda has to make her own choices."

Caterina fell silent. Was she the only one who cared what became of Leda? It felt as though a part of her own body were lost, floating somewhere out in the open lagoon.

There was a soft knock at the door, and soon after it opened. A hunchbacked nun entered, carrying a gilded porcelain teapot, cup and saucer, and milk pitcher set on a tray. Arcangela! Caterina smiled, relieved to see a friendly face.

"You remember our Caterina?" Marina asked the misshapen nun, who kept her head down while serving her abbess. Now she looked up with squinting eyes and grinned at Caterina.

"*Bellissima!*" she exclaimed, coming closer to embrace her. Caterina warmly reciprocated the hug.

"How are you?" Arcangela asked, eyeing her from head to toe. "Are you married—and with children?"

"Married, yes," Caterina answered. "But no children." Arcangela's face fell. Just as it had been so many years before, it seemed to Caterina she always fell short of Arcangela's dreams.

"Still"—Arcangela recovered herself—"how good it is to see you back. Will you be staying long?"

"No," Marina answered before Caterina could. "Our friend will be leaving soon."

"Perhaps you can return for Carnival?" Arcangela pressed. "We can play *biribisso,* like in the old days." She gave Caterina one of her *please-love-me* smiles.

"Yes, of course," answered Caterina, meaning it in the moment. How good it was to see an old friend who had always been kind and wanted the best for her.

"*Poverina,*" Marina sneered, the minute Arcangela left the room. "That she still loves you so much."

Oh! Caterina was sick of it. Being made to feel that anyone who loved her was making a mistake.

"Where were we . . . ?" Marina asked now, slowly pouring tea for herself. "Oh, yes. Have you ever wondered *why* I sent Leda home with *you?*"

"No—not really," Caterina lied.

"She reminded me of you." Marina's voice became playfully cruel. "Our innocent Caterina, pregnant and in love. Only—

who knew at the time how madly in love you really were? *Murderously in love.*"

Sharp sunlight angled in the window and raked Marina's face. Her skin looked yellow, the blood and beauty all gone. Caterina knew she had done this to her. She bowed her head, accepting her deep guilt.

"Yes . . . I asked you to take care of Leda to punish you," Marina went on, slicing out Caterina's insides. "To make you relive your past. To remember what you once lost—and consider what you did to me."

"I understand," said Caterina, mumbling into her lap. She felt naked, entirely unmasked. Yet, from somewhere deep within herself, she found another layer of courage. She knew she would never have another chance like this. She seized it.

"I've wanted to tell you for such a long time—" she said, lifting her head to look directly into Marina's eyes, "how sorry I am for what I did to you. I was out of my mind. Nothing you could ever do would punish me as I've punished myself all these years. Can you forgive me, Marina? I beg you to forgive me—with all my heart."

Marina drew in a slow, surprised breath. The room grew silent, except for the distant echoes coming from the hallways. Caterina had no idea what to expect from this old rival, enemy, lover, and friend. This woman who had betrayed her, and whom she had betrayed.

Marina regarded her for another minute or two. Then she spoke, her voice soft, almost a whisper. "What's done cannot ever be undone, Caterina." She paused. "Still—we both have done things that we regret."

Caterina waited for more, and when more did not come, nodded her acceptance. Marina dropped her eyes and went back to her writing.

Feeling light-headed, Caterina stood to go. She had come out to the convent seeking only one thing—to find Leda. Instead, she had received something else. It wasn't forgiveness. Far from it. But it felt as though Marina had lifted something away from her.

What's done cannot ever be undone. Still—we both have done things that we regret.

The secret of what Caterina had done had felt like a sharp stone in her hands. Hiding it in shame from everyone, always trying to rub it smooth.

For the first time in twenty years, she began to sense what it might feel like to be free.

CHAPTER 86

Caterina surrendered to sleep on the way home from the convent. Sweet wall of exhaustion: Her mind could not fight it. The rhythm of the long oar in and out of the waves, the sense of someone else taking care of her for a few hours—she stopped worrying about Leda and let the gondolier take her home.

Home. She felt sure Leda would be there by now. If she had not been at the convent, she must be at home.

"Where have you been? I'm starving!" she imagined Leda teasing her when she saw her climbing the stairs. Caterina smiled to herself in the gondola, picturing her little loving rituals for Leda: making her favorite pasta dishes and buying her sweets, smoothing her twisted sheets and blankets, laying a hand on top of her head to kiss her before she went to sleep.

But when Caterina got home, the rooms were as silent as when she had left. The sun had disappeared and the lagoon looked gray outside the windows. It gave the sad feeling that the day was already ending, the best parts of it gone. Caterina sank into a chair. Worry clamped down on her all over again.

Her stomach growled and reminded her to take care of herself. She went to the kitchen and cut an apple and some bread. She gobbled her food, as she often did when she was alone. Some bread got stuck in her throat. By the time it finally cleared she had hiccups, and had lost her appetite. She went back to her chair to wait again.

Caterina heard the outside door slam shut. She sat upright. She strained her ears, and after a minute, heard the soft, shuffling sounds of leather slippers on the stone staircase.

She jumped up and ran to the door, pulling it open.

"Sweetheart!" she cried out. Leda was struggling to climb the last remaining steps. Caterina ran to help, putting her arm around the girl's back. "Where in God's name have you been?" she demanded. "Are you alright?"

Leda's eyes were ringed with purple shadows. She looked pale, but gave Caterina a weak smile. Caterina led her inside. Leda went over to her chair by the windows, and fell into it with a huge exhale. Caterina perched right near her on the footstool. She felt she could not get close enough—never wanted to know that awful distance between them again.

"I—I went to find the little painting of the Madonna," Leda explained.

"The little painting?" Caterina had no idea what she was talking about.

"The little painting that you once showed me. Near the Frari. The one with the Madonna nursing the baby in the stormy landscape. You said expectant mothers always went to see her. I felt I needed . . . help."

Ah. Caterina squirmed a little.

"And—did she help you?" She decided not to ask what Leda needed help with. Maybe the magical Madonna had made it disappear.

"I never got to find out!" Leda gave a short laugh. "I got lost trying to find the painting again. I got very thirsty, and tired, and some painful convulsions started. I crouched outside the church of San Pantalon, and the priest found me. He sent for a midwife, who let me stay the night with her until the pains stopped."

"*Che consolazione!*" Caterina was grateful to these strangers who had looked after Leda. She had imagined gypsies and thieves preying on her, but instead, Leda had been met with kindness. "Do you think we should send for Dottore de la Motte?" she asked. "Is it your time?"

"Not yet," said Leda. "The midwife told me the baby's head has not yet started to lower. But soon."

Caterina smiled with relief at the news. Leda settled her hands on her belly and closed her eyes—she clearly needed rest. But Caterina was not ready for the girl to drift away from her yet.

"Leda—I—didn't know what to think when I discovered you were gone," she stammered. "I know you read that letter. I wondered—I wonder what you must think of me."

Leda opened her eyes; crushingly deep, so they seemed, and very blue. "I think that this vengeful Caterina is not the Caterina I know," she said.

"But it is," said Caterina, struggling to be honest about herself.

"Then—" said Leda, "I think . . . that we all make mistakes. *Che consolazione*, that yours did not end as tragically as it could have."

Caterina could not suppress a small smile, hearing this traditional Venetian phrase from Leda's lips. *Che consolazione.*

"Can you ever forgive me?" she asked, softly.

"Forgive you?" Leda echoed. "I think a better question is . . . can you forgive yourself?"

Could Caterina ever forgive herself? She wasn't sure. Her soul was a turbulent sea. But it felt, ever since Leda had come to stay with her and listened to her story, that maybe it would come to her one day—a new lightness and joy in life.

"Tell me," Leda said now, hoisting herself up to sit straighter in her chair, "how is it that Marina survived arsenic poisoning? And Giacomo—did he ever know what you had done?"

Caterina breathed in, readying herself to be completely truthful with Leda for the first time.

And for the first time to tell another soul the last part of her story.

CHAPTER 87

Murano, 1753

"Abbess Paulina, I must get some air."

"*Certo,* Caterina. You have taken good care of your friend."

I glanced at the table clock in Marina's room. It told me most of the day had passed, passed as long days with the sick do: with shuttered windows, murmured words, hopeful offerings of water, a cool cloth, maybe a bite of food. It had been six days since I had given Marina the arsenic-laced chocolate. Nobody knew what I had done. She was finally tolerating spoonfuls of the garlic- and onion-soaked beans the convent physician had prescribed. At times she sat propped up on pillows. But her eyes were dead. I had snuffed out her beauty, and her fire, too.

"Abbess, may I go, too?" I heard Laura, Marina's *conversa,* parrot me. Poor Laura. She had been servant to the Queen of the Convent—Marina Morosini, with her exciting comings and goings, her lovers, her money and influence—and now, it had come to this. A stinking room that made you want to run away. Even the canary was gone, rescued by Arcangela.

"Yes—yes," conceded the abbess. "Both of you go. I will stay until Vespers." It wasn't like Abbess Paulina to tend to the sick, but Marina was a rich noblewoman. The abbess couldn't afford to lose her.

"Caterina," Laura whispered as we closed the door behind us and I turned to go to my room. "I have a message for you."

"A message? From whom?"

Laura stepped closer and placed a folded piece of paper from her pocket into my hand. She was gone almost before I realized I was holding something.

I continued down the hallway, my heart beating wildly. Had someone figured out what I had done? Was this a threat? I opened the door to my room, closed it with shaking hands, and stood to read.

Come find me where you first saw me.

Giacomo. I recognized his handwriting immediately. Only no name, no place given. Cunning, as ever.

Come find me where you first saw me. What did he mean? My mind went first to Venice: our meeting at my house, almost a year before. But he knew I could not leave the convent.

Come find me where you first saw me. The day of Leonora Vendramin's profession?—after my miscarriage. Down by the water. The old tree.

I threw a wool cloak over my shoulders and slipped outside, running to my past. I had no illusions left. Too much sadness had killed our love. But I ran anyway, if only to touch my memories one last time.

The abbess, I knew, was preoccupied in Marina's room. Still, there were other busybodies at the convent I worried might see me. I ran through the cloister, finding it empty. Arriving at the top of the brick path to the lagoon, I looked across the empty winter lawn. All the nuns and boarders were inside, keeping warm. With one glance back, I ran down toward the water. Cold wind blew against my cloak and skirts.

I arrived within a few paces of the old tree. Its leaves were gone, just bare branches scratching the sky.

"Caterina!" I heard a loud whisper from behind its thick, knotted trunk. I stepped around, following the familiar voice.

"Giacomo!" I exclaimed. How worn he looked. His eyes, once dark and glittering, were dim, and sad. There were a few new lines in his forehead.

"How can you risk being here?" I asked, pulling my cloak around me and trembling. He was also wrapped in a thick cloak, with brown wool breeches showing beneath. No more bright silks.

"I had to come. I wanted to say farewell."

"Farewell?" I echoed, numbly. In a sense, he had said farewell to me long before. Only I had chosen not to hear it, and to keep fighting and fighting against the tide.

"I have brought you and Marina nothing but misfortune," he explained. "It is time for me to leave you both behind."

"But it is not all your doing—" I said, feeling sick he was taking responsibility for what I had done to Marina. Still, I had no intention of confessing to him. Let him believe I was an angel for the rest of his life. Let him never know what I had done.

"I never wished to bring either of you harm," he said, shaking his head in disbelief at his situation. "You must know that. Yet somehow—I have done just this. Marina is improving, I hear?"

I nodded. Tears began to well in my eyes. "Giacomo, must you leave us both behind on this miserable island?"

"I must, my angel. Please do not cry," he begged. "I cannot bear to think I have made you unhappy."

"Yes—you have made me unhappy!" I burst out. I began to cry, not able to keep myself from honestly showing him how I felt. "I loved you, we exchanged vows, and yet they meant nothing to you."

"Vows of eternal constancy are vows no man should make, even to the most beautiful woman," he said, fingering a wind-blown curl near my face. He looked disarmingly into my eyes. "I think we both have learned that—no?"

"No!" I shouted, shaking my head away. "Not, *no man should make*. You. Eternal vows *you* should never have made."

He sighed. "Perhaps you are right. It is me. All I know is—if I could have changed who I am for anyone, it would have been you. I loved you that much. But—what did I once tell you? A man cannot change who he is."

"Did you ever truly want to change?" I asked, searching his eyes. "Or was it all just a trick?"

"A trick? How can you accuse me of that? I wanted more than anything to be the husband you deserved." His face be-came angry. "I was turned away with scorn by your father. Made to feel unworthy. A nothing."

My heart, broken by him a hundred times, broke now for him. I held his once-beloved face in my hands.

"And if my father had not banished me?" I asked, pleading to understand. "If you had never set eyes on Marina?"

"'If,' 'if,' 'if,' Caterina," he said, turning his face away. "To think on all these accursed 'ifs' will only add to our misfor-tunes."

I was silenced. He did not want to examine the past, nor step with me into the future. That left only these last, fleeting min-utes. Tears slid down my face, hot and stinging.

"Do not cry, my angel," he said, giving me a wistful smile. "I did not come here to leave you sad. I came here to give you this."

He took a small, thick book out from his breeches pocket. "It is my copy of Dante's *Inferno*. Do you remember the verses I copied out for you, the night before you left Venice?"

"Of course I do," I said, wiping my eyes.

"Here, then, is the entire poem. I want you to have it." He

handed the book to me. Its leather cover was well-worn and soft, its parchment pages thin as onionskin. "Dante tells us that life is a journey: *'When I had journeyed half of our life's way, I found myself within a shadowed forest, for I had lost the path.'* I've squandered many opportunities in my life, Caterina. Along the way, I lost you, too. But I shall never forget you."

I held the precious book to my chest. "Nor I, you," I echoed.

A cold, orange sun was setting into the sea and the black branches above us shook against a darkening sky.

"Farewell, my angel," he said, bowing one last time to kiss my hand. "My only wife."

CHAPTER 88

Venice, 1774

"You never saw him again?" asked Leda. She reached out a hand to hold Caterina's. Caterina felt comforted by her touch and gave her a warm, sad smile.

"Never again. Giacomo was arrested the next year by the State Inquisitors for owning forbidden books on magic, and bewitching noblemen to get money out of them. As he had done to poor Signor Bragadin. He was locked up in the Leads."

"Imprisoned!" Leda exclaimed. "For how long?"

"The Inquisitors never tell prisoners how long their sentence is. And there was no trial. It didn't matter in the end—he escaped. He is one of only a handful of men who have ever managed to break out of the Leads."

"Escaped? How?"

"I only know what Pier Antonio told me, from gossip he heard around the city. Giacomo dug a hole in his cell with a pike, climbed onto the roof, and lowered himself down with a rope made of knotted bedsheets and napkins." Caterina laughed. His cleverness amazed her still. "A gondola took him to the mainland—and from there, it is a mystery where in the world he has gone."

"Can he ever come back?" Leda asked, with youthful hope. "Might he be pardoned by the Inquisitors one day?"

"Maybe, sweetheart," said Caterina. "Maybe one day."

Leda leaned back, looking very tired. She closed her eyes, and soon, Caterina heard her soft breathing.

Caterina breathed in her own huge relief. Crossing herself, she thanked God for bringing back her beloved girl.

CHAPTER 89

"You still haven't told me," Leda playfully chided Caterina a few days later, "if Zulietta married Stefano Cavallini."

They sat together in their usual chairs overlooking the shining water, unwrapping the clothes and linens they had bought together on Burano. The time when a little person was going to need them was drawing nearer.

"She did." Caterina paused and smiled at the memory. She still could not believe what had happened. Perfectly behaved Zulietta . . . had in the end defied every expectation of her.

"Did she end up poor?" asked Leda, incredulous. "She does not seem to be."

"They did not have much to live on for the first few years—true," Caterina explained. "Zulietta's father refused them her dowry. That was no surprise. But once Maria Maddalena was born, he relented. Zulietta was his only child, and the center of his life. I imagine he decided it was not worth holding on to his anger, when he loved her so much."

"And Stefano lives off her wealthy family?" asked Leda, struggling to make sense of it. It was far out of the ordinary, especially for someone noble born, as Leda was.

"Stefano eventually became prosperous in his own right," Caterina corrected her, feeling pride in him.

"As a farrier—truly?"

"Indeed," Caterina said. She was enjoying surprising Leda. "Over time, his reputation as someone gifted in the cure of horses grew. He even tends to the Arabian horses owned by the royal family in Naples. Because of his work, he travels often—leaving Zulietta at home with the children. This saddens her . . . but overall, I think she is happy. Does she not seem so to you?"

"Oh, she does," agreed Leda. The story seemed to make Leda happy, too. She gazed with soft eyes out the window.

Caterina worried seeing her lost in a daydream. Better to keep her focused on real life before her. "Leda," she asked, "have you thought of a name yet for your baby?"

"Yes, I have." Leda turned to answer. Her eyes became filled with mirth. "Cleopatra."

Caterina started to laugh. "You're going to name the baby Cleopatra?"

"Only if it's a girl!" Leda went on teasing. "If it's a boy, it will be Pompey."

"Oh Lord!" Caterina shook her head. "Poor baby."

"But seriously—" Leda changed their joking mood, "I have been thinking. I want to name the baby something that reminds me of you. Of how much you've helped me, when I have no living mother."

Caterina was lost for words and blushed with pleasure.

"If it is a boy, I am thinking of Carus," Leda continued, "and for a girl—"

Leda paused midsentence. Caterina looked at her puzzled, then realized the words of a song were floating up to them from outside the open windows.

O graceful, lovely eyes,
my beloved eyes,

living rays from heaven,
so bright and clear . . .

Leda went white and froze. Then she clutched her pendant.
Coraggio.

"What is it? Leda? Do you know the song?" It was a man's
voice, melancholic and full of longing. He seemed to be pleading.

. . . since you desire so much,
to see me languish, to see me die,
lovely eyes that I adore . . .

Leda struggled up from her chair and stood to lean out the
window. Caterina went to stand beside her, her arm around her
shoulders.

Just below them, a man about twenty-five years old was
playing a small harpsichord. The instrument sat on a wood
table, and Caterina could see that its parts were hinged, so that
it could be folded and carried. The man was well-dressed, in a
burgundy silk suit, but his shirt and cravat looked unironed
and grayed. Long locks of his dark hair fell in his face as he
sang.

. . . oh look at me a little
and rejoice in my fire.

"Filippo!" called out Leda when the song ended. Tears had
sprung to her eyes and were running down her face. Caterina
held her tightly.

"Leda!" Filippo looked up. His eyes were dancing with happiness. "I have found you!"

"But how?" Leda called. "How did you know I lived here?"

"Let me come up and I will tell you everything," Filippo

called back, laughing. "I will say—I have visited many convents since I arrived in Venice a week ago!"

Caterina dropped her arm from around Leda's shoulders. She felt swept up in the happy scene. Filippo's words had sounded so true, his voice even catching a few times as he sang.

"Do you want to invite him inside?" she encouraged Leda.

But Leda stood rooted where she was. Something held her back.

"I—I can't," she said, taking a step away from the window. "How can I trust him ever again? He took my father's money and ran away and left me. Why is he back now? For *more* money?"

Caterina's face fell. She realized she had no wise words to offer Leda. No one had ever come back for her . . . after breaking her heart.

"Will *you* go and speak to him for me?" Leda asked, startling her. Leda sat back down and was wringing her hands feverishly. "Ask him how he found me here . . . and what he wants from me?" Her tears started again.

Caterina's eyes were wide, but she wanted to show some maternal confidence. "Of course," she answered. She smoothed her dress and went to get a *fischu* to tuck into her bodice before going downstairs.

She gave Leda a reassuring hug on her way out. The girl's face had turned very pale again. It reminded Caterina of the poem Giacomo had given her, about the lovers Francesca and Paolo . . . their faces pale with longing, frightened by the truth of their desire. But Leda seemed determined not to be conquered by love. Instead, Caterina saw her pull the shutters closed on Filippo.

CHAPTER 90

Caterina approached Filippo as he was packing up his harpsi-chord. She had never seen anything like it before: the three sections of the instrument folded lengthwise to make a box with a carrying handle. A small crowd had formed around him to hear the song, but now they were dispersing. Filippo knelt down, making last adjustments to the box.

"Filippo?" Caterina touched his arm lightly to get his attention.

"Yes!" He startled, jumping up. He smiled with relief at the sight of her, recognizing her from the window.

"I am Caterina Capreta. I have been looking after Leda since she had to leave the convent."

"*Grazie, Signora,*" he said with a deep bow. His face turned red with embarrassment that Caterina clearly knew all about him.

She noticed sweat running down his forehead. "Will you come have a cold drink with me?" she asked. "I want to talk to you . . . about Leda."

"*Certo, Signora.*" He lifted the heavy instrument box, and walked slowly with its weight in his hand. They made their way to the nearest café along the water.

Filippo took a seat gratefully. Caterina noticed one of the soles of his shoes was torn. He looked as if he had been walking for days. She felt compassion for him, but also did not fully trust him. He was seductive with his love song—yes. But her cooler reason had returned.

"Tell me, where have you been living since you left Florence?" she asked, trying to hide any judgment in her voice. *Where did you run?*

Filippo fixed his eyes—one the tiniest bit crossed—on her before he spoke. Just as Leda had said, it made Caterina feel that he was noticing only her. The noisy café with its voices and clattering dishes seemed to recede around them.

"Vienna," he answered. "Leda's father threatened to ruin me if I stayed in Italy. I panicked."

A waiter came by and offered them fresh river water. He set a chilled carafe and two glasses on the table. Filippo poured with a trembling hand, and Caterina noticed his long, musical fingers gripped around the neck of the carafe.

"I realized very soon that I had made a terrible mistake," Filippo continued, wetting his dry lips with a glassful of water. "I had to come back for Leda. I wrote everyone I could think of, seeking employment in Venice. I knew she was here—locked away in a convent. After several months, the librettist for the Italian opera in Vienna helped me find a position playing in the orchestra here at Teatro San Moisè."

"But—how did you find us?" Caterina asked. *And—why?*

Filippo's face brightened. "Ah, Signora. It is quite a story. Of course—the only convent I knew was the Pietà, because of its music conservatory."

Caterina nodded. Yes, the singing orphan girls at the Pietà. They were famed all over Europe.

"I asked one of the *maestri* there to help me. He gave me the names of a few other convents where Leda might be. But I tell you—none of those nuns were too happy when I showed up looking for her!"

Filippo chuckled and poured himself more water. Caterina drank hers, and glanced up to the closed shutters of her house. She knew Leda must be in torment inside, waiting for her return.

"After a few days my gondolier took pity on me," Filippo went on. "He told me, *Gondoliers know all the secrets in Venice. Tell me what she looks like.* And sure enough—he found a gondolier who remembered her." Filippo smiled at the memory of his good fortune. "This gondolier recalled, in early spring, taking a beautiful girl with purple-tinted hair from Santa Maria degli Angeli to this neighborhood. He showed me your house."

Ah. Leda's dyed hair. Long since returned to its natural brown. Caterina could not restrain a small smile, remembering the odd boarder she had taken home from the convent only six months before. She stole another glance up to her windows and saw Leda was now peeking out from the shutters, watching them.

"Filippo," she said, pulling her eyes away from the windows before Filippo turned and got lost staring up at her, "Leda worries she cannot trust you again. You accepted her father's money. She wonders whether you are only back for more—"

"No! I am not!" Filippo's voice was anguished. "The opposite is true. One of the reasons I came back is to return all the money to Leda. I should never have taken it." At these last words, he lowered his eyes. Caterina was sympathetic to his shame. She knew the feeling well.

"Signora—" he continued, facing her worst doubts about him, "if I were after money, why would I come back for Leda? I'm sure her father will cut her off if she ever agrees to marry me. It will be a hard life for us, maybe—I will never be rich. But I am making my way. My contract with the orchestra is for the fall Carnival season. It is a good start."

He nodded confidently as he spoke, showing Caterina he believed in himself and his talent. She liked that.

"It's not money I am concerned about," Caterina said. This was true; money had never meant much to her. "More importantly—will you stay with Leda and your son or daughter if life *does* turn out to be hard? Or will you run away again?"

Filippo flinched, as if she had surprised him with a hidden blade. But he quickly recovered. "You have my word, Signora. I am determined to take good care of my family. I will work hard to give them a good life."

Caterina gave him her first smile. She felt reassured, sensing that while Filippo had been scared away by Leda's father— surely—he was back to stay. But forgiveness? That would have to be Leda's own choice.

"Filippo," she suggested, "why don't you tell me a place where I can bring Leda to speak with you? This way, she can decide whether she wants to come—or not."

She glanced up to the windows one last time, as if seeking Leda's approval of her plan. But the shutters were now closed.

"Signora—what a good idea!" Filippo stood up so excitedly, he came close to knocking his water glass off the table. "Ask her to meet me at Teatro San Moisè tomorrow at one in the afternoon. The musicians will have all left for *pranzo*. We will have the theater to ourselves."

Oh—that eager smile, Caterina mused, watching him closely. There was nothing she missed more from her own youth than seeing that smile on a lover's face.

CHAPTER 91

"Are you sure this is a good idea?" Leda asked Caterina in the gondola cabin the next afternoon, crossing the Grand Canal on their way to Teatro San Moisè.

Caterina squeezed her hand. She understood why Leda was afraid to take a risk right now. The baby changed everything.

"At least listen to what Filippo has to say," Caterina encouraged, as Leda took several long, deep breaths. Caterina had insisted on not sharing any details of her conversation with Filippo the day before. She wanted Leda to make her own decisions.

Only one thing Caterina *had* told her—no matter what, Leda would not be going back to the convent. No. Caterina had decided this the frightening day the girl had disappeared. Leda's home, together with the baby, was with her and Bastiano—if she needed it.

Leda rested her head on Caterina's shoulder during the short ride, eyes closed, but not sleeping. Occasionally, Caterina saw her finger her pendant, her lips moving in some sort of prayer.

The boat bumped to a stop at a set of old oak mooring poles.

It took two gondoliers to hoist Leda out and onto the quay. Then, Caterina and she began their walk to the theater, arm in arm.

"You never finished telling me," Caterina said, to distract her, "the name of the baby if it is a girl. Carus for a boy, and for a girl—is it Cara?" Caterina smiled. She liked the sound of it. *Dear one*.

"No," Leda answered her with a mysterious smile. "Guess again."

"Caruska?"

Leda collapsed in giggles. "No! That is the ugliest name I ever heard!" Men and women walking by stared at her, not only because she was beautiful, and laughing, but because she was unusually far along in her pregnancy to be out in public.

"*Caterina*," Leda said, composing herself. "If the baby is a girl, she will be Caterina."

Caterina felt a huge rush of joy, and turned to kiss Leda's cheek. Leda tightened the link of their arms.

They passed the church of San Moisè with its busy façade of carved fruit garlands, *putti*, and saints. It was excessive but cheerful, which fit Caterina's mood. They rounded the corner and found a sunny courtyard filled with cats enjoying buckets of scraps that had been lowered down from windows above. Caterina spied the theater at the far end of the courtyard. She and Leda made their way across, and Caterina pulled open its huge entrance doors.

The foyer inside felt deliciously cool, with pink marble columns and a black, white, and pink inlaid geometric floor. Mounted on the gold-coffered ceiling was an enormous painting showing the Muse of Music holding a lyre and floating on a cloud. To Caterina, it made the room seem open to the sky.

The jewel-like foyer reminded her of being inside Teatro San Samuele many years before, with Giacomo. She had not gone back to any theater since. When they were first married, Bastiano used to offer to take her to the opera, but she always refused. She had not allowed herself to be happy with him. Now she vowed to go more often—Filippo's song had reminded her how much she loved to hear singing, to experience the human voice opening her heart.

Caterina guided Leda noiselessly through a door and into the main chamber of the theater. Inside was all black, except for the single figure of Filippo in the orchestra pit at his harpsichord, tinkering on a tune by lamplight. Strings, flutes, oboes, and horns lay on empty chairs scattered around. On the stage, Caterina could make out the looming silhouette of some stage machinery. And—looking out of place, a simple wooden cradle.

Caterina signaled to Leda she would wait at the back of the theater, and hid herself in the dark behind a thick column. She peeked around and watched Leda walking heavily down toward the pit.

Filippo sprang up from his instrument the moment he saw her. He led her up the short flight of steps onto the stage, and showed her the cradle. He went down on one knee in front of her. Taking both of Leda's hands in his, he covered them with kisses. Caterina saw him explaining himself, but she could only hear murmuring. It seemed to her that Filippo looked into Leda's eyes as if they were the very living rays of heaven he had been singing about below her windows.

Finally, Filippo stopped speaking. He bowed his head and waited for Leda's verdict. Leda placed her hand alongside his cheek and lifted his face to see hers. She was smiling. Filippo, seeing he had been forgiven—that he was loved by his beloved— jumped up, embraced Leda, and consumed her with ardent kisses. At the sight of their passion, Caterina became awkwardly aware she was spying. She slipped out of the theater.

Once outside, her heart swelled with happiness. *Leda— reunited with Filippo.* She breathed in the joy of it. The baby would have a mother and father who loved her. Or him. But she hoped it was a girl. A girl named Caterina. Whose name said, *Caterina Capreta helped me find a safe place in the world.*

I have done more good than harm in my life, Caterina told

herself now, *and perhaps that is all I, or anyone, can ask of themselves.* She felt the last, terrible burden of her past lift away.

As she made her way home, she was hardly aware she was smiling. She reached a bridge near Campo San Moisè and a handsome man, about her age, gave her an appreciative glance. She smiled even more, meeting his gaze for a brief, flirtatious moment.

I am not so very old after all. Young enough to still receive second glances. Young enough to enjoy the rest of my life.

She surprised herself by thinking tenderly of Bastiano, maybe for the first time in their long marriage. She felt new appreciation for him, thinking of how he had quietly helped her with Leda. He was kind and careful, and loving in his own way. Somewhere in her heart, she knew, she did in fact love him.

She glanced back to see if the handsome man on the bridge was gone. He was. He had reminded her a little of Giacomo. She stopped for a second, and closed her eyes. The early September sun gently warmed her face. She touched her cheek, remembering the sweet echoes of Giacomo's fingers on her skin. And wondered if somewhere far away, he ever closed his eyes . . . and remembered her too.

HISTORICAL NOTES

This is a work of fiction built on events told by Giacomo Casanova in the third and fourth volumes of *The Story of My Life*. Casanova began his memoirs around 1791, when he was already well past sixty years old. The memoirs—totaling an incredible 3,600 manuscript pages and never published in his lifetime—were therefore written many years after the events described took place. While he claimed he invented nothing, he must have had to do some fiction writing himself. He adored this project above any other he had ever undertaken, claiming he did it "to laugh at myself." He happily wrote thirteen hours a day, which passed like thirteen minutes for him. "What pleasure in remembering one's pleasures!" he wrote in a letter from this period, lamenting only that he had to mask the names in order not to "expose the affairs of others."

Casanova describes meeting a young girl he calls "Signorina C.C." in 1753, soon after his return to Venice after several years abroad. (He had been forced to leave his native city already by 1748, for beating an uncooperative prostitute with a broom and slicing off a dead man's arm and putting it in someone's bed as a joke.) Casanova is immediately enchanted by "C.C." as much for her beauty—he describes her as having alabaster skin set off by black hair and large black eyes—as for her whole personality:

> What chiefly struck me was a lively and perfectly unspoiled nature brimming over with candor and ingenuousness, a gay and innocent vivacity, simple and noble feelings—in short, a combination of qualities which showed my soul the venerable portrait of virtue, which always had the greatest power to make me the slave of the object in which I believed I saw it.

Caterina's brother "P.C." disgusts him, and particularly his attempt to sell his sister to him. Casanova claims he felt sorry for her, but actually never tells us whether he ever paid any money for her company.

The identity of the young girl "C.C." was uncovered by the Italian scholar Bruno Brunelli Bonetti in 1937. He pieced together the puzzle from a record in the Venetian State Archives that referred to "Sig. Pietr' Antonio Capretta" (the spelling of the name is variant) and Giacomo Casanova and several bills of exchange. If "P.C." in the memoirs could be tied to Pier Antonio Capreta, then "C.C." was his sister, Caterina. When the father's initials "Ch.C." perfectly matched up with their father, Christoforo Capreta, Bonetti knew he had the right family.

Later, the French scholar Jacques Marsan found Caterina's birth and marriage records in Venice. It's true she was only fourteen years old when Casanova met her, born December 10, 1738. Her large home was somewhere on the present-day Fondamenta della Misericordia in the northern part of the city, but it did not survive. I put her as a girl in my favorite house in Venice, the fifteenth-century Cà Dario in the neighborhood of Dorsoduro. The story's details about its upper loggia and small, walled garden are drawn from what can still be seen in Campiello Barbaro today.

For Casanova, Caterina was an angel and he never wavers in this view of her. Even as their story becomes complicated and she is banished to the convent, suffers a miscarriage, and discovers his affair with her friend "M.M.," Casanova quotes letters (whether real or reconstructed, he makes clear there were many letters written between them) that betray no jealousy at all. In fact, she exclaims joy over his new affair:

> I am not at all sorry either that you love her or that she loves you, and I pity you so much for being cruelly reduced to making love at a grating [that is, being kept apart by the bars in the visiting parlor] that I would gladly let you take my place. I should make two people happy at one stroke.

According to Casanova, "M.M." also considers Caterina an "angel incarnate" for not hating her, when M.M. is the reason Casanova no longer loves Caterina. It was this all-too-happy state of affairs that set the wheels turning in my imagination and led to this story telling about Caterina's hidden feelings and actions. How could she not have been devastated?

The identity of Caterina's rival "M.M." has proved a more complicated puzzle. The initials coincide with quite a few noblewomen in convents on Murano during this period: no less than eight at Santa Maria degli Angeli alone. The strongest candidate was proposed by the French scholar Pierre Gruet in 1975. Marina Maria Morosini would have been twenty-two years old in 1753, just as Casanova reports. Even more, Casanova wrote a friend saying he planned to refer to his lover Marina in the memoirs as "Mathilde" because the name has the same number of syllables and vowels; the friend wrote back and suggested he simply use "M.M." Marina Maria Morosini became the abbess at Santa Maria degli Angeli sometime in the period 1773–1799.

That Marina was poisoned by Caterina is probably a fiction. However, it is consistent with what Casanova tells us about the end of his affair with Marina. He records that in January of 1755 she "fell ill and her life was in danger." When he saw her at the convent on February 2, "her face displayed the signs of approaching death." She suffered fever and delirium and—just as bad—"her confessor was hastening her death by his boring sermons." Unexpectedly, by the end of March she had recovered. But by this time, Casanova admits that "my passion for M.M. was declining." Soon after, Casanova moved on to Tonina, the daughter of a *conversa* at the convent with whom he had stayed during Marina's illness.

Around the time of his affairs with C.C. and M.M., Casanova caught the unwelcome eye of the State Inquisitors in Venice, a governmental body set up in 1539 to tighten security in the Republic. The spy Giovanni Battista Manuzzi was set after him. The reports are full of juicy accusations: that Casanova cheated at cards, bewitched people to get money out of them, and that nothing could be more "monstrous" than his thoughts and talk on the subject of religion. He was arrested on July 26, 1755, and put in the Leads. He made his famed escape on October 31, 1756. He was eventually pardoned and allowed to return to Venice on September 14, 1774.

Caterina's brother Pier Antonio was imprisoned again in Venice in 1764 and 1767, on charges of swindling. He fled at some point to Szeged, Hungary, and there assumed a new name, Antonio Atterpach. He was arrested yet again in 1779 on similar types of charges—falsifying letters of exchange—and in the course of the arrest, was stabbed seventeen times. He was escorted to Pisa (the Grand Duchy of Tuscany at this time was ruled by the House of Habsburg-Lorraine) and sentenced to prison or forced labor. This is the last historical record of him.

Leda Strozzi, Zulietta Pasini, Giorgio Contarini, and Stefano Cavallini are all fictional characters. However, Giorgio was inspired by the portrayal of Peter III in the memoirs of Catherine the Great of Russia during this period. She describes the seventeen-year-old Grand Duke as being "very childish." He spent a lot of time in "pursuits unbelievable for one his age, such as playing with dolls." My story's details about how a non-noblewoman such as Zulietta could marry into the noble class in Venice are based on historical facts. Membership in the noble class—the only class allowed to rule in the Venetian Republic—had been essentially closed since the year 1297. Only rarely were new members added, and the government remained an aristocratic oligarchy until it fell to Napoleon five hundred years later.

The letter Casanova sends Caterina smeared with his semen is based on Andrea di Robilant's account of such sticky tokens of love sent by the nobleman Andrea Memmo to Giustiniana Wynne in Venice in the 1750s. The details about Caterina's miscarriage come from Casanova's own story, supplemented by surgeon and man-midwife medical books of the period. (A "man midwife" was the term used to distinguish such practitioners from the "ignorant women" who attended births.) Sadly, the story about the peasant woman whose child was born rotted like paper is true. It was recorded by Guillaume Manquest de la Motte in Paris in the year 1746.

Caterina married the lawyer Sebastiano Marsigli on February 5, 1757 (M.V.). She was widowed sometime in 1783. There is no record of any children.

A fragment found among Casanova's many papers indicates that he did see Caterina again sometime after 1774. He wrote he was saddened to find her "a widow, and unhappy." He was forced to leave Venice in 1783—in trouble again—and this time he never returned. After several years spent wandering, he took a job as librarian to Count Joseph Charles de Waldstein at his castle in Bohemia.

Two letters from Caterina—or more accurately, cryptic notes—also survive among Casanova's papers. The handwriting is shaky; she is an aging woman by this time. She refers to books he is sending to her, though she does not name them. They seem to have shared some sort of long-lasting interest in reading together. The note mentions payment of a few *lire* for the items.

In the end, we can never know what was in Caterina's heart. But Casanova believed that she continued to love him. He claimed that she only got married after his escape from prison and subsequent exile—"when there was no longer any hope that I would ever be seen again in Venice."

Giacomo Casanova died in Bohemia in 1798.

The date of Caterina Capreta's death is unknown.

The convent of Santa Maria degli Angeli was suppressed by Napoleon in 1810 and destroyed in 1832. As late as 1919, the little door in the garden wall through which the nuns escaped was still there.

ACKNOWLEDGMENTS

Some years ago, walking with a friend, Linda Fisher, in Mount Auburn Cemetery, I shared an idea I had: to write a novel about Giacomo Casanova and his young lover, Caterina Capreta. I wanted to tell her story.

I'm busy with work and family, I explained, shrugging. *I'll probably never write it.* To which Linda gently challenged, *Why not?* Those words stuck. Soon after, I started to write.

Patricia Fortini Brown, John Butman, Celia Latz, Chiara Peacock, Emily Rubin, and Monika Schmitter read and encouraged my early efforts. *Mille grazie,* as they say in Italy, to the amazing women in the Concord Writers' Group, who read several more: Jeannine Calabria, Sue Curtin, Becky Sue Epstein, Katharine Esty, Fran Grigsby, Maile Hulihan, Elisabeth Townsend, and Marti Thomas Webster. I can hardly thank enough Judy Sternlight, my incomparably skilled, tactful, and positive-minded editor. Sitting on a high rock with Judy in Central Park, with her dog Ruby by our side, talking over the final scene, is a memory I will hold on to forever: the fusion of our imaginations, dreaming of the eighteenth century, sunlight at our backs.

My agent, Elizabeth Winick Rubinstein, believed in this story, and I am immensely grateful for her help in leading me to my editor at Kensington Publishing, Alicia Condon. From our first phone call, I knew the book had found its right home.

Thank you to my family: my parents, Sumner and Phyllis Myers; my husband, Michael; daughter, Ginevra; dog, Lyra; and cats, Shura and Clementine. These people and animals make me feel special, loved, and supported in my dreams each day.

*Please read on for an excerpt from
Barbara Lynn-Davis's next fascinating
work of historical fiction . . .*

RAPHAEL'S MUSE

Rome, 1514

"By Christ's body, can't you move any faster? I'm starving over here!"

Margherita reached into a basket of fresh, crusty bread, clasping her fingers around a darkly baked loaf. She was hungry herself—the bakery would be closing soon for the midday meal, but customers were still clamoring inside the small shop.

"That's the smallest one," the stooped old man grumbled. "I want a bigger one."

Margherita put back the loaf and grabbed a larger one. She pulled the fabric of her cotton chemise over her breasts as she reached; otherwise the men always peered in as she worked.

"*Ecco, Signor.*" She smiled at the old man. She was alone working today, her father tending the wood-fired oven located off the back courtyard, unaware what Margherita experienced most days in the bakery, selling.

The old man counted his coins. "How many more for you, sweet bitch?" he asked. Margherita froze.

"That's enough," Margherita heard a younger man say, saw him step beside the old man, and nudge him gently away. This younger man was in his mid-twenties, and hardly the sort to play the hero. Margherita noticed his large, sensitive eyes, his fair skin, his long neck. He had a slight moustache and chest-nut-colored hair to his shoulders. He struck her as a dreamer.

"*Prego, Signor,*" she asked him, feeling the color rise in her cheeks, immensely grateful for his intervention but not wanting to acknowledge any further what had happened.

The young man stood staring at her face. Margherita was used to that, to be honest. Men's eyes simply went to her, un-able to resist. Her long, dark hair, which she always kept tied up in the shop, her almond-shaped, gypsy-dark eyes. She didn't see her beauty as a gift, but a nuisance, attracting unsought-after and often rude attention. Having no status—a baker's daughter, with the baker himself not usually present—she was fruit all too ripe for picking.

"Signor?" she asked the young man again. Other customers were becoming impatient and beginning to push their way to the front of the line.

"Is there any honey cake left?" he asked Margherita.

"*Mi dispiace,*" she answered, shaking her head. "Wait!" She remembered, seeing the disappointment on his face. "There was one that got stuck in the pan—I left it by the oven—but I can sell it to you if you do not mind it will not be well-shaped."

He put his hand to his heart and bowed to accept her offer, and Margherita was surprised to see various colors—blue, red-brown, and green—embedded under his nails. His hands were rough, not what she expected from this slightly built, almost delicate-looking man. She guessed he was one of the painters working to decorate that awful Chigi house nearby—the banker was the richest man in Europe, it was said. Didn't he have any-thing else to spend his money on, Margherita had wondered, than banquets and paintings?

"*Un' attimo,*" Margherita raised a finger to reassure her other customers, patted the money purse tied around her waist, and ran out to the courtyard to the nearby *forno*. Her father had left—he usually walked home earlier than she did, to begin cooking for them, some soup, maybe some pasta, nothing fancy. On the large pine table, Margherita spied the honey cake she had given up on a few hours earlier. She quickly cut off the worst of its broken edges to make an awkward triangle shape, and ran back through the courtyard to sell it to the painter. She'd decided she would ask half-price. Probably, it had not been worth angering her other customers to fetch it—*sometimes, you make shortsighted decisions,* she chided herself.

Returning breathless in the doorway to the bakery, Margherita stopped suddenly. There was the painter—behind now, not in front of the counter, selling to her customers, reaching for the loaves of crusty bread, the last pieces of rosemary *focaccia* topped with fat green olives. His fingertips were oily from fragrant olive oil, and the pigments under his nails now shone vibrantly. He looked over and opened his palm to her with the coins inside, as if to say, *Where do you want me to keep these for you?* Margherita's mouth hung open.

"Signorina?" A customer near the doorway startled Margherita back into action, asking for a dozen pistachio *biscotti*. Side by side, for ten, fifteen minutes, Margherita and the painter sold the rest of the baked goods. Margherita looked over to him occasionally, smiling to tell him her gratitude, but he mostly avoided her gaze, as if entirely wrapped up in the fascinating business of selling to hungry, irritable people. Once or twice their arms touched as they reached for items, and they both laughed and blushed. Margherita noticed she didn't feel compelled to pull her chemise to cover herself as she worked. Instead, she let herself simply be herself.

Finally, the last customer was gone and the baked items all gone, too. Margherita's father was a genius—a frugal genius—at calculating just how much to bake so nothing was ever wasted.

And just how many people to hire—that is, none—to help his only daughter run the shop.

"*Grazie, Signor . . . ?*" Margherita said to the stranger as she locked the front door and he handed her the money he had collected.

"Rafaello." He smiled, bowing slightly.

"Margherita," she introduced herself. She hoped this was not the last time she would see this dreamer-painter, whose eyes— deep, dark, and seeming to take everything in—met hers.

About the Author

Beth Kery lives in Chicago where she juggles the demands of her career, her love of the city and the arts, and a busy family life. Her writing today reflects her passion for all of the above. She is the *New York Times* and *USA Today* bestselling author of *Because You Are Mine*. Find out more about Beth and her books at BethKery.com or Facebook.com/Beth.Kery.